A Narrow Return

A Narrow Return

Faith Martin

ROBERT HALE · LONDON

ISBN 978-0-7090-9476-0

Robert Hale Limited
Clerkenwell House
Clerkenwell Green
London EC1R 0HT

www.halebooks.com

2 4 6 8 10 9 7 5 3 1

Typeset in 10.75pt/14.5pt Palatino
Printed in Great Britain by the MPG Books Group,
Bodmin and King's Lynn

CHAPTER ONE

It was a beautiful Sunday evening in mid-March when Hillary Greene turned the corner onto a very familiar part of the Oxford canal. Up ahead, she could just make out the first glimpse of the few rooftops and chimneys that marked the small hamlet of Thrupp, which was less than a mile from Kidlington, in the heart of Oxfordshire's Thames Valley.

She throttled down the engine of the Mollern, her narrowboat and home for more years now than she cared to remember. Even though she was doing the speed limit – all of a giddy 4mph – she was in no hurry to arrive, and preferred to savour the moment.

Although spring didn't officially arrive until the twenty-first, the weather was doing one of those funny little twists and turns that England did so well, and not even a cold breeze came across the open, khaki-coloured water. Some of the willows were just beginning to bud, giving the towpath that slightly frothy, lacy edge of green that lifted the heart, and confirmed that winter was indeed well and truly over. And as she approached the first of the houses, the yellow drifts of the first opening daffodils seemed to echo a cheerfully sunny yellow agreement.

A newly arrived and early chiffchaff called away to her right, but she doubted any of its potential female mates would have arrived from the continent just yet.

She spied a mooring opening up not far ahead and about fifty yards down from the canal-side pub, The Boat. She checked to make sure that it didn't have any private-mooring warnings, then

5

expertly brought her boat to the side, turned off the engine, and stepped casually onto the side. It didn't do to poach someone's spot, as she'd very quickly learned during her year and a half of touring.

The boat behind her had lights on inside and she could sense movement, but the boat in front was dark and silent, and had that just-starting-to-look-neglected air about it. But then, a lot of canal-dwellers spent the winters in a more conventional home, preferring the benefits of snug central heating and double glazing.

Anyone watching her go about tying up the Mollern would have seen an attractive woman in old snug-fitting jeans and a cornflower-blue jersey, who moved with an economy of move-ment that would have told them she was no novice to narrowboat living. She was curvaceous but lithe, with a just-past-the-shoulder cut of bell-shaped auburn hair.

Her home secure, Hillary turned and eyed the pub thought-fully, then gave a mental headshake. There was plenty of time yet to be acknowledged and welcomed back into what had once been her local.

Instead, she went inside and set about fixing up a scratched meal of tinned ham, boiled eggs and salad, which she ate in soli-tary splendour in the tiny room at the prow of the boat that passed for her living area.

It felt odd to be back in Thrupp. For the past year and half she'd been touring Britain's waterways in her boat, writing a novel which was now finished but was hardly ever likely to see a publisher's desk, and generally getting the 'hang' of retirement.

Or not.

With the big 5-0 breathing down her neck within the next few weeks, ex-Detective Inspector Hillary Greene had finally had to admit defeat. She was bored and restless, and badly needed to do something more meaningful to occupy her time than being a tourist in her own country. And tomorrow she would no doubt have to weather the I-told-you-so blandishments of her old boss, Commander Marcus Donleavy.

She sighed and washed away her plate, before settling down in front of the small TV. She turned over from an old Morse re-run, and found an adaptation of a Jane Austen novel on BBC2. Settling down with another sigh, she sipped her glass of bog-standard supermarket white plonk and wondered, not for the first time, if she wasn't making a big mistake in coming back.

Who was it who'd said that you could never go back? She poured herself a defiant second glass of wine and muttered that whoever it was deserved a good kick up the backside.

Monday morning bright and early, Hillary dressed in a dark blue skirt and jacket, feeling oddly uneasy in her old work clothes. Since retiring, jeans and t-shirt, baggy cardigans and comfortable jerseys had been her uniform. Life on the canal, especially in winter, with all the mud and damp that went with it, was hardly conducive to sartorial elegance. She then had to hunt around for a pair of 'proper' shoes, since she'd worn nothing but trainers for what felt like forever. Her toes instantly objected to being confined in the black leather flatties, and she mumbled something dire into her morning cup of coffee.

And that reminded her. She was going to have to stop this retirement-acquired habit of muttering to herself. Anyone catching her at it could justifiably wonder if she was going doolally.

She checked her appearance in the mirror, realized she'd forgotten her watch, and then had to have another hunt around for it. Timekeeping was another thing she was going to have to get used to again. On the boat, meandering from spot to spot, it hardly mattered what time you got up, or ate, or anything else. Now routine would once more become the norm.

She scowled at her reflection in the tiny mirror. Just why the hell was she putting herself through this, anyway? She had plenty of money to see her through to her cranky old age, and it wasn't as if she needed the hassle of going back to work.

Still, fifteen minutes later saw her heaving her bicycle from the roof rack of the Mollern and pushing it along the towpath towards the lane. She cast another quick glance at the pub, and wondered if the landlord's son still had Puff. She'd sold him her car, an ancient Volkswagen Golf that she'd christened Puff the Tragic Wagon – because it was – when she'd left the police service. Now, depending on how things went, she might need to buy another second-hand car, and she felt a distinct pang of something that might have been nostalgia for her old rust-bucket.

She sighed, and with a glance at a cloudy but mercifully rain-free sky, put the toe of her newly-polished, black leather shoe to the pedal and set off. Luckily, she didn't have to go far. She was hardly a born cyclist or a die-hard keep fit fan, but Thrupp was barely a mile from the Thames Valley HQ and as such, was well within her limits. And she had to admit to feeling a certain amount of malevolent satisfaction as she was able to pedal righteously past all the stalled traffic at Kidlington's many traffic lights.

She turned into the familiar car park of her old stomping ground barely ten minutes later and then had to stop and think where the bicycle racks would be. Before she'd always parked Puff in the first empty car parking space she found. But she eventually found the right place, and padlocked her bike into place. She had no illusions about it being safe enough outside a police station; more than twenty-five years on the job had taught her a lot about criminal cheek.

She ran a quick hand through her hair to check that it wasn't too windblown, then began to unbutton her long raincoat as she walked towards the doors. When she stepped into the lobby, it felt like coming home. Which was hardly an auspicious start, considering she was not sure of whether or not she'd be staying or even what sort of reception she was going to get.

Not that she'd left under a cloud or anything. But the death of a former colleague during her last case still tended to leave a bad taste in her mouth.

'Hey up, look what the cat's just dragged in, fellahs. No, hold on, now I come to think of it, no self-respecting cat would even think of dragging you in.'

The booming, happy voice of the desk sergeant brought an instant smile to her lips. Over the years, the banter she'd shared with the men who manned the desk had more than once kept her sane when she felt like tearing her hair out.

'Less of the cheek, you,' she said, heading towards him, noticing a small gaggle of constables clustered off to one side, who'd fallen silent at this sally, and were now watching her with interest. 'I'm a member of the public now, you're supposed to show some respect.'

The desk sergeant roared with laughter. 'Never showed you none when you were a DI, guv,' he pointed out when he got his breath back. 'Don't know what makes you think I'm likely to start now.' Hillary grinned and leaned against the counter, resigning herself to a long-winded catch-up session. Desk sergeants were not noted for their taciturnity. 'Here, I've got a bone to pick with you,' the sergeant rumbled on. 'We had bets around here about how long it'd be before you came back. I had a tenner on you showing up last autumn. What the hell kept you?'

Hillary sighed. 'Go on then, get it over with,' she said, and let him rag her for a while about her taking early retirement, and now her reappearance. The gaggle of uniforms stirred and murmured as it began to filter through to them just who it was who had returned to HQ. Some of them knew Hillary on sight, of course, but most of the others were new, and all of them knew her name.

Her notoriously bent husband, her medal for bravery and her unbeaten arrest record made sure of that. And since walking away from the job, she'd become something of a legend.

But one of them watched her with far more interest than the others. His eyes were cat-green and observed her every move-ment and facial expression. How old was she? If she was retired she had to be getting on a bit but she looked gorgeous. He'd swear that hair was real and not out of a bottle, and her figure was perfect. Not stick-thin, like some girls, but with proper curves.

'Well, I'd better get on,' Hillary said, after she'd listened to all the station gossip the desk sergeant could muster – which was plenty. 'The boss is expecting me.'

'Ah Commander Donleavy,' the desk sergeant said, in mock-hushed tones. 'Never seen his hallowed portals myself.'

Hillary grinned. 'I'll tell him shall I? Maybe he'll invite you up for tea and biccies.'

The sergeant was still guffawing over the likelihood of that as she took the stairs two at a time and disappeared out of sight without even breathing hard.

The man with the cat-green eyes smiled briefly. For a wrinkly she certainly seemed fit enough.

Hillary Greene sat in the hallowed portal of Commander Donleavy's office and sipped her coffee. Brewed by his ever-loyal secretary in his own pot and made with Brazilian beans no less. There were no biscuits, however.

'I can't tell you how pleased I was to get your letter,' Donleavy was saying, pausing to sip from his own cup. He was wearing his trademark silver-grey suit, which went so well with his neat coiffure of silver-grey hair. And if his silver-grey eyes were sparkling rather more brightly than usual with hidden mirth, it was hard to call him out on it. For he had indeed said, all those many moons ago, that she would be back.

And here she was. Back.

He handed her a folder. 'Here's all the data you'll need. Salary rates, forms to sign, official ID and what have you.'

Hillary blinked. 'Hey, hang on a minute, sir,' the respectful term for him slipped out without her noticing, but Donleavy's eyes gleamed even brighter. 'I haven't even made up my mind I'm going to do this yet.'

Donleavy nodded. 'I've placed you with Superintendent

Crayle's team,' he carried on as if she hadn't bothered speaking, making her choke on her superbly percolated coffee.

'Bloody hell, sir, now you *are* being premature,' she managed, once she'd stopped sounding like a strangled parrot. Her eyes were still watering from her coughing fit, so she put her cup down and reached for a tissue. 'I only said I wanted to come in and see how the land lies. I hope you've told this Superintendent Crayle that nothing's fixed yet.'

Donleavy smiled savagely. That wasn't quite what he'd said to Steven Crayle.

'I'll show you your new office after we've finished our coffee, shall I?' he gave her a salute with his mug and smiled benevolently as she scowled back at him. As if he'd give her even the remotest chance of wangling out of it now! In all his years as a copper, Hillary Greene had been by some way the best natural detective he'd ever met. She had the ability to sift facts and spot the ones that mattered, and in interview, she was second to none. She had a way of understanding people – perps, victims, suspects – that had them eating out of her hand and confessing all. He'd fought tooth and nail to keep her from early retirement and didn't admit defeat gracefully. And now that she was back and cautiously sniffing around the mouse hole he was determined to secure her services before the other cats even knew she was back.

Let alone the mice.

'Let me tell you about the Crime Review Team,' Donleavy railroaded on. 'Basically it's set up to review cold cases with a new and bang-up-to-the-minute eye. Which means, of course, computer whizz-kids mostly riding a desk and crunching numbers and running programmes through databases. A crony of the chief constable is overseeing all of that. But within the CRT is a more investigative sub-branch, which takes on specific cases that need to be investigated using more tried-and-true methods.'

Hillary nodded, seeing the sense of what her old boss was saying. 'And this Superintendent Crayle is in charge of this set up, yes?'

'Right, and this is an area which should be right up your alley. You never were one to stay behind a desk and delegate, were you? Working for Crayle, you'll be hands on from start to finish,' Donleavy said smoothly.

Hillary smiled, knowing full well what he was doing. Namely laying tempting bait and hoping she'd fall for it. And it was good bait, damn him. The thought of getting out and about interviewing people, gathering facts and trying to solve the puzzle on hand was exactly what she'd lived and breathed for.

'And I'd be given a set of cases, and left to work them as I see fit?' she asked, determined to get a full picture of exactly what was on offer before committing herself to anything.

'That's it. He's divided his staff into small teams, each with its own set of cold cases. In each of these teams, he's tried to match up a retired or ex-copper with the young wannabes. Oh yes, and some part-time retired forensic officers hold a watching brief and overall view.'

'Wannabes?' she asked, puzzled and in spite of herself, curious. She had to watch Donleavy, she knew. He was a wily bugger and used to getting his own way. If she didn't watch it, she'd be back at work tomorrow instead of in the two or three weeks that she had originally planned.

Marcus Donleavy grunted. 'Oh don't get me started on that!' He sighed heavily then shrugged. 'As you'd expect, with the government cutbacks biting us so deeply in the arse nowadays, Crayle's budget is paper-thin. Most of the resources are eaten up with trying to keep the immediate crime figures down – so cold cases hardly get a look in. And youngsters who want to join the force are facing one hell of an uphill struggle just now. It's not like it was when you left us. Admin are actually cutting the numbers of staff we have, let alone hiring on new ones. How the government thinks we can still provide what's needed on half the....'

Hillary picked up her cooling coffee and let him get on with his moaning. She agreed with every word he said, but didn't need a lecture on it. Instead she let her mind wander a bit.

It felt good to be back, both in Thrupp and back in her old station house, but that didn't mean she was ready to jump head-long into the thick of things just yet.

Oh yeah, a little sneering voice piped up in the back of her head.

'So when Crayle put forward the proposals for the training programme, the accountants jumped at the chance.'

Hillary blinked. 'Huh?'

Marcus smiled bleakly. 'Simply speaking, youngsters who want to join up are now looking for back-door methods to get in. Some are becoming community officers.'

Hillary nodded. They did good work – men and women, not police officers but with some authority, who worked mostly in the cities, pounding a beat, being visible and trying to take on the mammoth task of prevention, rather than actual policing. They did an invaluable job taking on the lesser and more time consuming peace-keeping work, thus leaving trained officers to tackle the more serious issues.

'Others are taking courses in specialist areas. Family liaison training, rape-crisis management, that sort of thing,' Marcus went on. 'And now, we have Crayle's wannabes, as I call them. Most of them are still at uni, or in a gap year, or are looking for employment. They work on a volunteer basis, but get basic part-time pay if they put in a certain number of hours. Plus they get on-the-job training, all of which is supposed to put them in a better position to land a proper placement when the time comes. Even this government must finally come to its senses and realize that we can't keep law and order without the manpower, and the means to start a new recruitment campaign.'

Hillary sighed. 'In other words, we're getting the foot soldiers without paying them a proper wage for it,' she translated bitterly.

Marcus Donleavy grimaced, but was secretly pleased to hear that word 'we' creeping back into her vocabulary. So she still thought of herself as a copper. Well, that didn't surprise him. She had the job in her bones. It only surprised him it had taken her this long to get tired of civilian life and come back where she belonged.

'Exactly. So as you can see, Steven needs all the experienced help he can get. He was delighted when he heard that he was going to get his hands on you. So to speak.'

Well, perhaps not delighted, Donleavy mentally observed, but his smile never faltered.

Hillary sat up straighter in her chair. 'Now just hang on a minute, sir,' she said, her voice low and flat. It was a voice that Donleavy instantly recognized, and one that always made him pay attention.

'I haven't even made my mind up yet about whether or not I want to come back to work. I'm not even sure if working as a consultant will even suit me. I was used to being a full DI, and the Crime Review Team might not be the answer. I'm just here to dip a toe in the water, that's all. I might be on my way again tomorrow.'

Donleavy nodded. 'Of course, whatever you say Hillary,' he said, spreading his hands benevolently. Once Crayle had handed her her first case file, she'd be hooked. And then he could sit back and enjoy the show. He'd always admired the way Hillary Greene could crack a murder case. And he was rather interested to see how Steven Crayle would react to having a star in his firmament.

That Steven Crayle was ambitious, Marcus knew and approved of. He had a good university degree, and nowadays a failed marriage was par for the course and nothing to his detriment. He had good instincts in spotting a villain, could play the politics game, gave a good performance with the media, and had brains. Marcus was more than happy for him to climb high. But he could tend to be just a trifle complacent at times.

And he rather thought that being confronted with the station legend would do him the world of good. Hillary, if nothing else, would give him something to think about other than where his next promotion was coming from.

*

The Crime Review Team had their offices in the basement. Hardly surprising, Hillary thought with a gloomy sigh as she followed the commander down into the depths. A low-priority department would have to make do with the leftovers and be thankful. But high windows on a level with the parking lot let in a lot of natural light and banks of fluorescent lighting at least gave the bland cream walls and beige carpeting an airy appearance. Nothing could disguise the fact that it was a bit of a rabbit warren, though, with old-fashioned offices, cubby holes and nooks and crannies that told her that this whole floor had once been used as a storage facility more than anything else.

She thought of her old open-plan office on the third floor with a sigh of regret.

Donleavy first popped his silver head into what he called 'the hub' where computers ruled the roost. His appearance caused a bit of a stir amongst the sparse human population, and Hillary was introduced and given a quick run-down on the CRT's main purview – which was comparing cases in the hopes of finding matches, it seemed.

A rounded man, about two inches shorter than herself, who introduced himself as Sergeant Handley, explained how things worked.

'Say we have a rape case, two years old, come down to us from above,' he began, making Hillary wonder for a moment if he was some sort of religious nut, until she realized that he meant it rather more literally, when he pointed upwards towards the main offices. 'After two years, all inactive files come down from central to be processed,' he added. 'We then run a programme to see if the MO matches any other cases we already have on file – since, as you know, many rape cases that aren't solved in the first six months are serials.'

Hillary nodded. Date rapes, or rapes by a disenfranchised ex tended to be a one-off and were more often than not solved quickly. The problem came when you had a lone male targeting women unknown to him. Serial rapists, in other words. These were the hardest to catch because they had no other contact with the victim, and so the chances of tracing him were significantly reduced.

'So as soon as we get a new unsolved rape,' Sergeant Handley went on, 'we compare it with others with a similar MO and check on the physical evidence. You'll be surprised how many we can match up after a while. The sighting of a car or a partial registration plate in a similar case six or four years ago now matches that with one of the suspects in the latest case. Or a DNA sample from a case that's fifteeen years old and that couldn't be matched, now has a new suspect to type it against. And so on.'

Hillary got it. 'The more strands you have, from as many cases as you can identify, gives you more to go on, and thus a better chance of pinpointing a suspect.'

'Right. Often it's even easier than that. If a perp has done time, his DNA is now in the system. And so by regularly running any physical samples from our older cases, we often get a hit. And once a perp's in prison, he's more likely to cop to other crimes in the hopes of getting them written off as time served.'

'CRT comes in very handy when our solve-rates figures get reviewed,' Marcus put in drolly. 'I'm sure that's one of the reasons it even gets funded at all.'

The shorter man glanced at him nervously, not sure if he was being facetious or was being genuinely appreciative.

'You must get a good clearance rate,' she mused, and meant it. Collating and comparing cases, putting together all the facts and figures and getting a major overview of stacks of data must inevitably bring up patterns that wouldn't necessarily be noticed in the field. But this sort of thing wasn't her cup of tea at all. 'But I can't see it being of much use when you get one-off murder cases, for example.'

'Ah, that's where Superintendent Crayle's team comes in,' Sergeant Handley said airily. 'Not my department, I'm glad to say,' he added thoughtfully, and glanced almost lovingly at a computer that was churning out columns of tax-reference numbers. He had the look of one who lived in virtual reality and Donleavy was quick to thank him and let him get back to his cyberspace world.

Leading her further into the rabbit warren, he then paused before a door and gave a brief tap. On it, the words DETECTIVE SUPERINTENDENT STEVEN CRAYLE had been stencilled in black letters.

'Time to meet your new boss,' Donleavy said.

Hillary opened her mouth to tell him yet again that she hadn't agreed to anything, but he was already opening the door and ushering her inside.

The office was surprisingly spacious, with two high windows letting light stream in. Several large and colourful abstract paintings hung on the plain white walls, and a large, modern ash desk sat beneath the windows, to make the most of the natural light. And rising from behind the desk was one of the best-looking men Hillary had seen in an age.

Hillary looked at him and swore, very softly, under her breath.

He was perhaps just a little bit over six feet and lean in that elegant way some men have. They tended to move like Fred Astaire and could wear those bulky Fair Isle sweaters and yet still look sexy as all hell. He had a head of thick, dark brown hair worn a little long for a super, and dark brown eyes under arched dark brows. Clean-shaven, his square-jawed chin looked just a shade dark. He was obviously one of those men who had to shave at least twice a day or just give it up and grow a beard. High cheekbones gave him just a slightly Slavic look. At first glance he appeared to be about thirty, but very fine lines at the corner of his eyes told Hillary that she should add another decade to this. He was, quite simply, stunningly beautiful in a classic, masculine way.

He should have been modelling something on a fashion catwalk in Paris. As it was, he wore a plain dark blue suit with a white shirt and black enamelled cufflinks. His tie was electric blue with some sort of tiny motif in black, white and gold. And he still should have been modelling it on a catwalk in Paris somewhere.

Her libido abruptly sat up and took notice.

She silently told her libido exactly what it could do, and listened instead with a grim smile of agreement at what the sardonic voice at the back of her head was telling her.

Namely that this was just what she needed. Not.

'Commander,' Steven Crayle said, acknowledging Marcus first, his voice carefully neutral. And then he turned those velvet chocolate brown eyes to Hillary. They were guarded.

Most definitely guarded.

And the sardonic voice in Hillary's head picked up a gear. Great, not only was he gorgeous, he was hostile too.

Oh this just got better and better, her little voice said gleefully. Anyone with an ounce of sense would just turn around and scuttle back to her narrowboat and head for the hills.

Or even the Greater Manchester canal.

'And this must be DI Greene.' His voice was pure Oxford.

'Ex,' Hillary said flatly.

'Of course. You have consultant status now,' Steven Crayle smiled briefly. The smile didn't quite reach his eyes. 'Welcome to Hades,' he said, and put out his hand. Seeing her startled look he smiled again. 'Sorry, that's what the troops call this place. But I hope it's not as bad as all that.'

Oh, I wouldn't bet on it, Hillary thought grimly as she took his hand and felt her fingers tingle. He had a strong grip, and the tingles shot up her arm and onto pastures new.

She took her hand back quickly, and wondered if the heating system was buggered down here. It felt very hot all of a sudden.

She cast a brief glance at Donleavy. She looked faintly bored, politely interested and cautious. It would take someone who knew her very well to know that she was actually mad enough to contemplate kicking him in the shins. Hard.

Donleavy, who knew her very well, smiled jovially. 'Well, I'll leave Steven here to show you around,' he said and smartly left.

Hillary glared at the door closing behind his back and silently promised herself that he would get his.

Then Superintendent Crayle moved around the desk and walked up to her. He was wearing an expensive aftershave, or maybe cologne, one of those that smelt faintly of citrus or pine.

'Let me introduce you to your team.'

Hillary opened her mouth to tell him that she didn't have a team, and might never have a team, that she hadn't even made her mind up to come back to work yet. And even if she had decided to give it a go, he was probably the last man on earth she wanted to work with. Who needed the aggro?

Then she closed her mouth again.

Why bother?

She was back, and she knew it.

CHAPTER TWO

Superintendent Crayle led the way through the rabbit warren until he eventually came to a reasonably sized office for one. Unfortunately, it now housed three people, who all turned and looked at her when Crayle walked in. Or rather took one step in and then turned to let Hillary precede him.

She smiled briefly and nodded all around as Crayle made the introductions. There was a single large desk in the middle of the room, with one computer on it, and three chairs pulled up around it. Even then, the backs of the chairs rested against the wall on the far side. It felt stuffy and smelt of coffee and perfume.

'Age before beauty,' Crayle said with a smile, and held out his hand towards a sixty-something man who had a full head of pale grey hair and bushy white eyebrows. It was hard to see the colour of his eyes from across the room but they looked pale, and they regarded Hillary steadily. She liked him right away. It was rare to have gut instincts, but she already had him tagged as her right-hand man before he'd even said a word. 'This is James Jessop. He's been on the team now for five months, isn't it?' The older man nodded.

'That's right, sir.'

'He retired as a DS from Bicester nick nearly three years ago now it must be. Nearly everyone calls him JJ,' the superintendent made the introduction with a brief smile. Again, the smile didn't quite reach his eyes.

Hillary thought she could detect on the face of the older man a bit of a wince in this pairing of his initials, and walking forward to shake his hand she said firmly 'Jimmy is it?' and got a warm smile back.

'Ma'am, I'm glad to be working with you,' Jimmy Jessop said, and meant it. Although he'd never worked out of Kidlington HQ before coming to the CRT, he knew enough about Hillary Greene to have felt excited when the super had told them all yesterday that she'd be joining their team. As the token ex-copper, he'd been leading the team if it could be called that, until then of course, but he was more than willing to become second fiddle if he could watch and learn from a master like Hillary Greene.

'Well, we'll have to see how it goes, Jimmy,' Hillary said, still determined to be cautious. 'It might not be permanent,' but even as she said it, she knew in her heart that she'd already made up her mind.

'And this strapping lad is Sam Pickles. Sam's at Brookes, doing a BA in sociology and economics,' Crayle carried on, and a tall, lanky, sandy-haired lad with a smattering of freckles and round hazel eyes grinned back at her. At six foot two or so, he was just beginning to develop the stoop-shoulders that some tall people get, as if they're trying to reduce or apologize for their size.

She smiled at him and gave a mental nod. She'd soon get him out of that habit and teach him to stand up straight. If he was going to be a beat copper one day, he'd need all the advantages his size could give him.

'Sam,' she said, shaking his hand, and making a mental note to herself to teach him how to intimidate. With his size it should be a doddle. All he needed to do, really, was learn how to hide his basically friendly face behind a dead stare.

'Ma'am,' he said, somewhat awkwardly copying Jimmy's deference, and she smiled.

'I don't know whether or not that title is appropriate, Sam. I'm not a full DI now you know,' she added, glancing across questioningly at Steven Crayle. He'd know better than anyone what the etiquette was around here.

'We mostly tend to use Christian names,' he said smoothly, picking up on her unspoken query.

'Right. Hillary it is then,' Hillary said, not really liking it much. Which made her wonder. Had all her years being referred to as 'guv' given her a sense of superiority? So much so, that she now felt uncomfortable with her given name? The thought made her feel distinctly wrong-footed.

'And last but not least, of course, Vivienne Tyrell,' Crayle continued, and a hint of reserve in his voice made her turn swiftly to the final member of her team. The one, no doubt, responsible for the perfume.

Vivienne Tyrell was young, barely twenty, Hillary would have said, with long curling dark brown hair and big pansy-brown eyes, which were expertly outlined in mascara to make the most of her lashes, and with a subtle bronze-amber eye shadow to highlight her best asset. She wasn't quite as beautiful as she obviously thought herself to be, but Hillary had few doubts that she could still have her pick of men simply by beckoning them over with one of her gold-painted nails.

'Hillary,' she said promptly, and held out her hand perfunctorily. It was obvious that she was not impressed with this stranger being foisted upon her, and was making it clear that she wasn't going to do any toadying.

Which was fine with Hillary.

'Vivienne.'

'Well, let me show you to your office,' Crayle said, then gave a brief laugh. 'Well, I call it office. I think it was probably once a stationery cupboard. But at least it's convenient – just across the corridor here.'

Which was something of a blessing, Hillary thought, and wondered just how many times she'd get lost down here before she learned the layout of her new domain.

He showed her to a tiny room with a tiny window, a desk which just had room to house a computer (not the printer, which was underneath on the floor) and an old-fashioned beige-coloured filing cupboard pressed up against one corner like a cowering suspect. 'Sorry, but at least it's a bit of privacy when you need it,' Crayle said, looking around the beige-painted room. It wouldn't even have made a decent cell. Hell, the prisoners rights groups would be up in arms if any criminal was housed in such a bleak space.

He watched her look around, curious to see what her reaction would be. When she'd left here, she'd been used to the open plan office upstairs, with a lofty view, a roomy desk and an obvious amount of respect accorded to her by her peers. Down here, they were all but invisible to the vast network up above, and, being out of sight, were also mostly out of mind. It must be something of a culture shock for a high-flying DI to suddenly find herself as a civilian consultant in the humble CRT.

When Donleavy had first told him he'd got a letter from Hillary Greene expressing interest in the CRT, he wasn't sure whether to be glad or sorry.

And he still wasn't.

Although he'd worked out of first Abingdon and then St Aldates nick, he'd come to Kidlington HQ about six months before Hillary had retired, and knew all the scuttlebutt about her. He'd been here when the debacle with the Myers case and her ex-sergeant, Janine Mallow, had kicked off. It hadn't taken him long to discover that she was popular with both the lads and with the movers and shakers. The high esteem in which Commander Donleavy held her, for instance, more than proved that. And of course her gallantry medal and the way she stood by her people had earned her an almost legendary status with the rank and file.

But it was not that so much as her arrest record, which gave him reason to think. Once Donleavy had dropped the bombshell on him that she was going to be working for him, he'd quickly done his research, and he knew she had an arrest and conviction rate that had always kept her star riding high in the ascendant. And in murder cases in particular, her skill was enviable.

And he knew himself well enough to know that he was envious. Although his own record was pretty good, it made him uncomfortable to compare it to hers.

So it hadn't come as much of a surprise when Donleavy had called him into his office just before the weekend and all but ordered him to give her nothing but the murder cases. And he'd dropped strong hints about giving her a good second-in-command, with a decent team behind her as well. His reasoning being that the better her tools, the better her performance.

Which on the face of it, all seemed well and good, he supposed.

If she did well, it would reflect glory back onto the CRT and his department in particular, naturally. And since he wanted to make Chief Super by the time he was forty-eight, he could use all the kudos he could get. Even so, if she became too successful, she might start to hog too much of the limelight again.

And that would be a problem. When the bosses talked about the CRT he wanted it to be his name that came first. He was, after all, still a serving officer and relatively young. Hillary Greene, for all her assets, was now a retired civilian consultant.

And he would have to make sure that nobody, including herself, ever forgot that.

'This is fine,' she said, breaking him out of his reverie, and making his lips twist in a grimace.

'It's barely adequate,' he contradicted her flatly, 'but it's the best I could do,' he added, totally truthfully. Space down here was problematic at the best of times, and not even he could magic a decent office for her, Donleavy's pet or not.

She nodded, her expression utterly unreadable. And it popped into his head that he wouldn't like to play poker with this woman.

The overhead lighting was making her hair gleam a deeper red than usual, and as she moved behind her desk and sat down, she gave the printer underneath it an accidental kick, which brought his eyes down to her legs.

And very shapely they were too.

He quickly dragged his eyes back up. He had enough trouble with the Tyrell girl mooning over him. The last thing he needed was to attract any spurious sexual-harassment charges his way. Not that Hillary Greene was the sort who'd do that. Everything he knew about her told him that if he started making overtures in that direction, he'd be more likely to get a knee in his groin rather than a formal complaint lodged against him.

Not that that was ever going to be an issue, of course. He knew all about that poor sod Paul Danvers – the whole station house did. Her former boss, DCI Danvers had fancied her for years, and had never got anywhere, much to everyone's amusement. And Steven Crayle had no intention of becoming another butt of station house jokes.

'I'll just go and get you your first file,' he said, abruptly turning around and vanishing.

Hillary sat in her chair, her face thoughtful. Then she glanced around and grimaced. Well, one thing was for sure, she wasn't going to be spending much time in here. In fact, if she had been at all claustrophobic she'd already be climbing the walls. Then again, if she had been at all claustrophobic she wouldn't be living on a narrowboat.

She stashed her handbag in the large empty bottom drawer of her desk and turned on her computer. She'd need a password. She turned if off again, sighed, then looked up as Crayle reappeared.

'I thought you might like this now. You're not supposed to take it out of the building of course, but ...' he shrugged and gave a brief smile. Hillary got it at once. She could take it out, but don't get caught.

'Right, guv,' she said. She used his title without giving it a conscious thought but for some reason the simple acknowledge-ment of his status made him blink and take a quick breath.

'Er, right. I'll let you get on with it then. I take it you'll be starting straight away?'

Hillary smiled grimly. 'Looks like it, doesn't it,' she said dryly. So much for being cautious.

Crayle nodded and returned to his own office. There he poured himself a mug of coffee and sat down, drinking thoughtfully.

So that was the legendary Hillary Greene.

From her personnel file, he knew she was going to be fifty in just a few weeks' time, but she looked much younger. For some reason he just hadn't expected her to be so attractive. For days now he'd speculated about her, seeing her as a potential threat, rival, or even a possible liability. After all, she'd stood at the side of her old friend, Mel Mallow when he'd been shot dead, and on her last case, a former colleague had also died. But for all that, she didn't have the reputation of being a Jonah; but you never knew.

He shrugged off all this speculation about just another consultant on his team, and brought his mind firmly back to work. And with that, he smiled wolfishly.

Well, Donleavy had told him to give her only murder cases and who was he to disoblige a superior officer? In fact, it had given him great satisfaction to go through his back files and pick out the hardest, coldest, meanest ones that he could find.

Now he could just sit back and see what the station legend was really made of. And it would certainly be interesting to see how Donleavy's blue-eyed girl tackled the impossible!

Back in her stationery cupboard, Hillary Greene stared down at the slightly grimy folder on her desk. The case file was thick, as she supposed most of the cold cases would be, since the investigation had already been done and dusted. No doubt this was just the basic brief. There were bound to be boxes and boxes of other stuff relating to the murder victim stored away somewhere. All of which would have to be gone through carefully.

It felt odd to be coming onto a case where the victim had been dead for twenty years.

Nevertheless, it beat idling away her days, desperately trying to find something to do.

With a happy sigh, she opened the file and began to read.

Mrs Anne McRae, née Carter, born on 2 February 1956, had been found dead in her home in the village of Chesterton on 6 June 1991, by her 13-year-old daughter Lucy.

Hillary took a deep breath, trying not to imagine the kind of trauma that moment must have been for a young girl. Or how it must have blighted her life ever since.

The victim was married, with three children, the eldest at the time being a boy named Peter, aged fifteen, the youngest, a girl of eleven, named Jennifer. All three children had been at school on the day of the murder. The victim's husband, Melvin McRae drove a coach for a holiday firm, and had been returning from a continental tour on the day of his wife's death. His alibi had been closely checked, of course.

He'd spent the previous week in the Netherlands with his forty-or-so passengers, and had just returned to the UK that very day. He had been at the coach station, returning his vehicle at the time the pathologist had estimated as time of death.

Questioning of all forty passengers confirmed that he'd been with them all that day, and had dropped the last five people off at the final drop-off point in Oxford at 2.45 p.m. The office and garage staff confirmed that he'd arrived in their depot at Weston-on-the-Green at 3.05 p.m.. This wouldn't have given him time to go home to Chesterton and kill his wife, even if he had found somewhere inconspicuous to park a large grey and white touring coach. Even his mileage and been checked and confirmed – there had been no little detours.

Melvin McRae had still been at the garage, going through his time sheets and paperwork when a uniform had come to inform him of his wife's death and to escort him back home. The bobby who'd picked him up, a 50-year-old veteran whom Hillary remembered from her youth as having a wise head on his shoulders and not being someone easily fooled by good acting or superb lying, had been in no doubt that his shock and grief had been genuine.

'Exit the husband,' Hillary mused out loud, then clamped her mouth shut. Hard. At least in her solitary splendour in her stationery cupboard nobody had heard her talking to herself.

She sighed, and returned to the file.

Anne McRae, according to the path report, had died some time between two and five o'clock in the afternoon. She'd last been seen in the back garden by a neighbour around lunch time. She lived in a small cul-de-sac of council houses, which were probably mostly privately owned by now, and had been there since her marriage, so the whole family was well known. Cause of death was blunt force trauma to the head, but there were no surprises there. The murder weapon, a wooden rolling pin, had been found beside the body, bearing traces of her blood, hair and brain tissue.

Hillary studied the scene-of-crime photos and grimaced. Unfortunately, the surface of the rolling pin wasn't much use for fingerprints, as most were smudged, and the only partial prints they could identify belonged, not surprisingly, to the family members.

DI Andrew Squires was SIO, and from what Hillary could tell over the course of a solid three hours' reading, had done a good and thorough job on the McRae case.

Which was a relief. The last thing she'd wanted to find was a shoddy job.

But Squires had very quickly discovered everything there was to know about the victim, and as far as she could see, had covered every lead doggedly.

Married at just eighteen, Anne had her three children in quick succession, but had retained her youthful looks and figure with regular keep-fit sessions at a local sports hall. From the photographs of her, she had been an attractive blonde woman, five feet four inches tall, with green eyes and a large smile. She seemed to be both popular and well-liked by her neighbours, had a healthy number of friends and outside interests, and volunteered a few hours a week at a charity shop in the nearby market town of Bicester.

Perhaps not surprisingly, given that her husband's job meant that he was away for weeks at a time, Squires had been keenly interested to find out if the lady had indulged in adultery and quickly discovered that indeed she had.

With her own sister's husband no less.

Hillary gave a silent whistle, guessing at once where this was going to go.

And sure enough, Anne's elder sister Debbie, married to one Shane Gregg, quickly became Squires's prime suspect. It didn't take him long to discover that Debbie, elder, plainer, and less popular than her sister, had always resented her younger sibling. She had no alibi for the time of her sister's murder, and, living in Bicester, had easy access. She was resentful and bitter on interview, and subsequently left her husband within weeks of her sister's murder. But the lack of both physical evidence, and witnesses thwarted Squires.

As Debbie had, of course, visited her sister's house on numerous occasions – Christmas and so on – any traces of her in the house hardly proved conclusive one way or another. And although Squires pressed her hard there was no confession. Worse still, although house-to-house went on for weeks afterwards and wide publicity was given in the local press asking for any witnesses to come forward, nobody was ever found who could place Debbie Gregg at her sister's house on the afternoon that she was killed.

Not that Squires concentrated on her to the exclusion of everyone else, Hillary noted with approval. It was very easy for a investigator to become obsessed with a fixed idea, or – the gravest of all sins – start trying to force evidence to fit around his pet theory. But Squires hadn't succumbed to the lure of either of these.

The lover, the victim's brother-in-law Shane Gregg was gone over with a fine-tooth comb as well. But he'd been at work in his office in Summertown all day. The manager of a car sales showroom, he'd had witnesses in the form of his secretary, and several forecourt salesmen who confirmed that he hadn't left the premises all day. He even ate in his office, since he'd been keen to sell a fleet of cars to a Japanese computer outfit that was relocating to Oxford and wanted some top-of-the-range vehicles for its executive staff and didn't want to miss their arrival.

So, exit the lover.

Squires had even made sure that all of the victim's children had been in school all day – they all had – and as far as possible, ruled out any of the neighbours. Nobody seemed to have – or would admit to having – any kind of a grudge against the victim.

Nothing was stolen from the house. A single strand of unidentified hair was found on the victim's body, the DNA of which couldn't be matched to anyone in Anne's life.

According to the husband, the victim's behaviour hadn't changed at all; she was outgoing and busy and happy right up to the end. There'd been no threatening letters or phone call, no sign of a stalker, or a disgruntled ex-boyfriend in the wings.

As far as Squires could ascertain, Shane Gregg had been the victim's only extra-marital affair, and Debbie Gregg had sworn up and down that she didn't know about it.

From his case notes, it was clear that DI Squires didn't believe that, although he was inclined to believe that the husband, Melvin McRae, had had absolutely no idea about his wife's affair.

Here Hillary broke off and sighed. That was the trouble with reading something years old. She wanted to see the husband for herself and assess his reactions with her own two eyes. But of course, all of this had happened two decades ago. The man would have had twenty years to grow calluses over his emotional wounds and become inured to his loss.

She was used to being on the spot and in the moment, but now she felt distanced and wrong-footed. She was seeing this only from Squire's perspective, and although she hadn't, as yet, any reason to doubt him or his conclusions, it wasn't the same as making her own observations and deductions.

She couldn't wait to get out there and start doing stuff herself.

She stretched her arms and arched her back, hearing her bones click. She wasn't used to sitting still for so long, and, needing to stretch her legs, got up and walked across the corridor and poked her head into the other room.

'What do you do for lunch around here?' she asked vaguely, and Sam Pickles held up a tupperware lunch box, from which he extracted a sandwich.

'We nearly always bring our own,' he said, unnecessarily.

'I was just thinking of going up to the canteen, guv,' Jimmy Jessop said diffidently.

Hillary silently blessed him and wondered if he used the term 'guv' simply out of habit, or if he had sensed her unease earlier.

'Has it improved any in the last eighteen months?' she asked with a grin.

'Doubt it, guv,' Jimmy said with grin of his own. 'There's always the Black Bull.'

'Done. Sam, Vivienne?'

'Not me, guv, I've already eaten,' Sam Pickles said at once, picking up on Jimmy's wording without seeming to notice. 'Besides, I've got seven more folders to get through and get back to Sergeant Handley before I can clock off.'

'I'm not here this afternoon,' Vivienne said quickly.

Hillary nodded and went back to her cupboard to get her bag. This part-time thing that her fellow team members took for granted was going to take some getting used to, she mused. And she tried to remember that she wasn't living in the good old days any more. She didn't have hot and cold running constables to order about and see to her every whim now.

'You got a car, Jimmy?' she asked, meeting the older man back in the corridor.

'Yes, guv, but it's nothing much.'

Hillary laughed. 'It's got to be better than my transport. I've only got a push bike at the moment.' Seeing his surprise, she smiled. 'I live on a narrowboat. Moored up in Thrupp. Getting a

31

car is going to have to be a top priority, I can see. You don't know anyone with a reliable second-hand banger for sale do you?'

'Not off hand, guv, but I'll keep my eyes open,' he said obligingly.

Hillary thanked him as they set off for the car park, where it turned out that Jimmy Jessop owned a dark green five-year-old neat hatchback, which he drove with casual but impressive skill.

'Something about the way you walk and talk reminds me of the military, Jimmy,' she said as they headed out onto the main road.

'Yes, guv. I joined the army when I was twenty, and then got turfed out when I was thirty-five. They like their grunts young and fit. I joined the police force straight away. Left when I was sixty.'

Hillary nodded. 'Married?'

'Was, guv. The wife died a few years ago.'

'I'm sorry.'

Jimmy Jessop shrugged. 'That's life, I suppose. Anyway, after retiring with all these plans – me and the missus were going to go on a cruise, get an allotment, you know, all that sort of thing.' He sighed and touched his brakes as a prat in a Mazda cut him up at the traffic lights. 'I suddenly found myself on my own in a nice little flat out by the canal, with nothing to do but twiddle my thumbs all day long. Turns out I can't grow a cabbage to save my life, so I gave up the allotment, and when I saw CRT advertising for us old codgers, I jumped at the chance.'

'Regret it?'

'Not so far, guv,' Jimmy said cautiously and Hillary grinned. As she'd suspected, he was a man after her own heart.

In the pub, Hillary began to pump him gently for information about Pickles and Tyrell and – even more delicately – about Crayle.

'Sam's going to be all right, guv, I reckon,' Jimmy said, over his ploughman's lunch. 'Bright lad, a bit green still, but he's got enough stuffing in him to make a go of it. The little madam's another matter. She's one of these butterfly types, must have had a dozen jobs since leaving school and can't stick at any of them.'

Hillary grinned. 'Not a Vivienne fan then, hmm? I thought those big brown eyes of hers would melt butter at fifty paces.'

Jimmy Jessop grinned and bit into a lump of cheddar. 'I dare say they could at that. But she's been wasting her time trying to melt the super and not having much luck, which has come as a bit of a nasty shock for her. Still, better that than her trying it on with Sam. She'd have that lanky loon in a puddle at her feet before you could spit.'

Hillary nodded. 'What's Crayle like to work for?' she asked neutrally, and trying not to feel too pleased at the fact that Steven Crayle, unlike most men, seemed able to resist temptation when it was flaunted under his nose.

Jimmy Jessop leaned back in his chair and took a sip of his half a shandy. 'Clever, I reckon. And ambitious, of course, that goes without saying. But he knows what he's doing. In spite of his looks, he's been a decent enough thief-taker in his time. Divorced now for a few years, with a couple of kids, nearly fully grown. He's straight with you, I'll say that for him, but I wouldn't want to get on his bad side. All in all, I've worked for worse.'

Hillary snorted. 'Tell me about it.'

Jimmy Jessop said nothing. He knew that she and a certain superintendent had crossed swords in the past, with the Super in question now licking his wounds up in Hull, and his career prospects in tatters.

He looked at her over his drink and thought that here was another one that he wouldn't want to cross either. Not that she wasn't a totally different kettle of fish from Crayle. Steven Crayle would make a great muckety-muck one day, but give him a copper like Hillary Greene any day. He was still looking forward to working with her, and the more he got to know her, the more relaxed he felt.

'So, what case has he given us?' Jessop asked, picking up a

cherry tomato with nicotine-stained fingers and munching it thoughtfully.

'Anne McRae. I'll let you have the file when we get back – you can have Vivienne copy the relevant parts of it and get up to speed.'

'Oh she'll love that,' Jimmy chuckled over his shandy. 'So is it a rape case?'

'No. Murder. I take it they get priority?'

'Yes, guv.'

'Fine. I'm going to be out in the field a bit, re-interviewing witnesses, that sort of thing. I'll need to give Sam some good work experience, but I was hoping you might like to ride shotgun too every now and then.'

Jimmy Jessop's pale eyes glittered. 'Any time, guv,' he said happily.

Hillary nodded. 'Right then. Back to the cupboard – sorry, office. I've got to get some admin stuff sorted out – get my ID and salary sorted. But first thing tomorrow we get cracking. And until I get a car, I was hoping that you wouldn't mind acting as chauffeur.'

Jimmy Jessop didn't mind that in the least.

That night, Tom Warrington worked up a sweat in his dad's garage. Tom had turned the workspace into a reasonable gym, complete with a boxer's sparring bag, a rowing machine, weight-lifting apparatus and various other pieces of equipment, all designed to increase his muscles.

His Dad approved. Although he was proud of his son, and the police uniform that he wore, he and his mother couldn't help but worry about him. It was a bad world out there, and the news was full of coppers who got knifed and shot and beaten up by scum.

He certainly didn't begrudge leaving his car out in the rain so that his only child could keep fit.

He brought a cup of tea out for him now, and stood watching him work. He danced around the boxer's punch bag like that

Muhammad Ali in his heyday. And John Warrington nodded with approval at his son's bulging biceps and the force that went behind each thump. Just let any snivelling little drug dealer take on his Tom and he'd soon regret it all right.

'Here you go, son,' he said, putting the mug down on top of a set of rounded iron weights.

'Thanks, Dad.' Tom stopped sparring to walk over and take the mug, careful to unwrap the protective bandages around his knuckles before picking it up.

'You heard anything about that promotion yet, son?' John asked. 'I'll be glad when you're out of uniform and off the streets.'

Tom Warrington's cat-green eyes narrowed just slightly in impatience. 'I told you, Dad. It isn't easy to break through into the detective squads any more. Cut backs and all. But my sergeant is behind me, and he says I aced the test,' he lied, 'so it's just a question of waiting for some opening to come up. In the mean time, I don't mind walking the beat.'

'OK, son. Don't stay out here too long though. You've got early shift tomorrow, you need to rest.'

Tom nodded, and did in fact begin to wind down his evening workout. Not because he listened to his father, of course. But because he had other stuff to do.

Living at home with your parents at the age of twenty-six was a bit naff, but with house prices like they were, there was no way he could afford a place of his own. And nobody wanted to share a flat with him. For all he gave the impression to his parents that he had a load of friends down at the nick, and was very much 'one of the lads' Tom Warrington was a bit of a loner.

Upstairs, in his bedroom, he turned on his computer and began to google.

He printed off page after page, and photo after photo, and pinned them up on the cork boards around his room. He kept the door to his bedroom locked at all times, of course, telling his parents that he had confidential police files in there, and had to be careful. In reality, these only existed in his fantasies.

Now he pinned up a 6-year-old photograph taken from an old article in the *Oxford Times*.

In it, Hillary Greene was receiving her medal for gallantry.

Tom Warrington sat back in his swivel chair and slowly looked around the room. Images of Hillary Greene looked back at him. Just that afternoon he'd volunteered for a stint in the ever-unpopular admin department, where he hoped he'd be able to photocopy her personnel file. That would be a real coup.

Until then, he was patiently and painstakingly building up his own dossier on her.

So far, he'd liked all that he'd found out about her. Except for the husband, of course. Finding out all about that bent, no-good tosser had been like discovering an ugly worm in an otherwise perfect apple. His memory niggled away at Tom, making him doubt her, and he hated that.

He so *didn't* want to doubt her. This time he wanted perfection. He couldn't bear another disappointment, like all the others.

And she was so close to being perfect. Choosing an older woman had been a really clever move on his part.

She was beautiful.

Experienced.

Clever.

Accomplished. When he'd found out about her degree in English Literature from Oxford it had made him almost glow with pride.

Not only was she all that, but she was like a celebrity back at HQ. Everyone was talking about her return.

She only had the one thing blotting her otherwise perfect image.

A bad marriage. No, worse than bad – a catastrophic marriage.

It was a pity that Ronnie Greene was already dead, Tom thought, his green eyes glittering with frustration.

He'd rather have liked to have been able to kill him himself.

CHAPTER THREE

Jimmy Jessop pulled off the main Oxford to Banbury road when he saw the signpost for Thrupp up ahead and found himself on a narrow lane, leading to what seemed to him to be little more than a cluster of cottages. Although he'd lived in Kidlington itself for several years now, he'd never had reason to visit the tiny satellite community, based on the Oxford canal.

It looked pretty and peaceful, almost out of time with the modern world just a few moments away and he understood at once why someone, faced with the stresses and pressures of a demanding job, would want to live here.

He parked on the grass verge, allowing room for cars to pass, and wandered down to the canal. On an overcast March morning, it looked grey-green and uninviting, although some rushes were starting to spring verdantly at the edges, promising beauty to come and a curious moorhen drifted by, eyeing him warily.

Most of the narrowboats that were moored along the towpath for as far as he could see were either brightly coloured or boasted traditional 'canal art' – painted panels of crudely cheerful scenes, mostly floral, in vibrant reds, greens, blues and yellows. But one narrowboat, moored further down, was a different proposition, being painted predominantly in a soft blue-grey, with a black-painted roof and attractive white and gold trim. As he approached it, he could see that the side panels on this boat had simple, well-executed paintings that all depicted herons. A quick glance at the name on the pointed end confirmed that this was indeed the 'Mollern', his new guv'nor's boat.

He stood beside it, not sure what to do next. A total landlubber, he was not sure of the protocol. Did he shout, 'Ahoy there' like someone from a pirate movie? Jimmy didn't much see himself as Johnny Depp. On the other hand, he didn't fancy stepping onto the boat at all without permission. And the wide hinged door allowing entrance looked to be made of metal, and he didn't fancy rapping his knuckles on it.

Instead he bent down a bit, and said loudly into the nearest window, 'Morning, ma'am.'

A movement at one of the curtains caught his eye, and Hillary's face briefly appeared, then withdrew. A moment later she climbed out of the back, and slipped the padlock around the door. She was dressed in a pencil-line black skirt with a matching black jacket and an apricot coloured blouse. She looked both smart and professional but also competent and comfortable. She smiled a welcome, and stepped neatly off the boat and onto the gravelled towpath.

As they walked to his car, Jimmy brought her up to date on what he'd discovered about the original inquiry's main suspect so far.

'Debbie Gregg, now aged sixty-two, and divorced,' Jimmy recited from memory, although her dossier was locked up in the boot of his car, and could be consulted before they started the interview if need be. 'Her husband, Shane Gregg died in an RTA three years after the divorce – no suspicious circs – and she's remained unmarried since. She moved from the former family home to a place in Brackley. Nothing known against her since.'

In other words, Hillary mused, she had no criminal record, and hadn't done anything to bring herself to the attention of the police since her sister's murder.

'She have a sheet before the killing?' she asked curiously.

'No, guv.'

They reached the car and Jimmy retrieved the dossier and gave it to her before getting behind the wheel. As he'd half-expected, she spent the travel time to the Northamptonshire market town where Debbie Gregg now lived reading everything that Squire's team had been able to get on her.

When they finally pulled up outside a small semi-detached council house on a large estate, Hillary repressed a small sigh of satisfaction. So, the hunt was on. There was no denying it – she'd missed all of this: The comradeship she was beginning to build up with Jimmy; the sense of purpose to be gained in bringing some kind of closure, if not justice, to that most feared of all human sins – homicide, talking to witnesses, ferreting out the truth, putting the pieces together, and seeing if she could get a clear picture of what had actually happened the day that Anne McRae had lost her life.

It felt damned good to be back!

She climbed out and glanced around. The estate was neat and tidy, with a few middle-range cars parked in the driveways, and most of the gardens were colourful and well tended. It wasn't exactly luxury living, but it was hardly a high-rise in a slum either.

'She didn't do too badly for herself, considering,' Hillary said thoughtfully. She knew only too well how a close brush with murder could tarnish and destroy lives for years afterwards. The family of murder victims never got over it, and even those who were suspected of being the instigator of a crime could feel the effects rippling down through the years. Jobs that were never offered when their past came to light; offended neighbours who made their feelings all too clear. A lot of people so tainted took to drink, or became bitter and antisocial. And a good proportion of them ended up addicted to drugs, or out on the street. Or walking them, looking for punters.

It would be interesting to see how Debbie Gregg had fared.

'Somebody's in at any rate, guv,' Jimmy said, motioning towards the house. 'I just saw the curtains move.'

Hillary nodded, and they walked up to the gate. Jimmy lifted the latch and let her go through first. The courtesy was automatic for him, and Hillary accepted it as automatically. She rang the doorbell and waited. A moment later, it was opened cautiously a bare inch or so and a woman looked out at them from around the door chain.

'Yes?'

Hillary held up her ID card. Once it would have been a full police badge, with the words Detective Inspector on it. Now it was a white laminated card, with her picture and some sort of red-motif that identified her as a civilian consultant with the Thames Valley Police Service.

'Hello, Mrs Gregg is it? I'm Hillary Greene. I'm working with the Thames Valley Police. We're looking again into your sister's case, and I wondered if we could have a word? This is my colleague, James Jessop.'

The door closed in their faces, and for a moment, Hillary wondered if it was going to open again. And if it didn't, she'd have no other recourse but to turn around and go somewhere else. She now had no authority to demand entrance, nor did she have the authority to take someone in for questioning. Or even arrest them. For that, she'd need Steven Crayle.

Then came the slither of the chain and the door opened reluctantly.

Hillary wasn't surprised that the woman was so security conscious. Her sister had been brutally killed in the safety of her own home, and whether or not this woman was responsible for it, the knowledge that no one was safe, anywhere, anytime, would have been a lesson well learned.

'It's been so long since I had any of you lot on my doorstep,' Debbie Gregg said, standing aside to let them pass.

She was about Hillary's height, but three stones heavier, with the sort of curly blonde hair that spoke of perms and a cheap colouring agent. She wore full make-up but only a turquoise jogging outfit that had never been used for its original purpose. On her feet were those feathery kind of heel-less mules that

Hillary had always thought were designed to trip you up, rather than keep your feet warm.

'Better come into the living room then, I suppose,' Debbie said, ushering them into a small but comfortable room. A football magazine under a plain wooden coffee table told Hillary that she was probably living with a man, as did a pair of distinctly masculine slippers she spotted, resting under a recliner chair that faced a large wide-screen plasma TV.

'Take a seat,' Debbie made no offer to make them tea, but once they were both seated, side-by-side on a dark brown leather settee, took a chair opposite them. She gazed at them steadily out of pale, rather bulging blue eyes. 'So, what do you want then?'

Hillary smiled. The victim's sister was obviously somebody who liked to come straight to the point.

'Well, Mrs Gregg, as you may or may not be aware, all unsolved cases are never officially closed, especially serious ones, like your sister's. Every now and then, what with the technical advances being made and so on, the police service periodically re-evaluates certain cases.'

'And Anne's is one of them. Yeah, I get it. But that card you showed me said you was a consultant. Not a proper copper then?'

So, she'd actually read the card and thought about what it said, and what it meant, Hillary realized instantly. Not many people did that. It meant that Debbie, for all her outward appearance, was a shrewd and cautious operator.

She'd have to bear that in mind.

'I used to be a full DI before I took early retirement. And James here was a sergeant.'

Debbie nodded. 'I get it. They can't spare the full-time coppers, who've got enough on their plate trying to solve crimes that happened yesterday. So they've put the old war-horses onto it. Makes sense I suppose.'

'I can assure you, Mrs Gregg, that both myself and my team

will do our best by your sister,' Hillary said quietly. And meant it. If the other woman took that as a threat, it certainly didn't register on her plump, pleasant face.

Debbie smiled grimly. 'By that, you mean that you're going to try and fit me up for it every bit as hard as that other bastard did. Squires.'

Hillary shook her head. 'Nobody "fits up" anybody, Mrs Gregg, I can assure you. That's only in fiction and on the telly.'

'Yeah, right,' she snorted. 'You're not going to convince me that that bloke DI Squires didn't do his best to get me had up for our Anne's murder. I bet it's all written down in his notes somewhere. I could tell what he was thinking, you know, he didn't make no secret of it. And I'm not stupid. He kept bringing me in for questioning, pestering the life out of me, even though I kept telling him and telling him I didn't do it. He kept on and on at the neighbours and our friends, until even they began to have a go at me for it. As if it was my fault!'

Her voice, which had been rising steadily in volume, suddenly fell off, as she paused to take a deep breath.

Hillary said nothing, waiting for the tirade to continue. A lot of truth came out in anger, and she was more than ready to be the butt of Debbie's bile if it meant she let slip anything interesting.

Or incriminating.

But the silence lengthened, and the older woman took a few deep breaths, obviously making the effort to regain control of herself. And succeeded.

'I can't tell you anything that I didn't tell Squires at the time,' she finally said, her voice almost defeated now. 'I don't know who killed her. It wasn't me, and it wasn't Shane. I wasn't there that day she died, and no prodding and poking about now is going to prove otherwise. So go ahead, and do your worst.'

Hillary nodded. 'Tell me about her,' she said softly, making the older woman blink in surprise. If she was expecting a hardheaded interview as she had probably endured many times before, she was in for a surprise.

Hillary had her own approach for belligerent-cum-wary witnesses like this.

'D'yah what?'

'Your sister Anne. What was she like?'

Debbie shrugged. 'She was my sister,' she said simply. 'There were four of us at home then. Don the oldest – he's dead now. Then me, then Mark, and then Anne. She was the baby of the bunch.'

'Ah. And spoilt to bits, I bet,' Hillary said knowingly.

''Course she was. Apple of Dad's eye. And she was so pretty, Mum used to love dressing her up in dresses and doing her hair in ribbons and whatnot. Funny, because when she got older....' Debbie rolled her eyes. 'Went punk she did.' And she giggled. It sounded strangely girlish coming from a woman in her sixth decade.

'She had the best of everything then?' Hillary persisted, keeping her firmly on track.

Debbie's blue eyes shot back to Hillary's face with a knowing gleam. 'You trying to get me to say that I resented her, like? That I was always jealous of her and so secretly wanted to do her in? Just like that bastard Squires said.'

'No, not at all. You can be exasperated with someone and still love and care for them,' Hillary said soothingly. 'That's what families are all about, isn't it? Or at least, mine is.'

Debbie took another hard, long breath, then nodded grudgingly. 'True enough, I suppose.'

'Tell me about her marriage. To Melvin, isn't it? Were they happy together?' Hillary kept any trace of a challenge out of her voice, and the other woman started to relax.

'Oh yeah. Well, I always thought so, anyway. Melvin had a good job, and he weren't bad looking. She had the kids, never seemed to want for anything. Why shouldn't she be happy?' Debbie asked, and there was an edge of bitterness now that was unmistakable. 'Anyone else would have been. But she had to have more, didn't she?'

'It hurt, didn't it,' Hillary said softly. 'When you found out about her and Shane – your own husband. Isn't that the ultimate betrayal? The one we're all scared of? That someone we love will go behind our back with someone else we love and trust?'

Debbie smiled and shook her head. 'At it again, huh? But I'm telling you, like I told Squires before. I didn't know about it, did I? Not until she was dead, and you lot dug it all up. They kept it very quiet, they did. Must have been very crafty about it, because I hadn't got a bloody clue, had I? How thick am I?'

'It's nothing to be ashamed of, you know,' Hillary said quietly, leaning forward on her seat to create the illusion of sympathy. 'If your husband cheats on you, especially with your own little sister, you are allowed to feel hurt and betrayed and angry. I know I would.'

Jimmy, who so far hadn't said a word, sat and watched and marvelled. He knew Hillary Greene's own husband had shagged anything that took his eye, and yet nobody would ever guess it from the way she was handling this witness. None of her own personal history showed.

He'd heard before that Hillary was a marvel with witnesses and now he could see the magic working for himself. It was as if Debbie Gregg was being prised open like a walnut, and she was already beginning to talk freely.

'Well, of course it hurt. I'm only human, ain't I? But even if I had known about it, it doesn't mean to say that I'd have hit the poor cow upside the head with her own rolling pin and killed her, does it?'

'Nobody has said you did.'

'Squires thought so!'

'I'm not Detective Inspector Squires,' Hillary said firmly, holding the other's woman's eye. 'And your sister's case is now my case, not his. You can tell me anything you like, and I won't judge you. It's not my job to do that. Only to try and find out who killed Anne.'

Hillary let that sit for just the right amount of time, and then added softly 'You'd like to see Anne's killer caught, wouldn't you?'

Debbie sighed, her eyes wandering around the room restlessly. 'It's been twenty years,' she said flatly.

Hillary nodded. For the first time, she was avoiding giving an answer. And that was very interesting in itself. Why not come flat out on one side of the fence or the other? If she was guilty, then a vehement affirmation that of course she wanted the killer to be caught must have sounded like a good way to go. And if she was innocent, but still full of self-pity and defiance, then why not go the other way, and sneer and say that she couldn't care less one way or the other?

But this sudden caution on the part of the witness set Hillary's radar off with a loud ping.

And not knowing what was behind it, made knowing how to proceed a bit tricky. When in doubt, Hillary had found from past experience that it was best to circle around, and come up with a different angle. She could always ask the question again another time.

'It gets easier to cope with, after such a long time, is that it?'

Debbie shrugged. 'It never goes away, but it gets easier, yeah. At first, I knew that everyone was looking at me and pointing the finger. Word gets around, everyone knew the cops kept pulling me in. "No smoke without fire" that's what they were all thinking. It's why I had to move away. Came to this place. It got easier then. And people forget, mostly. Oh, they know around here that I had a sister murdered – you can't keep that a secret for long. And every now and then I catch one or two of them looking at me funny. But mostly nobody bothers me. And I've got Colin now. That helps.'

'Your fellah?' Hillary prompted. 'Known him long?' Could her husband not have been the only one in their marriage that was playing around?

'Yeah. Colin works up at that racing car place. In maintenance, like. We've been together six years now.'

Hillary nodded. So he hadn't been in the picture when Anne McRae was murdered then. Scratch Colin.

'That's nice. Your husband Shane died in a car crash, that right?' she changed the subject abruptly. Sometimes a sudden switch could startle a straight and condemning answer out of the unwary.

Debbie's red-painted lips twisted into a sneer. 'Drunk,' she confirmed flatly.

'Oh. Was that as a result of what happened to Anne, or was he always a bit …' she pantomimed lifting a glass to her lips and Debbie sighed.

'No. It was Anne all right. Give the devil his due, he wasn't a boozer before it all happened. But it sent him right off the rails. And it was the end between us, of course. I'm just glad we didn't have no kids. That would really have done it.'

'And was not having kids a bit of an issue?' she probed delicately. And when Debbie frowned at her, obviously not understanding her meaning, added softly, 'do you think he really wanted kids? Was that why he strayed – with Anne? Or was he always a bit of ladies' man?'

Debbie shrugged. 'Who knows? He swore up and down at the time that Anne was the first. But by then I didn't trust him. Why should I believe him?'

'And why do you think Anne let it go on?' Hillary asked, genuinely curious now. 'Was she bored with Melvin, did she secretly want to get caught, and use it as an excuse for a divorce? Or was she just a bit of a thrill seeker? Some people aren't happy unless they're living life on the edge.'

'Anne was used to winding men around her little finger, that's all,' Debbie said angrily. 'She wasn't happy unless someone was paying attention to her, admiring her, listening to her, doing her bidding. She used to run that family of hers as if she was a sergeant major in the army. She had Melvin well trained, I can tell you that. I bet he never strayed – he wouldn't dare! And even the kids jumped to it when she said. There was only room for one person in the spotlight, and that was Anne.'

Hillary nodded. It was always fascinating to have a picture of the victim slowly take shape. From crime-scene photographs of a dead woman, a living, breathing human being was gradually taking shape, with all of her foibles, weaknesses and secrets being dragged into the light.

'She must have made enemies then. A woman like that,' Hillary said softly.

Beside her, Jimmy almost smiled. Wily as a fox, this new guv'nor of his, no two ways about it. It was a pleasure to watch her work.

'You'd think so, wouldn't you?' Debbie said, her face twisting into a wry grimace. 'But for all that, she could charm the birds out of the trees, as Dad used to say.' She laughed bitterly. 'More likely she just learned that you could catch more flies with honey. She was like that. Always got what she wanted, but made you feel like *she* was the one doing *you* the favour. Know what I mean?'

Hillary did. 'Yes, all the reports in her file say she was popular with neighbours and the like.'

'That was Anne. Mind you, she had her good points too. You gotta be fair.'

'Working at the charity shop, you mean?'

'What? Oh that, yeah. No, I wasn't thinking of that so much,' Debbie mused with a sigh. 'She only did that because she was bored, and it got her out of the house. No, I just meant that she was a good mum, for instance. She might have kept a sharp eye out on her kids, but they'd always feel safe and cared for, you know? And she'd help you out if she could, if you had any problems, like. She didn't begrudge giving you her time or making an effort if you needed it. Once, when I had flu, she practically nursed me through it for the first three days and nights.'

Again her eyes wandered restlessly around the room. 'It's still hard to believe she's gone. Even now I sort of half-expect to hear her voice on the phone when it rings, or to see her come walking through the door.'

It wasn't the first time Hillary had heard family members say something similar about a lost loved one.

'I'm sorry,' she said quietly.

Debbie's eyes turned her way again. 'S'all right. Like I said, it's been twenty years.'

'And you really have no idea who killed her?'

'No, I really don't.'

'You never got any feeling that something wasn't right? When was the last time you saw her?'

'The weekend before she died. We went over there for Sunday lunch. And she seemed much the same as ever.'

'She wasn't upset, or depressed, or angry about anything?'

'No, not so's you'd notice. Melvin was abroad, but then he was always abroad, driving that coach of his here and there. I think it used to nark her that he was always "on holiday" when she was stuck back at home. I tried to tell her, it wasn't as if he was really on holiday, was it? He was working, driving all them hours. I think she resented him living in hotels and seeing all them foreign sights. But like I said to her, he went to the same spots time after time. He always said it just got plain boring after a while.'

'But apart from that? She wasn't acting oddly, or upset by anything?'

'No, just the usual niggles. Family life, all that. I think her Peter was in a snit, because he kept having a dig about something, but Anne just ignored him. And Jenny was playing up merry hell about not getting some sort of game that she'd really wanted for her birthday. Anne finally got narked with her and told her that if she didn't pack it in, she wouldn't be getting it for Christmas either. But nothing like what you're thinking. I didn't get the impression she was afraid that some mad axe-man was out to get her or anything.'

Hillary nodded. 'And she never talked to you about any men in her life?'

Debbie snorted with sudden laughter. 'Well, she wouldn't,

would she? Seeing as it was my husband that was the man in her life at the time.'

With a wry smile, Hillary had to concede that she had a point.

'So, what do you think?' Hillary asked, as they returned to the car a little while later. Hillary had taken her through that day again, when her sister had died, but Debbie Gregg had nothing new to add. She'd been at home with no witnesses to confirm it. She had nothing new or different to say, and her responses were almost word-for-word what she'd said to DI Andrew Squires, twenty years ago. But there was nothing necessarily suspicious about that. It might smack of rehearsal, but then again, she'd probably said the same thing over and over so many times, that now it was stuck in her head like a groove in a vinyl record.

Jimmy slid in behind the wheel and shrugged. 'Hard to say, guv. She didn't seem to be all cut up, but like she said, it's been twenty years. She seemed straightforward enough, but then, more often than not, they do, don't they?'

'Killers?'

'Right.'

'So you agree with Squires? You think she did it, but there just wasn't the evidence there to prove it?'

Jimmy settled himself more comfortably behind the wheel and shrugged. He was too canny to commit himself so soon. Besides, he had a feeling that Hillary liked to keep an open mind about things, and would probably prefer it if her team did the same. Which was fine by him. 'It's hard to say, guv. It's early days yet.'

'A pity the husband's dead,' Hillary agreed. 'I would have liked to have heard about the affair from Shane Gregg's point of view. Would he have given us a similar picture of our victim, I wonder?'

'I doubt it, guv. In my experience, a man tends to look on the woman he's with through rose-tinted glasses. Well. For a while, at any rate,' he added phlegmatically.

Hillary grinned.

'So where to now, guv?'

'I'd like to go and take a look at the house where she died. I know the family don't still live there, but it won't hurt to get a feel for the place.'

'Right, guv. To Chesterton then.'

Melvin McRae had not lived in Chesterton for nearly twenty years. After burying his wife and the mother of his three children, he'd put the house up for sale and moved to a neat little semi, not far from St Edburg's Church in the nearby town of Bicester.

He was still living there that morning, when the letter plopped through his letterbox.

He'd retired from driving the coach two years ago, but had taken a part-time job in a newsagents, more out of loneliness than out of any need for money. His second wife, Shirley, worked full time as a hairdresser in the unisex salon a few shops down, and every lunch time, they'd meet up for a bun in Nash's. They'd paid off the mortgage on their house, ran a reliable second-hand car, and if they didn't eat steak and caviar every night, had no complaints. A divorced woman with two grown kids when they first met, he and his wife lived what most people would describe as a mundane, uninteresting life, but it suited them both.

That morning had begun as every other morning had, with Melvin rising first and making tea and toast, the appetizing smell of browning bread being enough to bring Shirley down eventually. He'd read the paper after she'd left for work, and had been working on the less-than-taxing crossword puzzle in a best-selling tabloid when he'd heard the postman.

And along with the usual bills, guff and advertising material, he had produced an official-looking long white envelope bearing the Thames Valley Police Service logo in one corner.

Now Melvin McRae sat at the kitchen table, the remnants of his breakfast still on the countertop by the sink, and read the piece of paper in his hands for a second time. Again, the words seemed to swim in and out of focus and he forced himself to read it yet again. It was that hard to take in.

But they were looking into Anne's death again.

Eventually, with hands that shook just slightly, he let the single page rest on his knee.

He looked around the kitchen, as if seeking help, but the McRaes didn't have even a cat to relieve the sudden emptiness of the house or offer comfort.

'Why now?' Melvin heard himself ask out loud, and shook his head.

But the question hung there, ominous, vibrating in the air of the still kitchen.

Had they found new evidence?

Had a witness come forward after all this time?

Had someone confessed? No, that wasn't possible. He was being stupid.

The letter was frustratingly sparing in its details. It simply informed him that the murder of his wife, Anne McRae had been reopened and was being actively investigated by the CRT. And that he could expect to be contacted by a civilian consultant to the police in the near future.

He got up on legs that felt just a little shaky and walked to the sink to refill the kettle. He didn't really want another cup of tea, but he wanted to do something with his hands.

He stared out over the small neat garden as the kettle began to drone. A chaffinch was on the bird table eating some seeds Shirley had put out yesterday.

Anne.

It had been years now since he'd thought about her – truly thought about her. At first, she'd been with him every moment of every day. And all the baggage that she brought with her. The horror of that moment when he'd been told she was dead. Killed. Murdered. The shame and humiliation when he found out about her and Shane. Memories of the funeral, the publicity, the questioning, the kids, bemused and bewildered and crying for their mum.

The kids.

'Oh hell, no,' Melvin McRae said softly, and sitting down abruptly at the table again, he began to cry.

Chesterton was a fairly large village, and sprawled itself without any real cohesion across flat farming land. For ten minutes, Hillary Greene and Jimmy Jessop drove around it, trying to get their bearings.

'I reckon it must be in one of these cul-de-sacs, guv,' Jimmy finally said, pulling back onto the main street. 'I didn't see any street signs back there for Cherry Tree Crescent, did you?'

'No, but wasn't there a blind turn-off back up here a bit. Yes, just here, see it? Perhaps this is it.'

A few moments later they were parked up at the end of a cul-de-sac that did indeed proclaim itself to be Cherry Tree Crescent and climbed out of the car. There were about fourteen small houses in number, all detached but set close together in a sweeping semi-circle around a central grassed area that did in fact, boast three cherry trees.

The houses had probably been considered modest affairs back in the 1990s, but would probably now sell for a sum that would have made Anne McRae's eyes shine with delight.

'Nice enough area,' Jimmy said, glancing around, as a pair of amorous robins flitted past them.

'Yes. What number were they?'

'Eleven. That one there.' Jimmy pointed.

Number eleven looked like all the others: yellow-bricked, grey-tiled and double-glazed. A small front garden held host to a forsythia bush that was just beginning to flower. 'They'd have back gardens stretching back almost to the road, I reckon,' Hillary said, remembering from the file that a neighbour had seen their murder victim working in the back garden on the afternoon of her death.

'Don't suppose there's any way around to the back?' she asked, setting off for the end house. But they were in luck, for a narrow pavement did in fact circumnavigate the area. A near twenty-foot tall wooden fence screened the houses from the road beyond, so no one driving by could see into the windows. At the rear of the houses, most of the gardens were also protected from prying eyes by wooden fences, but she could imagine that the linear boundaries were probably a bit less stark. Privet hedges maybe, or lattice-work festooned with climbers. It would have been easy for neighbours to chat across them, and see one another from their own windows.

They went all the way around and back out to the front again. On the other side of Cherry Tree Crescent was a scrubby-looking field being cropped now by some placidly grazing sheep.

'Not much passing foot-traffic,' she said flatly. 'No wonder DI Squires had so much trouble finding witnesses. Unless you had business here, nobody had any reason to be passing by. And the houses can't be seen from the road.'

Jimmy nodded. 'Doesn't look the sort of place you'd expect a young mother to be coshed to death, does it?'

'No,' Hillary said thoughtfully. 'It doesn't.'

'You're thinking it's unlikely to be a random thing, guv?' Jimmy guessed.

'Yes,' she agreed flatly. She and Jimmy both knew that a fair number of young women who were murdered were simply in the wrong place at the wrong time. That they were unlucky enough to catch the attention of a mental patient tossed out of an asylum and onto the non-existent mercies of the care-in-the-community. Or fit the hit-list of some psychopathic misogynist who plucked his victims at random. But whoever had killed Anne McRae had had to come to this place, come to her own home, to kill her.

'She knew him. Or her,' Hillary said softly. 'She had to have done. This can't have been a random killing by a passing stranger.'

Jimmy nodded. 'We're looking at nearest and dearest then?'

Hillary sighed. 'But not necessarily that near, or that dear. Don't forget, she felt safe here. If someone she only knew casually, or in passing, called at her door, she'd probably have invited them in without thinking about it. Unless she had reason to be afraid of them, and then she might try and shut the door in their face. But forensics found no sign of a struggle, right?'

'Right, guv. She was just standing at the table, making a fruit pie. Someone just grabbed the rolling pin off the table and bashed her. So it looks as if she was taken by surprise.'

Hillary sighed.

'Seen enough, guv?'

'Yeah. Back to the office.'

After her two unexpected visitors had left, Debbie Gregg sat in thought for a while, then got up, got changed, and left the house. She didn't have far to drive to reach Banbury, but finding a parking spot that she didn't have to pay for was the usual hassle. As it was, she had to walk nearly a quarter of a mile to her destination.

The ugly red-brick building that she walked to housed more than fifty poky flats, and depressed her instantly. The street lamps were all broken, dog shit lined the sparse grass verges, and the whole place stank of unemployment, despair and resentment.

She pushed open the lobby door, which was supposed to be kept locked but never was, and trudged wearily up three flights of steps that reeked of urine.

She knew better than to try the lift.

Once she reached her destination, she rang the bell and waited. Eventually, the door was opened. The woman who looked back at her did so without any sign of notable enthusiasm.

'Hello, Auntie Debbie.'

Debbie Gregg smiled and stepped inside. Having someone in

your home who was generally believed to have got away with murder, would be enough to cause alarm to most people.

But Lucy McRae, it had to be said, didn't look particularly frightened.

CHAPTER FOUR

' I haven't seen you in ages,' Lucy said, watching her aunt pace around the tiny living room, whilst she herself made some mugs of tea. Her kitchenette area boasted little more than a stove and a fridge tucked into one corner, and both appliances were filthy. A tiny sink and a breakfast stool pushed up against a solitary work surface comprised the rest of the less than lovely dining area.

At the age of thirty-three, Lucy had never learned to love housework. She loved fine clothes, and jewellery and expensive perfume and champagne and foreign holidays. And, in the past, had occasionally managed to indulge in them all – though sadly, not all at once. The thing was, they usually came with the men who paid for them all, and nowadays, men were getting less and less easy to come by. Lucy still kept her figure by religiously exercising, and any precious pennies she earned went on face creams, make-up and flattering clothes, all of which she needed to lure the next male. Spending money on detergent was a waste of time as far as she was concerned.

'No. Well, we're not really a family that keeps in touch much, are we?' Debbie said, moving aside a fashion magazine and sitting down in a cheap velour armchair, made even shinier by age. 'I keep expecting to get a wedding invitation though, from either you or Jenny. Don't want to settle down, is that it?'

Lucy smiled and poured hot water over the tea bags in badly chipped mugs. She had long blonde hair that she carefully looked after and large green eyes – her best feature. But she was wise to take such good care of herself, for already the slight signs of ageing were beginning to creep in: the odd crow's foot here; the slight thickening in her thighs that portended the dreaded cellulite. Trust Aunt Debbie to pick up on her insecurities with a question about matrimony.

'I wouldn't mind getting married,' she said glibly. If he had a few million in the bank, she added silently. And didn't want kids.

Lucy was never going to have kids. Ever. The thought made her shudder.

'I'm surprised you're still here. Weren't you moving out to somewhere in Cropredy, the last letter I had from you?' Debbie said, reluctant, now that she was here, to actually broach the reason for her visit.

'I did. I mean I was. Gerry, the bloke I was going to live with, died,' Lucy said flatly.

Well, he overdosed, to be more accurate, but she wasn't about to say so. It still made her angry whenever she thought about Gerry. Middle-aged, divorced, with a good job in real estate, he was going to be her meal ticket for life. He had a nice house in a swanky village, a big car, and with two grown kids, didn't want any more. He'd been ideal. But the silly bugger obviously didn't know how to handle the coke.

'Oh luv, I'm so sorry,' Debbie said, then added, 'ta,' as her niece handed her the mug of tea.

Lucy, dressed in tight-fitting black leggings and a spangly blue top, sat down opposite her aunt and took a sip from her own mug, careful to avoid the chips. The last thing she needed was a cut lip.

'So. How's things with you and … er …' she sought in vain for the name of her aunt's fellah, and let her voice trail off.

'Colin. Col.'

'Right.'

'Fine. He's fine. How's Jenny and Peter? I get Christmas cards from Peter, but I haven't heard from Jenny in years.'

'They're doing all right. Well, Peter is, any way. You know Pete – fall in the proverbial brown stuff and he'd come up smelling of clover. But Jenny,' she put her hand in the air, palm flat down, and waved it from side to side in a gesture of doubt, 'not so much. She's made some bad choices in life, I can tell you.' Lucy laughed bitterly and looked around, then grimaced. 'I mean, I might have made a few corkers in my time too, but nothing compared to hers. But you know Jenny. She can't be told anything.'

Debbie nodded, then sighed, put her cup down on a ring-stained bit of cheap pine, and said, 'Look, love, the reason I'm here. I just had a visit from two coppers.'

Lucy blinked. For a moment, she couldn't understand why she thought her aunt could possibly think that she'd be interested. What was up? Been caught shop-lifting or something, had she? Or had the man she was shacked up with been found out carting things off from the back of a lorry?

And then, at the same moment that she understood, Debbie said, 'It's your mum's case. They're looking into it again.'

Lucy opened her mouth, seemed about to say something, then closed it again. Finally she took a sip of her tea. 'Oh. Well, I suppose it's about time. Not that they're likely to find out who did it after all this time, are they?'

Debbie met her niece's green eyes, so like her mother's, and sighed. 'No. I suppose not.'

For a few moments, the two women drank in silence, Debbie fiddling with her chipped mug and glancing everywhere around the room, except at her niece.

Finally, she nerved up the courage to speak. 'You're so like your mum in many ways, our Luce. You've got her pretty looks, and you've got her ways too. She was clever, our Anne, but she never made the most of it.' She took a quick look around the sorry flat, and said grimly, 'and you're just the same. Why haven't you got a job? You could work in an office, you're good on a computer. All you youngsters seem to be, these days.'

Lucy laughed. 'I don't like working, Aunt Debbie, you know

that. Nine to five, same thing, day in, day out, kow-towing to a boss, waiting for a bus, fetching coffees for twits with pimples and BO who want to grope you. No thank you.'

'No, you want it all handed to you on a plate I suppose, just like Anne.'

Lucy's eyes narrowed dangerously. She didn't like being lectured. Or having her lifestyle choices questioned. So she was on a downer at the moment, reduced to this tatty flat, but soon she'd be on the up again. And luckily, she knew just how to teach her aunt to keep her opinions to herself.

'So the police are looking at you again for it, are they, Auntie? That must be a bit of a pain. I bet you thought all of that was behind you, too?'

Debbie paled slightly and bent her curly blonde head defensively a little further over her steaming mug. 'I don't like it, that's all,' she said quietly. 'They'll be raking it all up again, you'll see. They should just leave it alone.' Then she lifted her head and looked at her niece sharply. 'You'll have to be careful, our Luce. Promise me you will.'

Lucy laughed grimly. 'Aunt Debbie, it's not me who has anything to worry about. We all know that.'

Debbie swallowed a mouthful of tea, but wondered. Was Lucy right?

She didn't know, that was the trouble. She didn't know anything for sure.

But she had to do something. Lucy didn't understand how dangerous it was not to let sleeping dogs lie. And that woman copper who'd come to her house – Debbie had recognized her all right. Or rather, she recognized her type. She was clever, that Greene woman. And persistent. And good at her job – Debbie would have bet her house and last shilling on that. She'd keep on digging and upsetting things, and hurting everyone with her questions about Anne.

Bloody Anne. Twenty years dead, and still causing everyone grief.

No, Debbie knew she'd have to do something to keep the coppers happy. Toss that Greene woman some sort of bone, give her something to chew over. She'd have to think about it.

In the meantime, she could only hope that her niece didn't do anything stupid.

Or Melvin either, for that matter.

Back at HQ, Hillary Greene reached for the phone in her so-called office, and dialled one of the numbers from the new updated McRae folder.

Sam and Vivienne had done a good job on it, chasing up all the information they could and accumulating new data. In twenty years a lot could change, and had. Witnesses died or moved away, and new addresses and phone numbers had to be found. People changed jobs, their circumstances altered. Melvin McRae, for instance, had moved and remarried.

But the youngsters had obviously worked hard – even Vivienne had done her fair share.

And first on the list was Melvin McRae's latest telephone number. She dialled it, but it rang for so long that she almost gave up, before it was at last answered.

'Yes?'

The voice was male and sounded distracted.

'Mr McRae? Melvin McRae?'

'Yes.'

'This is Hillary Greene, sir. I'm a consultant with the Crime Review Team, at Thames Valley Police Headquarters in Kidlington. You may have received a letter in the post, concerning you wife's – that is Anne McRae's – case? I wanted to know when would be a convenient time for us to meet.'

In his home, Melvin McRae sat down suddenly. He was in his living room, and through the window he could see the square tower of the nearby church. He swallowed hard.

Bloody hell, that was quick. He'd only just got the letter that morning. He thought he'd have more time. A lot more time.

Weeks, or at the very least, days. He wasn't ready for this.

'Oh, yes, right. Well, whenever you like really. But look, I don't want the kids upset, yeah? Do you have to talk to them as well? They were only nippers when their mum died.'

Hillary leaned back in her chair, reaching for her diary. 'I understand that, sir. We'll have to speak to them, of course, but I don't think we'll have to take up too much of their time.' And they weren't nippers any more she thought, but then, she fully understood that to their father they'd always be his children and in need of protection. Even when they were in their sixties and he was a doddering ninety-something.

Melvin sighed heavily. 'How about tomorrow then?'

'Fine. What time?'

They agreed on a time late the next afternoon, and Hillary hung up. She sat there for a few moments, wondering about Melvin.

Whenever someone was murdered, the spouse was always looked at first. It was inevitable. Nearly all of those not killed by strangers, were killed by family members, lovers, or close friends. And normally someone with a rock-solid alibi made Hillary look very closely indeed.

But she couldn't see how Melvin could be in the frame for this. Andrew Squires had done a good job checking him out, even going so far as to see if any of Melvin's holiday makers had known him beforehand, thus giving rise to the possibility of collusion. But none had, and no connection between any of them to each other had ever been found either. And the last group of people to be dropped off from Melvin's coach that day had been six in number, all comprised of married couples. So for his alibi to be false, it would require a conspiracy of at least seven people.

And that, as any copper would tell you, was just not doable. Forget about all the conspiracy theories that become so popular nowadays. It was hard enough for two people to share a secret and not come unstuck. Let alone seven.

Besides, why would six strangers agree to lie for him? Most

people could be persuaded by money, of course, but Melvin was hardly a man with enough dosh to tempt three respectable middle-aged to elderly couples to wander from the straight and narrow.

Besides, the coach's mileage had also been checked out. And then there were all the office workers and garage people who'd confirmed his timings and whereabouts.

No. Melvin McRae definitely had to be out of the picture. Unless he was clever enough to think of a way to get home and kill his wife in such a way that neither Squires, herself, nor anyone else working on the case had been able to figure out.

Which wasn't impossible, of course. There were a lot of very clever people about, and until she'd seen Melvin for herself and assessed him, she had no way of guessing at his possible intelligence.

Still, it was a long shot.

He could have had an accomplice, of course, but that presented its own difficulties....

She sat upright as a tap came at the office door and Steven Crayle looked in.

'Hello. I heard you were back. Just checking in to see how you're settling in, and if you need anything?'

'Thanks, no I'm fine. The phone's working, and I've been allocated a password for the computer, which is up and running. There's no room or a power point for a coffee pot, though.'

Crayle smiled briefly. 'I keep a stash of the good stuff in my office. South American blend. Feel free to come in any time you need a caffeine hit.' He draped his tall, slender frame against the doorjamb, and crossed his arms loosely across his chest. 'So, how's it feel to be back in the harness?' He looked long, cool and elegant in a black suit with a pale mint-green shirt, and bottle green tie.

'Getting into stride already, sir,' she said blandly.

'And the case?'

'Interesting.'

Crayle nodded, and his dark brown hair flopped a little over his forehead.

Hillary continued to gaze at him steadily.

'Well, I'll let you get on with it. Let me know if you run into any problems. My door's always open. I mean that.'

'Thank you, sir.'

'You *can* call me Steven, you know. I'm not exactly your superior officer any more.'

'No, sir. Sorry – Steven. I suppose you're not,' she said thoughtfully. Just my boss in fact, she added silently. And a lot of people called their boss by their first name, right? And probably harboured secret lustful thoughts too!

Crayle smiled, displaying even white teeth and took himself off.

Hillary let out a long slow breath, and swore softly to herself.

Then reminded herself again not to talk to herself out loud.

Steven Crayle made his way from his fiefdom in Hades and up to the lofty heights of the police canteen, on the third floor. It was late, and most of the lunchtime crowd had gone, but there was still a cluster of uniforms sat at some tables, discussing an upcoming football match at Oxford's stadium.

Most were expecting a little aggro from the visiting team's supporters and would be on duty to keep the peace. Crayle didn't envy them. He hadn't been on the beat for more than a couple of years, and he'd been glad to leave the experience behind him.

He selected the vegetarian option and took a seat, looking up in surprise as a shadow fell over him, and Marcus Donleavy took the chair opposite. The noise from the tables nearest to him dimmed suddenly, as if the lofty rank of the commander demanded they all suddenly start talking in whispers.

'Steven, how are things?' Donleavy asked amiably.

'Fine sir, thank you.'

Donleavy put down a plate of tinned salmon with a rather limp offering of salad leaves, and reached for the vinegar.

'I hear Hillary started work right away?'

'Yes, sir. Then and there, after you'd shown her around. Your idea, I take it?' Steven asked, careful to keep his voice neutral.

He wasn't sure whether to be amused or not at the speed with which Hillary Greene had been thrust into his professional life.

But Donleavy was already shaking his head. 'Nothing to do with me, Steven, I assure you. But I'm not surprised – that's Hillary all over. Most people would take a few days to settle in. But I image she's in the thick of it already.'

'Yes, sir,' Steven said, and since Donleavy continued to look at him steadily, bowed to the pressure and said pleasantly, 'I gave her the McRae case. Murdered housewife, back in 1990.'

'Ah. Excellent.'

'I was thinking that it would probably have been kinder to give her something a bit more recent, perhaps. Or not such a dead end. The original SIO on the case was pretty sure he knew who the perp was, but simply couldn't prove it. And after all this time, I doubt Hillary can do anything positive with it.'

'Oh don't you be too sure,' Donleavy said, spearing a bit of soggy salmon and chewing it doggedly. 'She's always at her best when she's up against it.'

'If you say so, sir,' Crayle said mildly, and turned the conversation to increasing the CRT's budget, a gambit that Donleavy parried with equal skill.

The group of uniforms who left the table nearest to them at that moment and moved towards the door attracted the attention of neither man.

But one of them left with excited green eyes, and a spring in his step.

So it was true, Tom Warrington thought, as he followed the others down the large, wide concrete steps and into the lobby. He'd heard that Hillary Greene and commander Donleavy were friends, with the Commander really rating her. And now he'd heard it from the horses's mouth, so to speak.

Tom had always admired the senior brass. Unlike a lot of the other lads, who were more than ready to talk disparagingly about them, Tom saw himself as one day joining their rank. And Donleavy was just the kind of man he was going to become one day. People looked up to Donleavy. And Donleavy was Hillary's champion.

Just one more proof, if proof was needed, that Hillary Greene was worthy of his devotion.

Now all he had to do was set about proving it to her.

In her flat, Lucy McRae said goodbye to her aunt, and stood in the doorway, hearing her footsteps ring hollowly on the stairway. Then the scent of urine wafted in, and she wrinkled her nose and quickly slammed the door.

She knew who was responsible for the smell, of course – that old duffer who lived two doors down. Drank like a fish, and was seventy if he was a day. She wouldn't put it past him and his weak bladder to piddle in the corner halfway up the stairs because he was too knackered to make it to his loo in time.

She really had to get a different flat. She could hardly bring any decent man back here. One look at this place would tell him just how desperate she was, and that gave any man the advantage over her. Not to mention putting him on the alert.

Lucy walked through to the single tiny bedroom and thrust open the wardrobe door, needing the comfort of checking her own image.

Yes, as she'd thought. She soothed down the top and nodded. Breasts still big and pert. Well, she needed a good bra nowadays, but then men liked a good handful, didn't they? Waist still good – not quite as waspy as when she'd been in her late teens and early twenties, but still good enough to give her a classic hour-glass figure. Hips and bum were as good as ever – her exercise classes saw to that.

Hair still long and blonde, face still good.

Yes. She could find herself another Gerry, all right.

But that still left the problem of the flat. She had to get the cash together to find somewhere halfway decent. A six-month lease would be all she'd need. Maybe in one of those posh little maisonettes up by the Cross? She could laugh and say she'd only taken one because she was a Lady Godiva fan. Although nobody was quite sure that the famous Banbury Cross was anything to do with her, of course. But it was a good flirting line.

How to get some cash together though, that was thing. She hadn't been joking with her aunt when she'd told her that she loathed working.

Suddenly, her thoughts sharpened, as the unexpected visit by her aunt gave her an idea.

She slowly closed the wardrobe door and wandered back through to the living room. There was *someone* she could tap for a 'loan'. There always had been. And of course, by loan, she meant no such thing. She just hadn't tapped this particular source before, mostly because it had never really been necessary. And also because something surprisingly squeamish in her nature made her reluctant to take such a big step.

But things were getting desperate, and surely now was the ideal time to do so? If Aunt Debbie was right, and they were reopening mum's old case, the pressure would already be on.

But she'd have to be careful. Not that she was in any danger, of course. Even so. Yes. She'd still have to be careful.

Thoughtfully, Lucy McRae reached for the phone and then hesitated. No. She needed to think about it first. Rehearse what she would say. And how she would say it.

Hillary walked from her stationery cupboard and through into the main office and glanced at Jimmy. Then she gave a reluctant mental shake of the head and looked at Sam Pickles instead.

'Sam, got anything on?'

'Nothing urgent, guv,' Sam said eagerly, ignoring the knowing, pitying glance that Vivienne shot his way. She'd been ragging him about Hillary Greene ever since Commander Donleavy had introduced her.

But so what if he was desperate to work with her and learn? That didn't mean he was like a dog panting after his master, like Vivienne taunted.

'Good. We need to question the family of Anne McRae, and I don't have a car yet. The son, Peter, lives just up the road in North Oxford. By the way – Sam, Vivienne, a good job on updating the files. I've just called him, and he's in this afternoon. Fancy coming?'

'Yes, guv.'

'Yes, guv,' Vivienne mocked him softly, but just loud enough for Hillary to hear her.

Sam Pickles blushed red, but reached for his jacket. Hillary rolled her eyes at Jimmy, who was grinning over some paperwork.

'Do you want to come too, Vivienne?' Hillary asked patiently.

'Sorry, Hillary, I've got a job on from Sergeant Handley.'

'Fine.'

Ten minutes later, she and Sam were approaching the Woodstock roundabout, Sam driving a neat little Mini Metro in racing-car green. Hillary was consulting the file.

'According to this, he lives in a place called Oakmead House,' she said, frowning. 'There's no number given, but I imagine it must be one of these big places up here somewhere.'

'Nice. He must have done well for himself,' Sam said, with more than a hint of envy in his voice. He himself would be lucky if he could afford a mortgage on a housing association semi, when he left uni, let alone one of these North Oxford mansions.

'What's that one? Does that begin with an O?' she asked, peering down a short but leafy driveway and trying to see the name carved into a piece of driftwood attached above a large oak door.

Damn it, she'd have to get glasses.

'Yes, guv,' Sam said, indicating to turn in, and making the car behind honk its horn in anger at the sudden manoeuvre. Sam gave it the cheerful finger. Hillary smiled.

'Practising for when you're in traffic then, Sam?' she chided, and the youngster grinned.

'Sorry, guv.'

The house had a short, gravel-lined drive, bordered by speckled laurel bushes. It was white-painted, with diamond-paned windows and would have sold for more than a million easy on the open market.

Sam was right. Anne McRae's only son had done well for himself.

Hillary walked up to the imposing oak doors and rang an old-fashioned black iron bellpull. Discreet chimes sounded from within. A large black and white cat emerged from the bushes, and pressed his cheek against her calf, purring loudly.

The door was answered quickly by a man with a lot of blonde hair and wide brown eyes. He wasn't quite six-feet tall, and was barefooted. Dressed in tight-fitting designer jeans with a plain white shirt worn outside the jeans, he looked at Hillary without interest, but his gaze lingered longer on Sam, who began to blush.

The cat rushed in, and disappeared up a wide wooden stair-case, set back in the hall.

'Hello. You rang earlier. About Mum's case?' he asked tenta-tively, and Hillary nodded, showing him her ID.

'Yes, yes, come on in. Please just follow the corridor down to the right. Do you mind talking in the kitchen? I'm just in the middle of a complicated recipe and don't want to leave it.'

'The kitchen's fine, Mr McRae,' Hillary said, and indeed it was. More than fine. It was huge, with marble work surfaces, an island with a double sink, a beautiful shining cherry-wood dining table with six matching antique chairs, and was outfitted with beau-tiful contemporary cupboards. A huge fridge and freezer were tucked discreetly away in one corner, and brightly shining copper pans hung from what looked like original wooden beams over a vast range cooker.

'It's one of Jamie Oliver's recipes, but I'm trying to give it my own twist.'

'You're a chef, Mr McRae?'

'Good grief no. Just an amateur. But Sebastian, my partner, is a bit of a foodie, and cooking relaxes me, so it suits us both for me to play mother. Coffee?'

Hillary accepted with alacrity. She had a feeling any beverage served up in this household would be good, and that was confirmed a few moments later when Peter McRae went straight to a percolator and set it working.

He returned to the island, where he began to slice aubergines length wise, and turned on a grill.

'So, you're opening Mum's case again, is that right?' he asked quietly.

'Yes. That is, it was never officially closed.'

Peter nodded. He glanced at Sam, who was sat at the table quietly taking notes, and turned back to Hillary. 'Have you got new evidence? You know, has he done it again or something?'

'No sir, not that I know of. Nothing like that.'

'Oh right.'

He put the vegetables under the grill, and began to wipe down the chopping board.

'Can you tell me about that day?' Hillary asked quietly. 'You were at school is that right?'

'Yes. I left school on the bus as usual, and went round to a friend's house. Brian Gill. Hell, I haven't seen him in ages. I wonder what he's doing now? Funny how you lose touch, isn't it? At the time, Brian was my best friend in all the world.' Peter sighed and shrugged. 'Anyway, we watched some telly, I can't remember what, then I went round home.'

'Brian lived in Chesterton as well?'

'Yes. Down the road a bit. Anyway, when I got home, Lucy was there – she must have gone home straight from the bus, I suppose. She wouldn't let me into the house. She was all pale and shaky and she talked funny. I realize now that she must have been in shock, of course. But at the time, I was a bit angry – you know, thought she was trying to boss me about.'

69

'So she was outside the house?' Hillary already knew all this from the original report, of course, but it didn't hurt to check.

'Yes. Standing just by the front door. I suppose she didn't want to stay inside the house knowing … well … she'd have seen Mum, and …'

He removed the browning aubergines and put them to one side, then moved to the fridge, coming back with some milk, cheese and cream.

'Seb loves his sauces. He's a curator at the museum on Parks Road. We've been together nearly ten years now. Can you imagine?' Peter laughed, but it somehow didn't reach his eyes. 'Where does the time go?'

He was obviously trying to change the subject, but she had to keep him to the point.

'I understand how painful all this is for you, and that you don't want to dredge it all up again, sir,' Hillary said softly. 'You were, what, only fifteen when your mother died?'

'Yes. But Lucy was only thirteen. I can't help but think that if I hadn't gone to Brian's house first, then she wouldn't have been on her own. She wouldn't have had to find our mum like that.'

'I understand. You feel guilty,' Hillary said simply.

'Yes. Well, there's not a lot more that I can tell you – I'm sorry. Lucy said she'd called the police from the phone in the hall, and I asked her what she'd done that for. Then she said something had happened to Mum, and she wanted me to take her to Mrs Wilkins's house. She was the woman who lived a few doors down. A nice old soul – Lucy always got on well with her. So I did, and we waited there, and the police came, and questioned us. Then Dad came, and they took Mum away, but we went to stay the night at a hotel in Bicester. We stayed there for a couple of days, in fact. I don't know why.'

'The police would have wanted to seal your house off until forensics had finished with it,' Hillary explained softly.

'Yes. Yes, of course that's it. I knew that. Or rather, I would

70

have known that, if I'd thought about it. But I tend not to think about it. About Mum, I mean.'

Peter continued to make a supper fit for his foodie lover, and answered everything Hillary asked of him. But nothing he said helped her, or gave her a better picture of their murder victim.

Which was not surprising, really. Peter still saw Anne from a 15-year-old boy's point of view. She was his mother, which meant a rather sexless person, who was the ultimate authority in the home, since his father was mostly absent. She was pretty, and let him watch football late at night if it was an important match; she washed his clothes and fed him and he'd had no idea she was sleeping with his uncle Shane.

They left just as rush hour began to set in, and then had to sit in traffic at the roundabout for ten minutes.

Hillary took the time to sit and brood. So far, all she was doing was covering the same old ground that Squires had already covered twenty years before her.

She just had to keep plodding on and hope that there was something out there that he had missed, and that she would recognize it when she came across it.

CHAPTER FIVE

Debbie Gregg rose early after a fitful night, and made her partner's breakfast. He was fairly easy to feed, and this morning's fare consisted of cornflakes, toast and marmalade, and a strong pot of tea. She herself could eat nothing.

She kissed him goodbye at his usual time, and then glanced at her watch. She had a part-time job in a dental practice in town, but she wasn't due to start until 1.30.

Best to get it over with now.

She picked up the phone, and reached for the card the woman copper had left with her yesterday. She rang the CRT department and was instantly put on hold. Nervously, Debbie paced about the room with the phone in her hand, going over and over again in her mind what she wanted to say, and how she wanted to say it, and then abruptly sat down.

She gave a short bark of near-hysterical laughter. This was just like Anne, to be ruining her life, all over again.

'Hello? Mrs Gregg?' Hillary Greene's voice in her ear made Debbie jump and she leaned forward, hunching her shoulders protectively and suddenly wishing that she still smoked. Right now, she could just do with a fag.

'Yes. You called round my house yesterday. About my sister's case,' she heard herself rasp, and took a deep breath.

'Yes, I remember who you are, Mrs Gregg,' Hillary said softly.

'Well, I've just remembered something, see. Something we probably talked about yesterday must have triggered it off in my mind, because at about half past three this morning, I suddenly woke up and thought of it,' she lied, then wondered if she was talking too fast, and tried to relax a bit.

She had to spin it, so this canny copper would swallow it.

'It's funny how things like that can happen, isn't it? I mean I wasn't thinking about our Anne, particularly. But even if you think of something else, I suppose your subconscious mind carries on worrying about it. Chewing it over, so to speak. Or that's what they say, isn't it?'

On her chair, Debbie cringed. Now she was definitely waffling. Why the hell didn't she just say what she'd phoned to say and get it over with?

'Yes, it very often happens that way,' Hillary replied patiently. 'Why don't I pop over to see you and we can talk about it? It won't take me much more than half an hour or so to get there.'

Debbie shot off the chair and began to pace again.

'Oh there's no need for that,' she said quickly. 'I mean, it's a fair old way to come, and it's probably nothing. Well, nothing important. It's just that—'

'If it's all the same to you, Mrs Gregg,' Hillary said, doing something she very rarely did, which was to interrupt a witness in mid-flow, 'I'd rather do this in person. I'll start out right away, and should be there by ten.'

There was something in her voice that didn't brook much argument, and Debbie felt her temper flare for just a second, before she quickly got it under control. Her mother had always said that her eldest daughter had her infamous Granny Webber's temper, and would often regale her with tales about the trouble her grandmother's temper had led her into.

Determined not to lose it, she swallowed back the angry retorts that crowded into her mouth, and took a deep breath instead. The last thing she needed right now was to start a barney with the likes of this one. She had to remember just who she was dealing with. She might have her Granny Webber's temper, but she also had her famous instincts, and they were all telling her that

Hillary Greene was no Andrew Squires; she might have been able to run rings around Squires. She wasn't half so confident that she could do the same with the competent red-head.

'OK fine, but I still think we can just use the phone. It won't take me two minutes to say my piece,' she persevered, careful to keep her tone light.

'About ten then, Mrs Gregg,' Hillary said, and suddenly Debbie was left with just that annoying disconnected telephone buzz in her ear.

She hung up with an explosive bang and prowled about some more. Damn, she needed a fag. But Colin wasn't a smoker either, so there were no fags in the house.

She swore and paced some more.

Back at HQ, Hillary stuck her head in the communal office, but only Jimmy was in.

'I need a lift to Brackley again. Debbie Gregg's just phoned with some new information for us.' And added softly, 'Or so she says.'

Jimmy didn't need to be told twice.

As he drove to the small market town in Northamptonshire for the second time in as many days, Hillary stared thoughtfully out of the window.

She'd been determined to do the interview with her witness face to face simply because she needed to watch Debbie Gregg's body language. People lied to you all the time – and they lied even more if you happened to be a cop investigating a crime. And it was far easier to get away with it on the telephone. But face to face, she'd be able to watch the older woman's eyes, her hands, the way she sat, and be in a better position to gauge whether or not any hesitation in her voice meant prevarication or a genuine attempt at recall.

And if it did turn out to be nothing important after all, as she was so careful to maintain – well, they got paid for the petrol. And any time spent out of that stationery cupboard that was masquerading as her office, the better.

When they pulled up outside Debbie's modest little house, Hillary saw the curtain move and knew they were expected. Nevertheless, Debbie let them ring the doorbell, then wait a few moments before she answered the door.

Playing a power game, or just taking time to get all her skittles lined up in order? Probably both, Hillary decided, as the door opened, and a totally blank-faced woman looked back at her.

'Hello again,' Hillary said pleasantly. It took effort to school your face into showing no expression at all, and she wondered exactly what it was the older woman was trying to hide.

Debbie nodded, and glanced beyond them. It was a dull but dry day outside, not too cold, but there was nobody out and about. She shut the door firmly behind them. Again, there was no offer of tea or coffee, and she led them straight through to the same room as they'd occupied yesterday. She waited until they had seated themselves, once again side by side on the sofa, then sat down herself. Hillary wondered if she was the only one feeling like she was trapped in a time warp.

'I've got to go out soon,' Debbie lied, still annoyed by having to do this face to face.

Ever since visiting her niece yesterday, Debbie had been wracking her brains for something to feed to the cops to keep them off her back. It had to be genuine, otherwise the sods would probably do her for wasting police time or something, and in the end, what she'd remembered wasn't much of a crumb, but it should give them something else to gnaw on.

Or so she hoped.

'It was just after Anne's funeral. You know, it was delayed a bit, because of the coroner holding on to the body for so long,' she began cautiously.

Hillary nodded. 'That sometimes happens.'

'Yeah. Well, it was written up about in the local papers, like, and they had a photographer there, at Anne's funeral. It upset Melvin something terrible, it did, to have some strange bloke snapping away as if he was at a wedding. Sorry, that's not the point, is it.'

Debbie's eyes once again began to wander around the room. Hillary had noticed this habit yesterday, and had wondered then if it was a way of deliberately avoiding eye contact. Now she was far more inclined to think it was a nervous habit of long standing.

And not necessarily significant.

'Anyway, I was in Tesco's, doing a bit of shopping, when this woman came up to me. Funny enough I knew her, sort of, because she used to work on the tills – in Tesco's I mean, although she didn't then. When she came up to me, I mean. I suppose she'd found a better job somewhere else, but still did her shopping there,' Debbie gabbled confusingly, but Hillary was following what she meant. Just. What Jimmy, who was taking the notes must be making of it, she wasn't sure, but she could trust him to keep quiet until later.

'Yes, I understand,' Hillary said. 'Go on.'

As if aware that she was making a hash of it, Debbie suddenly coloured and bit her lip. 'I'm just explaining things, so's you'll know why I remembered her name, even though I didn't know her.' She sighed and gave a brief laugh. 'It was because when I used to see it on her name tag, you know, the ones they wear on their uniform lapel, it was the same name as a girl I went to school with. Diane Burgess.'

Debbie paused for a breath, then glanced at Hillary briefly before turning her gaze back to inspect a lacklustre print on the wall behind her. 'It wasn't the same Dianne Burgess that I knew, of course. She went to Australia with some bloke she married. I'm just explaining, like, how I came to know a stranger's name. Well, not a stranger, exactly, like I said, I used to go to her till, some-times, and we'd chat a bit.'

'I understand,' Hillary said again, wondering why Debbie, who yesterday had been rather defiant and not exactly garrulous, now felt the need to say quite so much.

'Anyway, I was in the bakery section, looking for some of these rolls I liked, when she sort of sidled up to me and said how sorry she was for all my trouble. Meaning Anne, of course. That was all anybody meant, back then.'

Debbie's tone took on a bitter note, and as if aware of it, she suddenly shook her head.

'Anyway, usually when people came up wanting to "pay their respects" – and what a laugh that is – what they really wanted to do was pump me for information, or get a cheap thrill talking to a murder suspect.' Debbie's lips twisted into a grim smile. 'Anyway, I was just about to say something pithy and leave her to it, when she suddenly put her hand on my arm and said she knew what I was going through. Well, that stopped me in my tracks.'

'Yes, I can see how it might,' Hillary agreed. 'So let's just make sure I've got this right. A woman called Diane Burgess, who used to work in Tesco's, came up to you just after your sister's funeral and said she knew what you were going through?'

'Right,' Debbie nodded. 'So I said something like, "Oh, you've had someone in your family murdered too, then?" or something sarky like that. Well, of course, she blushed a little bit, because obviously she hadn't, had she? But instead of walking off in a snit, like most of them did when I told them what to do with their phoney pity, she looked around, quick like, to see if anyone was listening in on us, and then said, no, it wasn't that. It was just that she knew what it was like to find out that Anne had been sleeping with your husband.'

Hillary felt herself stiffen slightly. This was new information indeed, for Andrew Squires hadn't been able to find any evidence of Anne McRae's infidelity with anyone other than Shane Gregg.

'I see,' she said quietly, trying not to let on how interested she suddenly was. 'And what did you say to that?'

Debbie smiled grimly. 'Well, not a lot, as it happens. I mean, what can you say? It was embarrassing enough to have everyone know me and Shane's private business, and let me tell you, the whole world knowing that your husband's been shagging your little sister on the sly is humiliating enough,' Debbie again paused to take a deep breath. 'But to have some virtual stranger come up and commiserate with you because that self-same little sister has been banging her husband as well – well, that takes the wind out your sails, let me tell you. I mean, what *could* I do? Or say? I could hardly invite this Diane Burgess woman back to my place for a coffee so that we could have a good old chinwag and slag off Anne, could I? She'd just been murdered for Pete's sake! Besides, what good would comparing notes do either one of us?'

'So what *did* you say?' Hillary repeated patiently.

'Nothing much. I think I said sorry, as if it was somehow all my fault. And muttered something embarrassing and lame, like how I hoped things worked out for her. And then I scarpered.' Suddenly, Debbie gave a sharp laugh. 'Never did buy the rolls I wanted, neither.'

'And you didn't tell this to DI Squires?' Hillary chided gently.

'No,' Debbie said shortly. And seeing the red-headed woman's eyebrows rise in silent query, she sighed grimly. Bloody coppers were all the same. They all wanted their pound of flesh. 'By then, I'd wised up, hadn't I?' Debbie carried on grudgingly. 'Squires had had me down at the bloody station answering questions a dozen times or more by the time we'd buried Anne, and I'd got sick and tired of it, and got myself a solicitor. And every time he pulled me in, I kept quiet until my brief got there. And so by the time this woman came up to me in Tesco's I wasn't talking much to the cops any more.'

Hillary sighed. She could see how that could happen. And no doubt there was also a hint of one-upmanship in Debbie not passing on the information to the SIO in charge of her sister's case. It was human nature to get resentful and bloody-minded when pressed too far, after all.

Even so, she must have understood that it could have been significant. Debbie was not stupid. She must have realized that uncovering another lover for her sister meant that there was now another murder suspect for DI Squires to question.

Unless, of course, Debbie didn't care whether or not her sister's killer was ever caught. By her own admission, she was angry with Anne, and resentful of her youth and good looks. Perhaps keeping the information to herself was her way of exacting some measure of revenge.

'And then I just forgot about it, as time went on,' Debbie continued. 'It wasn't hard – there was so much going on back then. Me and Shane were splitting up and getting divorced. I was looking around for a new gaff, and what with one thing and another, I never gave it much of a thought until last night. I dare say you coming around and raking it all up again – about Anne, I mean – jogged my memory, like.'

'Well, I'm glad it finally did, Mrs Gregg,' Hillary said. 'It could be a very important piece of evidence.'

'Well, maybe,' Debbie said dubiously. 'Don't see how, though. I mean, I can't see her, that Diane Burgess, being involved. She was a bit of a mouse, if you ask me. And definitely not the sort to take a rolling pin to somebody.'

'Well, we'll certainly try and track her down and talk to her,' Hillary said. 'Can you remember anything else she might have said?'

Hillary carefully talked through the encounter once again with Debbie, but she could add nothing more. After all, as the exasperated older woman pointed out, it had all happened twenty years ago. She could hardly be expected to remember it word for word, could she?

In her inadequate flat in Banbury, Lucy McRae sat on the sofa, with the phone in her lap. She could put it off no longer. With a brief nod of determination, she dialled a number from memory, and listened to the ringing tone, half hoping it would go unanswered.

'Hello?'

'Hello, it's me,' Lucy said.

'Hello, you.'

'Listen I need to talk to you. The cops have been to see me, and—'

'Wait!' the other voice interjected sharply, and Lucy felt her stomach clench in a small spasm of anxiety. 'This is an open phone line. Anyone could be listening in. Be very careful what you say.'

'I know that,' Lucy lied huffily. She hadn't, in fact, given the idea that they might accidentally be overhead a passing thought. 'I'm not going to say anything stupid.'

'Good. Now what did they want?'

'What do you think?' Lucy said smartly. 'They're reopening the case. What else? Do you think I regularly talk to the cops or something?'

'Sarcasm doesn't become you.'

'Screw you.'

'Charming as ever.'

Lucy sighed. 'Look, I didn't call just to argue. We need to get together. To talk about this.'

'I don't see why.'

'Well I do!' Lucy shot back, beginning to feel more confident. After all, she had the upper hand here. 'Besides, I need to get out of this poky flat. Why don't we meet somewhere nice. It's been ages since you stood me lunch. What about that fancy restaurant we went to before – you know, the one run by that famous French cook – the one that's been on the telly.'

The speaker on the other end of the line sighed heavily. 'Fine. How about next week?'

'How about lunch time today,' Lucy countered.

'I have plans.'

'Cancel them.'

There was a rather ominous silence, and Lucy felt compelled to rush to fill it.

'Come on, you know whatever it is, it can't be more important than this,' she wheedled.

The silence lengthened.

'It is murder you know,' she said flatly.

'I thought you were going to be careful what you said,' the other speaker reminded her grimly.

'All the more reason to get together, then,' Lucy pounced. 'We can be sure we won't be overheard then.'

A long-suffering sigh sounded over the telephone line. 'OK. I'll see you at 12.30 at the restaurant.'

'You'll have to pick me up from the bus station. My car failed its MOT and I had to sell it, virtually for the scrap.'

'Ah,' the voice said simply.

Lucy smiled grimly. 'So I'm a bit cash-strapped.'

'Yes. I thought it might be something like that.'

'You always were quick.'

'How much are you going to touch me for?'

This time it was Lucy's turn to hesitate.

'You might as well tell me now,' the other speaker said. 'If you want me to bring cash, I've got to take a trip to a cash machine. The restaurant might take a credit card, but I don't suppose you'd like a cheque?'

Lucy laughed. 'You know me so well.'

'Yes,' the other voice said grimly. 'I do, don't I?'

'Well, there's quite a few things I need, actually.'

'Don't push it.'

'Well, I need more of a loan than just a few hundred in cash,' Lucy said, careful to keep her voice nonchalant. 'So actually, a cheque for, say, five thousand, would be nice.'

Silence.

When they got back to HQ, Jimmy set about trying to track down Diane Burgess. With only her name to go on, it might have been a bit of a pain, but the added knowledge that she'd worked in Tesco's in Bicester at the time of the Anne McRae murder case would probably help.

The supermarket was his first port of call, and he rang the head office to get the permission needed to access personnel records.

If that failed, there were other avenues. The tax people, census, and various Records Offices. If Diane Burgess was local, he'd find her. Of course, she could have married a local boy, and come from Bognor Regis herself for all he knew.

Jimmy sighed as he was put on hold by a computer-generated voice, and then sighed again as he was given a list of buttons to press, depending on various options. He listened to the end of the spiel, but as he'd expected, there wasn't an option for coppers who wanted to access data-protected files. He pressed the button to list the options again, and tried to pick out the one that would come closest to getting him to connected to someone who could actually help him.

As he listened to a machine talking to him, Jimmy Jessop wondered just what the world was coming to.

In her office, Hillary Greene – who had a fair idea of just what the world was coming to, and didn't much approve – perused the updated file for ex-DI Andrew Squires's current home phone number. She needed to speak to him at some point, and get his first-hand memories of the case, and his take on it. She could only hope that he wouldn't take her being handed his old case as some sort of comment on his ability.

Some people could become very possessive about what they saw as 'their' cases – especially the ones that got away from you.

But when she called his number, he was out.

Ex-DI Andrew Squires, as it happened, wasn't more than a quarter of a mile from where Hillary was sitting. The Black Bull had been his local for years when he'd been on the force. And since retiring, although there were several pubs closer, he still made his way there two or three times every week for a lunch time pint and a bit of a natter with any of the lads who were willing to pass the time of day with him.

So whilst Hillary was trying to contact him with a view to having just such a natter, he was watching his favourite pint of Hook Norton brew being pulled for him into a glass, and sorting out the change in his pocket.

The pub was filled with a mix of people on the job, and regular civilians. Andy Squires wasn't quite sure which camp he belonged to now. As a retired gent of nearly seventy, he was hardly a copper any more, and yet he didn't think of himself as being a civilian either. So when a couple of familiar faces came in, he raised his glass and his eyebrows, and was glad enough when they came up to him to greet him before ordering a pint for themselves.

One was a sergeant from traffic, Dave Olliphant, who was obviously clocking off from his shift. He was a good twenty years junior to Andy, but they'd been stationed in St Aldates for quite a few years before they both got transferred to HQ. The other man with him was a few years younger, and Andy vaguely remembered him as a green-behind-the-ears constable. He'd been seconded onto Andy's team once or twice when they needed extra manpower.

Andy couldn't quite remember his name. He wore a sergeant's stripes now, though, and must be coming up to retirement age himself, if he wanted to take it early.

'Bloody hell, where does the time go?' he said out loud, as he offered to pay for the round.

'Cheers, Andy,' Dave Olliphant said, taking a quick gulp of the precious nectar. 'I needed that. That bloody M40 will be the death of me yet.'

The man beside him grinned. 'You've been saying that since they built the bloody thing, Dave. And it ain't killed you yet.'

'Give it time. You remember Andy Squires, right?'

'Course I do. Will Hogg, sir. I was with you on the Burke case. Your final do, wasn't it?'

Andy leaned against the bar and took a swallow of his beer. 'Yeah. Got him for it too, I seem to remember. Aggravated assault. Got ten years. Should have got double that. Vicious little bastard.'

Dave sighed. 'Bloody courts are always too soft.' It was a familiar lament, and for the next ten minutes, the three men happily talked shop and slagged off solicitors they all knew and hated. The barman kept the pints topped up.

'You must be glad to be out of it,' Dave finally said, draining his second glass of beer, and waving off Fred's attempt at giving him a third. 'Driving,' Dave said and laughed. 'Wouldn't do to get nicked for driving over the limit by one of my lot. And there's one or two sods who'd be only too glad to do it, too.'

'Nah, never,' Will said laughing. 'You're universally loved and admired, you.'

'Buggered if I ain't,' the traffic man said. Then he glanced curiously at Andy. 'Still, I'm not the only one who has to watch his back, eh, Andy?'

Andy blinked. 'Huh?' Unlike Dave, he'd walked to the pub, and was well into his third pint.

'You know. CRT.'

'Huh?' he said again. The CRT unit had been set up only after he'd gone, and he had no idea what Dave was getting at.

'They've only gone and reopened one of yours, haven't they?' Dave said, who was well up on the current gossip at the station. 'Given it to Hillary Greene, no less.'

Andy may have been retired for some time, but even he knew of Hillary Greene.

'I heard she'd retired too,' he said, puzzled.

'She had. But she's working for CRT now as a consultant. And Superintendent Crayle gave her one of your cases to start her off with.'

'Which one?' Andy asked quickly.

'That housewife and mum who got it in her own kitchen. Bashed over the head,' Dave snapped his fingers in an effort to remember the name.

'Anne McRae,' the retired man supplied it quietly.

Andy had no trouble at all in remembering her name. He might not have had quite as good a solve rate as Hillary Greene enjoyed, but he didn't have that many failures either. So those few that had defeated him lingered on in his memory.

And few plagued him with more regrets than Anne McRae. A pretty young woman, and a mother of three kids, he'd badly wanted to give her justice. But that sister of hers had just been too damned lucky. No matter how hard he'd tried, he hadn't been able to bring it home to her.

'So, Hillary Greene's reviewing the McRae case,' Andy said slowly.

'Rather you than me, mate,' Dave said, slapping him on the back in commiseration. 'They say that Commander Donleavy reckons she can solve anything. It'll mean a bit of egg on your face, though, won't it, if she gets a result after all this time.'

Jimmy Jessop grinned in triumph and quickly scribbled on his pad. He had the phone pressed against his right ear, his shoulder hunched up to keep it in place, and was rifling through the file in search of his notes from that morning. Although he could use a computer, he still preferred the feel of paper.

'Right. And you say he's still doing the same round?' He listened to the voice on the other end of the line, and chipped in with the occasional 'huh huh' and 'right', before finally managing to get off the line.

He went straight through to Hillary's office. She was sitting at her desk munching on a banana, which was making do as her lunch.

'Guv, I've tracked down Diane Burgess. Well, actually, to be more accurate, I've tracked down her husband, Mark. And you'll never guess what he does for a living.'

Hillary swallowed a mouthful of banana, and said cheerfully, 'In that case, Jimmy, you'd better tell me.'

'He does a butcher's round. You know, in a van. I was just talking to his boss, who owns a chain of butchers' shops. Apparently, Mark Burgess has been doing the same round for near enough the past twenty-five years. And guess what village he goes through, regular as clockwork, every Thursday afternoon?'

Hillary smiled. 'Chesterton?'

'Right. Which means he would have been doing so twenty years ago. You reckon our vic used to buy her steak and kidney off him?'

'And more than that, if his wife is to be believed,' Hillary said dryly. 'You got an address for them?'

'Yes, guv. But there's no one answering the phone at the residence.'

'Hmm. You got details of his round?'

Jimmy grinned. 'Yes, guv. His boss was just giving me a right earful about him. A bit of a character it seems. I've got his schedule right here.'

He handed over his hastily scribbled list and Hillary looked at it and checked her watch.

'Hmm. He's due in Souldern in an hour,' she mentioned a small village not far from the border with Northamptonshire. 'What say we go over there and see for ourselves just how lean his minced beef is?'

Jimmy grinned.

CHAPTER SIX

Souldern was a small village nestled at the northern end of the Cherwell Valley, and at just gone three o'clock in the afternoon in the middle of the week, it seemed, like most traditional villages nowadays, all but deserted. With the majority of its residents away at work, it had an eerily abandoned air, and could almost have been the setting for some post-apocalyptic film noir.

But a fitful sun was trying to shine through the clouds, and innocuously cheerful birdsong filled the air. And when Hillary stepped from Jimmy's car, the only thing on her mind was the more prosaic need to go second-hand car shopping at the weekend. She couldn't keep relying on being chauffeur driven by her right-hand man.

In the centre of the village was a small pond, at the moment bereft of ducks, and parked up beside it was a white butcher's van, with the back doors standing open. Two middle-aged women were standing between the doors, chatting and laughing with a tall, well-built man with salt-and-pepper hair and a wide, handsome but somewhat florid face. He was well over six feet and just running to seed, but so far the muscle was still winning out over the flab.

'That would be our Lothario then,' Jimmy said cheerfully beside her, and Hillary nodded.

'We'll wait until he's got rid of his customers,' she said, and then rued that decision as the trio spent the next good ten minutes indulging in mutual flirting and banter. Eventually, however, the two women moved away and Hillary and Jimmy approached the van, both of them with their IDs at the ready.

'Mr Burgess?' Hillary asked pleasantly.

Mark Burgess had his back to them, and visibly jumped at the unfamiliar voice coming from just over his left shoulder. He swung around, a silver weighing pan still in his hand. Beside her, she felt Jimmy tense, then relax, as the butcher smiled and hastily put the pan down.

Hillary noted the old soldier's still-good reflexes, and felt reassured. Not that she'd expected any trouble, of course, but it was good to know that with Jimmy along, she could rely on his back-up. Now that she was no longer a fully fledged DI, and didn't have sturdy constables at her beck and call whenever she might need one, it was good to know that Jimmy had his wits about him. She'd taken a few self-defence courses herself, and between the two of them, she was confident that they could cope with almost anything that her new job at the CRT might throw her way.

'Yes, luv, what can I get you? Got on offer on best British steak at the moment.'

Hillary held up her ID.

'We're with the Thames Valley Police Service, sir,' she smiled briefly. 'But I might be interested in some of that steak anyway.'

Burgess looked surprised. 'Police? What's up? Been some burglaries about, have there? You know, come to think of it, I did hear about that from one of my customers over Fritwell way. But I've had this round for donkey's years, luv you can check. There's nothing dodgy about me.'

Hillary put her ID away in her bag. 'We'd like to talk to you about the Anne McRae murder case, Mr Burgess,' she said, still pleasantly, but getting straight to the point.

'Bloody hell, that was, what, twenty years ago now. At least.'

His red-complexioned face went a shade paler, and his eyes, a pale shade of grey, swivelled from Hillary to Jimmy and then back again. He was obviously expecting the male in the team to take the lead, but Jimmy merely looked back at him mutely, giving him no help.

'I understand she was a customer of yours, sir, back in the day?' Hillary asked firmly, again giving him a brief smile when he reluctantly turned his eyes her way again.

Hillary had dealt with men like this before. He liked his women kept firmly in one category – sexual availability. She would have bet her last pay cheque that this man was a serial philanderer who needed easy sexual conquests to bolster up a chronic lack of self-esteem. Perhaps he felt professionally thwarted; that running a butcher's van was a job for a butcher's boy, and thus needed to prove his masculinity in other ways. She wasn't a shrink, and didn't much care, but it was clear that, to Mark Burgess, any woman in a position of authority would automatically be a threat to him.

And it made her wonder. Had Anne McRae threatened his self-image in some way? From what she'd learned of their murder victim so far, she was a strong-willed woman, and used to getting her own way. She could well see how two narcissistic personalities might clash, with potentially fatal consequences.

'Well, yeah, she bought off me regular, like. I was well shocked, I can tell you, when I heard that someone had killed her,' Burgess confirmed warily. 'Why are you digging all that up again now anyway?'

'We periodically review old cases, sir,' Hillary said blandly. 'What can you tell me about her?'

The older man's eyes went back to Jimmy again, but the wily Jimmy Jessop was ostensibly studying a robin, which was singing its heart out in a just-greening weeping willow at the side of the pond.

'Well, she liked her lamb and pork. Bought a lot of chicken too, not so much beef or offal though,' Burgess said, being, Hillary was sure, deliberately obtuse.

Wearily, she smiled again. Smart alecs gave her a pain in the backside. 'I wasn't thinking so much of her dietary habits, sir, as her personal life. You and she were close, weren't you?' she added casually.

Burgess shifted from one foot to the other. 'Huh? What do you mean?' he asked nervously.

'I mean that we have it on good authority that you and Anne McRae were on intimate terms, sir,' she persisted doggedly.

'Hey, you can't go around saying things like that! I mean, it's libellous.'

'Slanderous sir,' Hillary corrected him mildly. 'Libel refers to written material. Slander is verbal.'

'I don't want a bloody grammar lesson,' the discomfited butcher said, rather loudly, then glanced nervously around the deserted streets. 'Who's been telling lies then?'

Hillary cocked her head slightly to one side, allowing herself to look slightly incredulous. 'Are you going to deny it then, sir?' she asked, her voice slightly raised in disbelief.

As she knew it would, her amused surprise instantly made Burgess feel acutely unnerved and full of self-doubt. She could almost hear his mind working, trying to pick out where the pitfalls were. Was he being stupid? Would any other man simply boast about it and make out it was nothing, having been caught out doing the horizontal tango with some bird who later got murdered? Or should he already be denying it, and threatening to bring in his solicitor?

'Well, I … What does it matter now anyway?' he temporized. 'It was all so long ago.'

'Yes, sir. Perhaps you can tell me about her. Were you her only bit on the side?' Hillary asked, letting the amusement grow. Then she shook her head. 'Oh no, sorry, of course you weren't. DI Squires, the SIO – sorry, that's senior investigating officer – at the time established that Anne was also having an affair with her own brother-in-law, wasn't she?' Hillary continued blithely, thus lumping the butcher into being one of a crowd. And a not particularly discriminating crowd at that. His ego wouldn't like that, she was sure.

'Here, you're making her sound like a right slag. But she wasn't like that, Anne wasn't. She was class. A real beauty, and everything,' Burgess said defensively, his voice level once again rising. His point being, of course, that he was to be commended on his choice. And, naturally, to point out that he had his pick of beautiful, classy women.

Jimmy watched the robin fly away and then turned back to looking at Burgess, his face bland. He had to hand it to the guv – she'd already got him worked up good and proper. Now maybe they'd hear something interesting.

'Oh, so you were in love with her?' Hillary asked softly. 'It wasn't casual. Were you going to leave your wife for her then, sir?'

'What? No, course I wasn't. I'm a happily married man, me. Nearly thirty years now,' Burgess contradicted.

'But not so happily married that you're above extra-marital affairs? Come on sir, you can't have it both ways. Do you make a habit of sleeping around?'

'No of course not!' Burgess lied huffily.

'So Anne McRae *was* special then, was she? Did you find out about Shane Gregg? Did that upset you, is that it?' she pressed him hard now.

'What, who?'

'Her other paramour, Mr Burgess. Did it dent your ego to find out that you weren't the only one? Did you quarrel with her? Perhaps things got out of hand. That can easily happen. The rolling pin was just lying there, to hand, and you picked it up and swung it before you even knew what was happening. Is that how it happened?'

Burgess staggered back, and sat down heavily on a tray of chicken fillets, lying in the back of the van. His face was now ashen.

'You're trying to say I did it?' he squeaked, looking frantically to Jimmy, as if hoping he would deny it. 'Me?'

He looked so astounded, his voice so comically squeaky, that Hillary felt the urge to laugh. She squashed it ruthlessly.

'Someone killed her, Mr Burgess,' Hillary pointed out calmly. 'And at the time of her murder, you and she were having an affair, and yet you never came forward. You must have followed the case in the local papers, you must have seen and heard the many appeals for witnesses and information broadcast on the radio and the local news stations. Yet you never came forward. That makes us wonder why, you see. It makes us ask the question, "What is he trying to hide?" You can understand that, surely?'

Burgess ran a shaking hand across his mouth.

'I'm not hiding nothing – honest! I just didn't come forward because, well, I just didn't have any information, see? I didn't know who killed her. I still don't.'

'What were you doing on the afternoon that Anne McRae died, Mr Burgess?'

'Eh? Well, I must have been working, mustn't I. Doing my rounds like, as I always do.'

'I need you to be a bit more specific than that, sir.'

'How can I be? It was twenty years ago, for pity's sake!'

Hillary smiled grimly. 'Come now, sir, that won't do. By your own admission you were having an affair with her. When you heard about her death you must have been shocked. Surprised. Stunned, even.'

'Of course I was. I said so, didn't I?' Burgess said edgily.

'And you must have followed the case keenly. Read all the newspaper reports, listened to the local gossip, all of that?'

'Well, that's only natural isn't it?'

'Of course it is, sir,' Hillary said smoothly. 'It's only human nature. It's also human nature to think about what it must have been like for her. To imagine her in her kitchen, cooking her family's tea, maybe hearing the doorbell go, and perhaps letting someone in.'

'I don't have much imagination, not like that,' Burgess denied flatly. 'Besides, I didn't like to dwell on it. On stuff like that, I mean. It makes me feel sick.'

Hillary nodded. 'But the day she died must have burned itself onto your memory, sir,' she carried on, not about to let it go. 'You must have seen that her time of death had been put at between 2.30 and 3.30, on the afternoon of 6 June. When you heard that you must have wondered just what it was that you were doing at that time. Everybody does that, sir. You know how Americans say that they know exactly where they were and what they were doing when they heard about Kennedy getting shot? Are you really telling me you didn't do the same when you heard about the death of your lover?'

Once again, Hillary allowed herself to sound incredulous.

Burgess flushed, sensing reproof, and responding to it like Pavlov's dog. 'Course I did.'

'So where were you?'

'In Wendlebury. That day, that time, I'd have been in Wendlebury. One of my regular villages.'

Hillary nodded. 'So you were working. Can you remember the names of the customers you served that day?'

'Now you're taking the piss,' Burgess said, with a flash of defiance. 'Course I don't. How could I remember that? Nobody would.'

His eyes moved away from her, but this time didn't seek help with Jimmy. Instead, his eyes settled on a group of daffodils by the pond. His lips tightened, and she knew what that meant. He'd made up his mind not to talk.

Hillary sighed. He was lying to her, of that she had no doubt. But it would be useless to press him on it now. Instead, she changed tack.

'So, what was Anne like? How did you and she get started?'

Burgess took his eyes from the daffodils and thought about it for a second or two. 'Well, she had regular orders, like, and after a bit, I got to know the sort of cuts she'd like best and I'd put them aside for her, so that she didn't need to come to the van to choose them for herself. So after I'd finished serving from the van, I'd take the meat to her door. She started offering me cold drinks in the summer, and then, well, you know. It went on from there. There was no harm in it. That husband of hers was always away on that bloody coach of his, living the high life in Europe and what have you. And she was bored there on her own, what with the kids in school and nothing to do all day. It was just a bit of harmless fun. We never hurt or bothered anybody.'

Hillary nodded. 'And did she ever tell you about any of her worries?'

'Huh? No, she didn't have any. I mean, what worries could she have?' Burgess sounded genuinely surprised. 'It's us men who have to work, and pay the bills and fix the gutters and what have you. What do women have to do but a bit of housework and take care of the kids when they're little?'

Hillary didn't even blink at the sexism. 'So she never said that there was someone bothering her, or that she was worried her husband had found out about you or anything of that sort?'

'Nah. She said her hubby wouldn't notice a mink in the sugar bowl unless it bit him.'

'And while you were together, you never saw or noticed anything odd? She didn't get phone calls that upset her, or anything like that?'

'No, nothing like that. She was fine – honest. She wasn't the jumpy or temperamental sort. And if some asshole had been stalking her, she'd get her hubby to sort him out, wouldn't she?'

Because that's what they were for, Hillary could have finished the thought for him.

Yes, she knew Mark Burgess's kind all right.

'How long were you together?' she asked curiously.

'A couple of months.'

'You were still having an affair when she died?'

'Well, it was petering out a bit,' he said, a shade reluctantly.

'Perhaps she was finding Mr Gregg more amenable,' Hillary asked, just to see what sort of a temper he had.

But Burgess merely grunted. Obviously, being dumped for his lover's own brother-in-law hadn't worried him that much, and

Hillary could guess why. With an ego as fragile as his, it should have rubbed him on the raw, and there could only be one reason why it didn't.

'Well, that's all for now, sir,' Hillary said turning away. Then she quickly swung back, 'I would appreciate it if you didn't discuss this conversation with anyone else, sir. We don't want people alerted or made curious unduly.'

'Don't you worry none about *that*,' Burgess muttered with feeling. 'I'm not about to go blabbing about something like this, am I?'

'No, I don't suppose you are, sir,' Hillary conceded.

''Sides, who am I gonna tell? The missus?' Burgess asked rhetorically, needing to get in the last word. Then, for good measure, he guffawed falsely.

As they walked back to the car, they heard the van doors slam, and a moment later, the van roared away past them and back up the hill.

Hillary sighed. She'd forgotten to get the steak. She could have done with a nice sirloin.

'What do you think, guv?' Jimmy asked.

'Well, I think he can remember exactly where he was when Anne McRae died for a start,' she surprised him by saying flatly. 'He was lying about that.'

'You do?' Jimmy blurted.

'Yes. And if you think about it for just a bit, Jimmy, I expect you'll get it too.'

Jimmy climbed in behind the wheel and unlocked the door for her. By the time Hillary was settled in the passenger seat, he was grinning widely.

'He was in bed with some other bored and lonely housewife, wasn't he?'

'In Wendlebury, I expect,' Hillary agreed. 'That's why he wasn't more disgruntled that Anne McRae had got bored with him. He was getting his ego stroked elsewhere. Well, that and other things that I don't even want to think about.'

She shuddered theatrically.

Jimmy sighed. 'So he's scratched from the suspect list?'

Hillary smiled widely. 'Oh, I never scratch anyone from the list, Sergeant,' she said, using his old title without realizing it. 'Let's just say he's demoted to somewhere near the bottom. For now.'

Jimmy nodded and turned over the engine. 'So where to now, guv?'

Hillary glanced at her watch. 'Now we go and see the cuck-olded husband.'

Melvin McRae opened the door to find a good-looking redhead and an older man on his doorstep. Neither of them being what he expected, he stared at them silently for a moment.

'Mr McRae? I'm Hillary Greene – we spoke on the phone yesterday?' Hillary prompted. 'This is my colleague James Jessop.'

Both of them held up their IDs, but Melvin barely glanced at them.

'Oh yes. Come on in. My wife's at work,' he said, confusing Hilllary momentarily, until she realized that he meant his current wife. For a moment there, she'd wondered if he was mentally ill, and then had a brief but disturbing image of Anne McRae's ghost beavering away in some office somewhere.

He showed them into a small but pleasant room, with a view of a large church.

'So, what can I do to help?' Melvin asked, indicating a couple of armchairs, but sitting down himself in a small, hard-backed chair beside a table. Once there, he leaned forward, letting his arms dangle along his thighs, with his large-knuckled hands hanging above his knees. He looked tired, as if he hadn't slept well, but he was neatly groomed and his clothes were clean and freshly laundered.

'This is really just a courtesy call, Mr McRae,' Hillary said, making Jimmy's mental eyebrows go up. So she was going to go with the soft-soap routine here, was she? Interesting.

'As you know, I've been assigned to re-investigate your wife's case, and I just wondered if you had any questions for me?'

Melvin shot her a quick glance. Whatever he'd been expecting from them, it hadn't been that.

'Questions? No. About what?' he asked, clearly confused.

'I just thought that you'd like to be given the opportunity to speak to me, sir, that's all,' Hillary said smoothly. 'Have you had any thoughts on who might be responsible for your wife's death in the intervening years?'

'No. I'd have been on to DI Squires if I had.'

'Inspector Squires has retired now, sir,' Hillary said softly. 'Anything you want to say, you can say to me.'

Melvin sighed. 'I just don't want you bothering the kids none, that's all,' he said finally. 'It really cut them up, their mum going like that. Young Jenny – well, it really sent her off the rails, even now, she's having a bad time of it.'

'We haven't even spoken to your daughters yet, sir,' Hillary said gently. 'And we will be careful. We don't want to rake up bad memories, and we'll be as brief as possible.'

'I know it's been a long time, and all that, and you probably think I'm fussing, but I know Anne would say the same.' Melvin looked at Hillary from eyes that were watering with tears now. 'Some people said a lot of bad things about Anne – you know, about how it turned out and all that business with Shane and what have you. But she was a good mum to her kids – they always came first. You can ask anybody – even her detractors have to admit that. She always put the kids first – like a tiger defending her cubs she was, a proper dedicated mum, and she wouldn't want you worrying them now, not even on her own account.'

'I believe you, sir,' Hillary said softly. 'Her sister says the same thing.'

'Debbie? You've already spoken to her?' Melvin asked sharply.

'Of course, sir, she was first on our list,' Hillary said simply, and putting no undue emphasis in her tone at all.

But Melvin McRae quickly gave a sighing grunt. 'Of course she was. Inspector Squires thought she did it, didn't he?'

'He said as much?' Hillary asked, surprised.

'No. He didn't have to. Debs was beside herself at one point. She was sure she was going to go down for it.'

Hillary couldn't detect much bitterness in the man's voice, and she looked at him curiously. 'Do you think she did it, sir?' she asked simply. And beside her she felt, rather than heard, Jimmy take a deep breath.

Melvin McRae leaned back in his chair and rubbed a hand wearily across his face. 'I don't know. I just don't. I don't like to think it. Debbie's family after all, isn't she? Anne's big sister and all that. You don't like to think someone you've shared countless Christmas dinners with has murdered your wife, do you?'

Hillary smiled noncommittally.

'On the other hand, Inspector Squires seemed certain. She had no alibi at the time Anne died. And she had motive.' Melvin shrugged. 'I just don't know. She swears up and down that she didn't, though.'

Hillary nodded, but she was not about to comment on that. The number of times she'd heard villains swear to their innocence didn't bear thinking about.

Still, it was interesting that Melvin McRae seemed to bear the chief suspect in his wife's murder no obvious ill will.

'Were you surprised to find out about the affair, sir?' she asked carefully. It might be more than twenty years since he'd first learned of his wife's infidelity, but it had been in such horrific circumstances it was bound to leave a massive scar.

'Of course I was. I couldn't believe it, not at first,' Melvin confirmed grimly. 'I was gutted.'

'You had no inkling?'

'No. I never thought Anne was like that.'

Hillary believed him. So he probably had no inkling about Mark Burgess either.

'Well, sir, if you can think of anything you want to tell us, you can call me any time.' She handed him a card with the CRT's number on it. Her name was scribbled on the back.

'Thank you.'

Once outside, they walked thoughtfully back to the car.

'DI Squires never liked the husband for it, guv,' Jimmy said, 'and I can't say I do either. Even without the airtight alibi, he just doesn't strike me as the kind. I know you never can tell, right? But still….'

Hillary knew what he meant. 'You get a feeling for it.'

'Yes, guv.'

'Well, I can't say as he's my number one suspect either.'

Jimmy grinned. 'But he stays on the list right, guv?'

'You're learning Jimmy.'

Back at HQ, Hillary and Jimmy found the communal office more or less deserted.

'You can send Vivienne and Sam out to Wendlebury tomorrow, see if they can track down any candidates for Mark Burgess's bored housewife,' Hillary gave out the instructions without hesitation, but Jimmy knew she wasn't trying to throw her weight around. She was, quite simply and inevitably, going to be the operational boss of this outfit, and he had no trouble with that. He didn't think Sam would mind either – she was obviously going to be a great teacher for him. He wasn't so sure about the young madam though.

'It won't hurt to get confirmation of Burgess's alibi,' Hillary continued, unaware of the ex-sergeant's thoughts. 'Don't forget, his butcher's van was regularly seen in Chesterton, so he could have parked it up somewhere and nobody would have thought much about it. Plus, he was known to the victim, so if he'd come calling, she'd probably have let him into the house, even if it wasn't one of his regular days.'

'Right, guv. That should please our Vivienne. It's been twenty years, so it's likely the woman in question has moved house long since, or even been dead for years. Talk about a wild-goose chase.'

99

'It'll be good practise at door-stepping for both of them,' Hillary said, without sympathy.

'Yes, guv,' Jimmy grinned.

'And you can set about getting a warrant to compare Mark Burgess's DNA with that one stray, unaccounted-for hair they found on the victim,' she added, lest he think he could get away with any of the scut work.

'Guv.'

'That should please the super at any rate,' she added, and when she caught his questioning look, added, 'I daresay having something solid, like DNA evidence to go on, will be right up his street. After all these years, we're going to be hard pressed working up a case with just witness statements and circumstantial corroboration.'

'Right. But he'll still go to bat for you if he thinks you've cracked it, guv,' Jimmy predicted.

Hillary blinked. She hadn't put Steven Crayle down as someone who'd be willing to go out on a limb for anyone or anything.

'If you say so, Jimmy,' she said blandly.

Jimmy opened his mouth to say something, then obviously thought better of it, and closed his mouth again. It was obvious that she didn't rate the super very much just yet.

But Jimmy reckoned she'd learn. She was smart. It wouldn't take her long to realize that, ambitious and careful though he undoubtedly was, Steven Crayle was also one of the good guys.

With a sigh, he set about finding a judge who'd be sympathetic to the cause of comparing a single human hair to a very light-weight suspect indeed.

But that evening, as the sun began to set, and the daytime staff at the Kidlington HQ began to make way for the night shift, Jimmy Jessop wasn't the only one contemplating the merits or otherwise of human hair.

Long silken strands of auburn hair, to be precise.

The locker room in the CRT was situated at the end of a particularly torturous set of rooms in the rabbit warren that was the basement. It was also a unisex affair, and Hillary Greene's locker stood beside that of Sergeant Handley, the computer-loving technophile and someone the newest member of CRT had not yet met, a Sergeant Sheila Young.

But neither Crayle nor Young's locker interested Tom Warrington much.

With a set of lock-picks that he'd 'confiscated' from a collar a few months ago, he set about opening Hillary's locker, and eventually succeeded only due to luck rather than to skill. He didn't know it, being an amateur, but he left clear scratches and marks of his lock picking behind on the new brass padlock. Blissfully unaware of this, he eagerly opened the metal door in the deserted room and was bitterly disappointed at the meagre pickings inside.

A spare coat hung from a solitary hanger, and a duffel bag proved to be largely empty. But a half-full perfume bottle had him spraying the air and sniffing appreciatively. The scent, like the woman herself, was classy, subtle and pleasing.

He reached up to the top shelf and removed her comb – a plain and simple black affair, and his heart tripped a little faster at the sight of the long, red hairs stuck in the comb's teeth.

He had to have it.

He pressed the comb into the top of his shirt pocket, where he could feel it resting against his heart. He was sure it was getting warm, setting his breath coming faster and faster.

A sound coming from a little distance behind him made him hastily close and re-lock the door, but it was only someone passing by the outer door on the way to the loos.

Tom was careful not to be seen as he left the locker room, and made his way back upstairs into the main area of the building, which was now largely deserted.

The comb in his breast pocket now felt hot and secret against his ribs, making him smile and want to shout for joy.

This was going to be so good. This time, he could feel it, things would finally go the way he needed them too. And she'd realize he was the man for her.

She'd better.

Tom Warrington didn't take rejection well.

CHAPTER SEVEN

D iane Burgess was a small woman, rounded and rosy-
cheeked, with a fading modest beauty that reminded
Hillary of everyone's generic favourite aunt. She lived in what
had probably been a council house at one point, but which was
now almost certainly bought and paid for, in a pleasant but dull
little cul-de-sac in Bicester's King's End.

The garden was neat and well tended, and when Hillary and
Sam Pickles introduced themselves at her doorstep, they were
immediately invited in.

Hillary could tell by the nervous, puzzled and just faintly
excited look on her face that her husband had not told them
about his interview with the CRT representatives yesterday. So a
visit from the police was the last thing she'd expected.

Hillary knew she was about to ruin the woman's day.

'Mrs Burgess, there's nothing to worry about,' she began
warmly if not altogether truthfully, as the older woman settled
them down in a small living room done out tastefully in shades
of mint-green and amber. 'We're re-investigating the murder of
Mrs Anne McRae. You may remember it?' she began cautiously.

Diane's rosy cheeks paled suddenly, and she put a hand up
nervously to her hair, which was mouse-brown, with streaks of
grey, and swept back in a rather untidy bun at the back of her
head.

'Oh, er, yes?'

'She was the mother of three who was bludgeoned to death in

her kitchen in Chesterton, about twenty years ago now,' Hillary prompted with a reassuring smile.

Diane blinked, her round pale blue eyes becoming gradually more and more frightened. They shot to Sam, who unnerved her further by looking away with a guilty expression that made Hillary want to kick him.

She hid an inner sigh carefully. Women like this always made her feel like a bully in a schoolyard, no matter how kind she tried to be. But she knew from past, and sometimes bitter, experience that pussy footing around wasn't always a kindness when dealing with life's innocents.

'I remember,' Diane said, her voice so low, it was almost a whisper now. She fixed those big blue eyes on Hillary like a dog expecting a kicking.

Hillary smiled bracingly. 'I don't suppose you knew her?'

'Oh no. But I read about it. We all did,' Diane said quickly, as if anxious to be seen to be ultra-honest and truthful.

'All?' Hillary asked casually.

'Oh, you know. My friends, the neighbours around here, my sisters and all. It was a local murder, you see, and not something that you expect to happen to us. I mean, someone like us. I mean, living here, and not in a big city. I mean, you expect drug pushers and, well, women who walk the streets to be in danger. But a housewife from Chesterton....' Her voice trailed off helplessly.

'Yes. I understand,' Hillary said softly. And did. Something like the murder of Anne McRae would have been totally outside of Diane Burgess's experience. When something that shocking and unexpected happened, rocking that little bit of your own personal world that you had always felt to be safe before, it tended to leave a scar.

'But you knew her sister, I believe?' she pressed on.

Diane looked puzzled.

'No, I don't think so.'

And she wasn't lying either, Hillary thought instantly. She knew this type of witness. All her life, Diane Burgess had respected the law – she'd probably been taught it by her respectable working-class parents, and then had it reinforced by her school teachers, and would no doubt have dubbed the same mindset into any children she may have had. Added to that, she was a genuinely timid soul, and they tended to avoid confrontation out of habit. More than anything else, she would be uncomfortable lying, especially to someone in authority. It was far easier for someone like this to simply tell the truth. It required less effort.

Hillary would have bet her first pay cheque – when she got it – that this woman was going to answer anything and everything put to her as honestly and as simply as she could hope for.

'You used to work at Tesco's didn't you? In the town?'

'Oh that was years ago.'

'But you used to serve Anne McRae's sister often. Her name, though you might not know it, was Debbie?'

Diane smiled and shrugged her rounded shoulders. 'I must have served lots of people.'

'But you remembered and recognized your regulars?' Hillary persevered gently.

'Oh yes. People are usually friendly, aren't they?' Diane said simply. And meant it.

Hillary nodded. Yes, she could imagine that most people were friendly with Diane Burgess. She was that kind of woman. Beside her, she could feel Sam practically beaming. No doubt she reminded him of his good old mum.

'I'm sure they are. And I think this is how you knew Anne McRae's sister. Maybe not her name, not as a friend, exactly, but as someone you were friendly with, say.'

'Well, perhaps that's so,' Diane said, sounding puzzled once more. 'But....' she broke off, and looked at Hillary a shade helplessly.

Hillary smiled. 'But what am I asking this for twenty years down the line, that's what you're wondering, isn't it?'

Diane blushed. 'Oh I wouldn't like to say that. I'm sure it must be important otherwise you wouldn't be here.'

Hillary nodded. 'Yes. It is rather important, Mrs Burgess, because, you see, Debbie Gregg remembers you. And she remembers one incident very clearly. It was just after her sister's funeral. She was in Tesco's, when you approached her to offer your condolences.'

Any colour left in Diane's face suddenly fled completely. A look of definite and unmistakable shock passed swiftly across her plump features and left them looking slightly foolish.

'Oh. Yes.'

'You remember the incident now as well?' Hillary prompted softly.

'Yes.'

'You felt sorry for her, and not just because of the murder of her sister. Isn't that so?'

Diane was once again looking at Hillary like a dog that was expecting an undeserved kicking from its master. Beside her, she could feel Sam shifting uncomfortably. She understood his unease, of course. Questioning hard-headed, cold-hearted villains was one thing. Badgering a nice lady was something else again. But he would soon learn that you couldn't pick and choose. If he wanted to become a copper, he'd have to.

'Yes, that's right,' Diane swallowed hard, and in her lap, her hands began to shake. She folded them together, fingers linked, and Hillary watched her knuckles turn white.

The sense of strain was now palpable.

'You told her that you understood what it felt like to be a wife who had been betrayed by her husband,' Hillary was careful to keep her voice calm, almost conversational.

'Yes,' the voice was back to a whisper now.

'You told her that you knew what it was like to have a husband fall under Anne McRae's spell too.'

'Yes.'

'Her specifically, I mean. Not just any woman willing to cheat with a married man.'

'Yes.'

'That your own husband, Mark, had in fact also had an affair with Anne McRae.' Hillary carried on, her voice soft and steady.

Diane continued to stare at her, like a helplessly hypnotized rabbit regarding a stoat. 'Yes.'

'That must have hurt, Mrs Burgess,' Hillary pointed out reasonably, her voice sympathetic now, and inviting confidences.

But all the other woman could manage was her usual, softly spoken, 'Yes.'

'How did you find out?' Hillary asked next, knowing that she'd have to get this witness talking. Monosyllabic answers simply weren't going to cut it.

'Oh, the usual way, I expect,' Diane tried for a brave smile, but it came off as being distinctly wobbly about the edges. 'A supposedly well-meaning friend told me, isn't that how it usually happens? She was a next-door neighbour, who had a cousin who lived in Chesterton, who told her all about how my Mark used to deliver meat to Mrs McRae's house in person. And took a half an hour to do so. She thought I'd want to know.'

Hillary nodded. 'As I said. It must have hurt.'

'It did. At first. But the kids were little, and he swore he wouldn't do it again.' She shrugged helplessly. 'What could I do?'

Hillary nodded. 'But you think he did do it again, don't you?'

'Yes.'

'With his other customers, as well as with Anne McRae?'

'Yes.'

'He's been doing it for years, hasn't he?'

'Yes.'

'And probably still is?'

Diane Burgess made another attempt at a brave smile. 'The kids are all grown up and gone now. I keep telling him that the next time I'll leave him. But I never do.'

'No,' Hillary agreed flatly. Someone like this wouldn't. It was just far easier to take the path of least resistance and turn a blind eye. After all, her husband had been a good provider – he'd held a steady job, his wages had bought off the mortgage on the house.

The kids had been well fed and clothed, and had probably done as well for themselves as their mother could have hoped for. Besides, women of this generation had been brought up to more or less expect men to wander, and it was up to women to turn the other cheek.

Hillary didn't blame her for her attitude and she certainly didn't judge her. After the farce of her own marriage, she knew she was in no position to cast stones. She'd been on the verge of divorcing her own husband, Ronnie Greene, a notoriously bent police officer, when he'd been killed in an RTA. And Ronnie, like Melvin McRae, had been a serial adulterer.

And when she'd finally realized the truth, she'd walked out on him faster than you could say that Robert was your mother's brother.

But Diane Burgess was not that sort of woman. Which was why Hillary was now reasonably sure that she wasn't facing Anne McRae's killer. Diane Burgess simply didn't have the gumption – or the passion – needed to kill a love rival.

'Did you ever think your husband might have killed Mrs McRae, Diane?' Hillary asked quietly instead.

At which the older woman gasped in genuine shock. 'Oh no. Never. Oh no, Mark isn't like that at all.'

Hillary nodded. In that, she rather thought Diane was right. She might not be the sort to take on a fight, but Hillary was willing to believe that, after forty years of marriage, she knew her own husband well enough.

Once back at HQ, Hillary wrote up her notes and dropped a copy of them into the internal mail to keep Steven Crayle updated, then checked in with Jimmy. She'd already packed Sam off to Wendlebury to see how Vivienne was getting on with trying to trace Mark Burgess's alibi, but it now seemed to be hardly a top priority.

'Guv, I've got a judge in mind for a warrant to compare Burgess's DNA to the hair found on our vic,' Sam said, 'but I'm having trouble running him to ground. He's always in court, or on the golf course.'

'I'm shocked.'

Sam grinned. 'I'll keep on it.'

'Right. Fancy giving me a lift into Oxford?'

''Course, Guv. Who we seeing?'

'Jennifer McRae, the victim's youngest.'

'Right. A bit of a troubled girl by all accounts,' Jimmy mused, shrugging into his raincoat.

Hillary nodded. As they trooped back upstairs and got into Jimmy's car, Hillary contemplated what they knew of Anne McRae's youngest child for herself.

Over the years, the file had been kept updated, of course, but it had been Sam and Vivienne who'd done the latest round, and they'd done a pretty thorough job, for novices. Of course, they'd used the computer for most of it, which in this case, had come up trumps, mostly because, of all the McRae offspring, only Jenny had a record sheet.

Mostly petty stuff – it had started off with shoplifting as a teenager. Then it had progressed into one or two soliciting charges when in her early twenties. She'd had two children by two different fathers by then, one of which had beat her regularly, until she'd found the courage to bring a complaint. He was currently serving five to eight at Her Majesty's pleasure, but was due out soon. Since then she'd been busted twice in possession of class 'C' drugs, no time served, and had received a rap across the knuckles for a few other, mostly civil disorders.

She was currently living in a council flat in Headington, in the nearest thing to a high-rise block of flats that the suburb of Oxford was capable of producing.

As Jimmy parked up in front of the building, Hillary felt her spirits droop. The building was typical of its kind, in that it had probably been some architect's dream of a suburban Utopia when it had been built back in the sixties. Then it had been all clean lines and fresh paint, a bold, brave new concept in social housing. Now the paint was peeling, a fair few of the big windows designed to let in all that natural daylight were broken and boarded over, and litter and dogs' mess stained the concrete pavements and walkways.

Several large-sounding (and probably illegal) dogs snarled and snuffled under the gap at the bottom of the doors as they walked past, and from more than one flat, came the sound of babies crying. To make it all that more dreary, the day had turned damp and grey and drizzly, and Jimmy winced as they climbed the fourth set of outer steps.

Seeing her notice, he rubbed one knee. 'Bloody cold damp weather plays havoc with 'em,' he admitted with a sheepish grin.

'None of us are getting any younger Jimmy,' Hillary said, making the old sergeant give her a disbelieving double take. Today, she was dressed in a sage-green skirt and jacket with a lemon-yellow blouse. Her rich auburn hair seemed to be the only spot of fiery life within miles, and Jimmy thought she looked smashing.

Getting old my arse, Jimmy thought indulgently. No wonder Steven Crayle noticed whenever she was around, he thought, with a sly grin.

She knocked on Jenny McRae's door and waited.

Nothing.

She knocked again.

Still nothing. They were about to turn away, when suddenly they heard a door open and close inside, and then the front door reluctantly opened. It was on a chain, and the girl who peered out at them through the gap looked tired and suspicious.

'Yeah?'

Hillary held out her ID. 'I'm with the CRT, Ms McRae. We're looking into your mother's case?'

'Oh. Right. Dad called. Said you'd probably be dropping by. Hang on a mo'.'

The door closed then opened again, and Jenny McRae stepped back to let them in. She was stick-thin, and had the pale pasty face of someone who didn't get out much. Her long hair was lank, and a dirty-blonde in colour. Or maybe it was just dirty, and once washed, would show through in a much brighter shade, like that of her dead mother's.

'The kids are in school,' she said defensively, in what, Hillary guessed, was a pure reflex. If she remembered rightly, Jenny had been prosecuted once before for allowing her children to be habitual truants.

'Yes, I'm sure they are,' she said soothingly.

The flat was tiny – there were, she suspected, only two bedrooms, meaning the children had to share one between them. The living room had enough room for one sofa and a single armchair. There was no television. A glaring omission, which probably meant that Jenny had sold it at some point in order to get a fix. The whole place smelt of faintly sour milk. The walls were painted an off-white, which had probably come courtesy of whoever had had the flat before her.

'Please, sit down.'

Jimmy left the cleanest cushion seat on the sofa for Hillary and perched on one arm for himself.

'So, what can I tell you, then? It can't be much,' Jenny said, sitting on the edge of the seat of the armchair, her hands twisting and turning in her lap. 'I was at the swimming pool when it happened. I used to be one of the sporty set, believe it or not, when I was at school.'

'And swimming was your favourite?' Hillary asked, willing to ease her into it slowly. She knew she had to be careful, she wasn't expecting the girl's memory to be the best and this one looked as though she had all the emotional stability of a roller coaster.

'Yeah. That and running fast. You know, sprints and stuff. Not that marathon or longer-distance stuff.'

'And that day, you were at the pool? Was that a school thing or a private arrangement?' Hillary asked, genuinely curious.

'Oh, private. My best friend was a girl called Maddie Morrison, and her mum was a keen swimmer too. Maddie liked messing around in the water, you know, playing more than exercising, but her mum was teaching me how to time myself doing lengths. I was getting quite fast – the coach at the pool was beginning to notice me and everything. Anyway, she picked us up after school that day, and then took me back home.'

'Your mother knew all about it, right?'

'Oh yeah. Mum and Maddie's mum were friends. Only that day, when Mrs Morrison took me home there were all these police cars there. And Mum was dead. I remember Lucy and Dad sitting with me in Mrs Morrison's car. And Dad told me that Mum was dead.'

Jenny McRae had pale green eyes, and they were staring mostly out of the window. 'Lucy said it would be all right. But it never was. All right I mean. It never was all right again, somehow.'

Jimmy Jessop shook his head with the barest movement of his neck, but Hillary saw it, and silently agreed with him. Looking at Jenny McRae, at the wasted life, the wasted body, the awful tiny flat, and the flat despair in her voice, it was enough to make anyone want to throw in the towel.

'We went to a hotel. Peter had a room with Dad, and I had to share with Lucy. I wanted to have the room with Dad, but Peter did. Peter always got the best of everything,' Jenny said resentfully, as if she was still eleven years old, instead of a woman in her thirties.

Hillary had to smile. 'You don't get on with your brother?'

'Peter's a piss artist. He always was, he always will be. It's not fair – he always lands on his feet. Just look at where he is now – living in some swanky place in North Oxford. The best bloody address in town. 'Course, that old fag that he's living with pays for it all – some sort of snooty academic. It's typical of Peter to end up as some rich old man's toy boy. He calls himself a landscape gardener. Hah! That's a laugh. All he does is plant some roses and bushes for his old man's cronies, and calls himself self-employed. It's a joke. He's just a tart. A male tart, that's all he is.'

Hillary let her rant. She'd come across this type of behaviour before – normal as pie one minute, raving the next. She'd calm down and then be off on another tangent soon.

'I'm hoping to speak to Lucy later on,' she said, hoping to divert her before she got really started.

'Lucy,' Jenny said flatly, slumping back in the chair. 'Lucy's all right, I suppose.' She didn't sound particularly sure. She had a sheen of sweat on her face, and her fingers were beginning to walk along the edge of the chair arm. She was getting jittery. Hillary wondered when she'd last had a fix.

'And I've already spoken to your father,' Hillary continued, her expression totally bland. 'He seems a nice man.'

For the first time, Jenny smiled. 'He is.'

Hillary nodded. Ah, she got it now. Jenny was Daddy's little girl, and she'd have bet the family jewels – if she had any – that Peter had been Anne's favourite. It was often that way in families – Dads favouring the girls, and mothers favouring the boys.

Which left Lucy, the middle child, out in the cold, so to speak. Hillary wondered if she'd felt the draught. When she talked to her later on, she'd have to find out.

The more she knew about the way the McRae family had functioned, the better. Even though the killer obviously wasn't part of the immediate circle, they were her best bet at finding the thread that might lead her to him. Or her.

'He's concerned about you,' Hillary went on. 'When he talked to us, he made it very clear that he didn't want his children to be upset by all this.'

Jenny suddenly beamed. 'That's Dad all right. He's always giving the kids pocket money, and if ever something breaks down around here, he comes and fixes it for me.'

And pays some of the bills too, Hillary would have bet. But wisely, didn't say.

'Did you know about your Mum and your uncle Shane?' Hillary asked instead, and as casually as she could.

'No! Bloody hell, no. None of us did,' Jenny shot forward on her chair again, the agitation back with a vengeance. 'Of course, I didn't really understand it at the time. I kept asking why Auntie Debbie didn't see us anymore.'

'Did you realize that your aunt was a prime suspect for your mother's death at the time?'

'No. I was too little, I suppose. A lot of stuff was kept from me. But I found out, anyway. From the kids at school – they used to tease me, of course. They read the papers, see, and kept them and showed me the articles. They said that my mother was a tramp – something they'd heard their own parents say, I suppose.' Jenny gave a sudden high-pitched yelp of laughter that made Jimmy visibly jump. 'You know, that puzzled me for ages afterwards, because I didn't know what it meant. I mean, to me, a tramp was an old man who couldn't find work who tramped about the countryside looking for handouts. And what did that have to do with my mum?'

Jimmy winced. Kids could be heartless little buggers.

'And thinking back to the days before it happened. Did your mum seem to change in any way?' Hillary ploughed on doggedly.

'No. I know what you mean, and I've thought about it a lot,' Jenny said, surprising Hillary somewhat. Druggy types weren't exactly known for their introspection. 'I lay awake at night for ages, looking back to see if there were any clues that I'd missed, but I don't think there were. She was just the same as usual. She was always pretty, that's what I remember. She always looked prettier than the other mums. And she was cheerful and funny, but you didn't backchat her. Of course, Peter was giving her grief – he always was. He thought he could get away with anything, and he was sulking about something, but Mum just laughed it off, the way she always did.'

Hillary nodded. It sounded right. Their victim might have favoured her only son, but she doubted he'd be allowed to get away with much.

'But if she did have a problem, do you think you'd know about it?' Hillary asked gently.

But Jenny merely snorted. 'I can't imagine anyone giving Mum a problem,' she said with a suddenly savage grin. 'She looked like butter wouldn't melt in her mouth, but Mum was tough. Tougher than Dad, for sure. Tougher than Auntie Debbie too as it turns out. Nobody told Mum what to do, I can tell you that. She wouldn't have cared if anybody had found out about her and Uncle Shane. She just did whatever she wanted to, and look out if you didn't like it.'

Hillary nodded, feeling her antenna begin to twitch. 'So if she had a problem with someone, she'd take the fight to them, you think?'

'Oh yeah. She wouldn't back off from anything,' Jenny said instantly. 'You can ask anyone who knows her, and they'd say the same thing.'

'Yes, that's the impression I'm gaining of your mother too,' Hillary agreed softly. 'Well, thank you, Jenny. May we come back if I can think of anything else that I might need to know?'

'Oh yeah. Any time,' Jenny said. She didn't sound particularly enthusiastic about it, but Hillary put that down to an aversion to having cops about.

Driving back to HQ, Jimmy wound down a window. 'Sorry about the draught, guv, but I've got to get the smell of that place out of my head.'

'I know what you mean.'

'Losing her mum really buggered her up, didn't it?'

'Absolutely.'

'You thinking what I'm thinking? About what she said about her mum?' Jimmy asked.

'About her being the tough one in the family?' Hillary shot back. 'Yeah, it opens up possibilities doesn't it? With her husband away for long spells, it makes sense that she was the one who took the reins, so to speak. And someone like that, someone so self-confident and used to taking charge might not be aware of the dangers in confronting someone.'

Jimmy nodded. 'Just what I was thinking. If someone was

threatening her or her family, she'd go at them no holds barred, not realizing that she might be walking right into something that she couldn't handle.'

Hillary sighed. 'Thing is, Jimmy, we've no idea what that might be – and there's lots of possibilities. If someone was threatening her kids in some way, she'd be vicious. But let's not forget she was playing the field – she had two lovers that we know about, and who's to say there weren't more? That's a minefield all on it's own. And if someone was trying to blackmail her, for instance, I can't see her simply rolling over and taking it lying down.'

'Then there's her marriage,' Jimmy said. 'She might not have been the faithful type, but I get the feeling she wouldn't have wanted to divorce her husband or upset the kids. If someone was threatening to tell Melvin about her, she'd have it out with them.'

'That leaves the field well and truly wide open, doesn't it?' Hillary said grimly.

Jimmy sighed heavily. The guv was right. So far they had nothing. Still, it was early days yet, and nobody was expecting a miracle. After all, the case was twenty years old, and colder than a witch's tits. The chances are it would have to go back into the unsolved pile when they were done, anyway.

But he doubted that anybody had told Hillary that. She wasn't the sort of woman who ever admitted defeat, and like a terrier with a rat, he couldn't see her letting this case go.

But she might have to. The sad fact was, that the majority of the cold cases that were looked at a second time, remained unsolved. And then you simply had to go on to the next one.

But he just couldn't see Hillary taking kindly to having her case snatched away from her and being ordered to forget about it and get on with something else. And that might very well be what Steven Crayle would have to do at some point in the near future. That was part of his job, after all. Jimmy grinned as he drove. And he was welcome to it. He only hoped he'd be around – but at a safe distance – to watch the fireworks fly when it happened!

It was nearly lunchtime by the time she got back, and Sam and Vivienne were already back at the office, Vivienne looking damp and displeased.

'No luck with Mark Burgess, guv,' Sam reported, without being asked. 'He still does the rounds there, and a lot of people have confirmed that he's got an eye for the ladies all right, but no one's willing to point the finger.'

'I think it's gross,' Vivienne said with a shudder. 'A middle-aged butcher, for Pete's sake. Some women have no class.'

Hillary bit back a smile. No doubt to someone of Vivienne's age and good looks, the thought of anyone over thirty and possessing a less than physically perfect body, having sex was the ultimate in bad taste.

Unless they looked like Steven Crayle of course, she corrected herself with an inner smile. She hadn't missed the goo-goo eyes the youngster had been giving their boss. She wondered, briefly, if he secretly enjoyed being the object of a young and pretty girl's desire, then abruptly cut the thought off.

He was a man. Of course he did.

'Up for a pint at the Bull, guv?' Jimmy asked, interrupting her suddenly sour thoughts.

'Give me ten minutes,' Hillary agreed readily. She went back to her stationery cupboard and picked up her bag and headed to the locker rooms. There she used the ladies next door and went to her locker. She noticed the scratches the moment she lifted the padlock into her hand and, with her own key paused a centimetre above it, blinked in surprise.

Slowly, she opened the locker and looked inside. Her spare coat was hanging just how she'd left it. Her holdhall, though still on the bottom shelf, had its flaps showing. But she had stashed it the other way around. Which meant that someone had moved it. Which meant it had almost certainly been gone through. Her eyes swept on, doing a rapid, mental inventory.

Her perfume bottle wasn't in the same place either.

And her spare comb was gone.

She stood there for several moments, baffled.

There weren't that many possibilities to explain it. The first and most likely, was that there was a thief about. Nothing new or surprising in that, of course. They were everywhere, just like rats. Seldom seen, but you knew they were there. And the fact that they were in a police station meant nothing at all.

She checked the padlocks on the lockers either side of hers, and then a few at random. Most of the padlocks were old and had their fair share of scratches, but none that looked new or recent.

So why would a thief target her locker specifically, and no one else's? She'd only be on the job for a few days – if robbery had been the motive, any self-respecting light-fingered tea-leaf would know better. They'd wait a few weeks before striking, giving her plenty of time to store more stuff here – maybe a spare handbag, gear, hell, even trainers or a watch. That way they'd be far more likely to come up with something they could sell on for a reasonable profit.

No. This was not the work of a thief.

But the comb was missing. Not her perfume, which was nearly a full bottle, and might have been taken to give to a girlfriend as a makeshift present.

But her comb. Which was something very personal.

Unless someone into voodoo wanted a strand of her hair, of course. The thought made her lips twist into a grim smile. If she suddenly started getting sharp stabbing pains, then she might consider the occult.

Until then, there was only one likely explanation.

She had picked up an admirer.

'Shit,' Hillary said succinctly.

Melvin McRae looked surprised to see Sam and Jimmy on his doorstep.

After their lunchtime drink, Hillary had asked Sam to take

Jimmy to re-interview Melvin, and find out if he knew about Mark Burgess, or any other casual affairs his wife might have had, whilst she borrowed Sam's car and went to interview Lucy McRae.

Melvin led the two men back into the pleasant living room overlooking the church. This time he poured himself a beer from the fridge in the kitchen before they started, and offered them tea.

'No thank you, sir,' Jimmy said politely. He was still full from his two lunchtime pints, and he'd made sure Sam had driven over here. 'Sorry to bother you so soon, sir, but we've uncovered some new information. Its might be rather painful,' Jimmy warned him.

'Oh?' Melvin said warily.

'Were you aware that your wife had had an affair with another man, sir? Apart from Shane Gregg, that is.'

Melvin drank slowly from his bottle of beer.

Finally he sighed. 'No. But I did wonder. I mean, when I learned about Shane. It had been going on for some time, you see, and neither me nor Debbie had any idea. Well, it made me wonder, that's all.'

Jimmy nodded. 'Yes. If she'd done it once, maybe she'd done it before. I can see how it might, sir.'

'So it was true?'

'Yes, sir. Do you know or remember a man called Mark Burgess?'

'Burgess? No.'

'He used to have a butcher's round. Still does.'

Melvin McRae shrugged. 'I left all that sort of thing to Anne. The shopping, buying food, keeping the house, feeding us, that sort of thing. I was away such a lot, you see.'

Jimmy nodded. 'So none of the neighbours ever mentioned anything to you, like? You know, trying to be kind. Well, trying to keep you in the picture. You see, sir, it seems unlikely that nobody knew what was happening.'

Melvin smiled grimly. 'No. But then again, most people like to keep themselves to themselves, don't they? Besides, everyone liked Anne. She was popular with the neighbours. Even our friends were more friends with Anne, than with me, if you see what I mean?'

Jimmy did. When it came to infidelity, they'd be more likely to side with Anne, is what he was saying. Probably most of them believed that Melvin McRae had more than his fair share of foreign birds when he was away on his coach tours anyway, so who was he to kick up a fuss?

'All right. Well, thank you, sir,' he said. He couldn't see that there was any point taking it any further. And it wasn't as if the man didn't have a solid alibi.

As Melvin McRae closed the door behind him, Jimmy only hoped the guv'nor was having better luck with her witness.

CHAPTER EIGHT

Hillary regarded the block of flats thoughtfully. Whilst not quite as insalubrious as the building that housed the youngest McRae offspring, it was a far cry from being what most people would describe as a des res. Red brick walls gave way to black roof tiles, both somehow managing to look like dreary smears on the landscape. None of the windows were broken or boarded over, but most were dirty, and needed a good wash. Where there was paint work it was cracked and fading.

Hillary wondered if Lucy McRae had always lived like this, or if it was a sign of recent hard times. According to her files, unlike her younger sister, Lucy had no previous record.

But that could just be because she'd been more careful.

Hillary walked to the door and saw that the intercom and locking method wasn't working. Anyone could just walk into the communal hall area, which she did, wrinkling her nose as the faint scent of human urine tickled her nostrils. Plain cream walls echoed her footsteps coldly back at her as she set off up the grey, not exactly clean, concrete steps, to the third floor.

And whilst there were no pitbulls snuffling threats under the door, or the sound of crying babies, the silence seemed somehow worse. She could imagine that most of the residents who lived there were first time buyers, and as such, nearly everyone was out at work. The building had an abandoned feeling that made her shoulder blades ache in a tight knot as she walked along the echoing landing, checking the door numbers as she passed by.

When she got to Lucy McRae's flat, she rang the bell and waited. She knew from the file, that Lucy was unemployed at the moment and claiming benefit, although she had held down a variety of jobs; but never for very long.

Commitment issues, maybe, Hillary speculated. Or maybe she was one of those people who just couldn't take instruction, and so was constantly running foul of their boss, believing as they inevitably did, that they knew better and could do better, given the chance.

The door opened, revealing a very attractive blonde woman, who gazed back at her blankly.

Hillary was slightly taken aback. Of all her children, Lucy resembled her mother the most. The photographs of Anne McRae, both alive and dead, were now burned into Hillary's memory, and here she was, almost alive again and in the flesh. The same longish blonde hair, and bright eyes, the same curvaceous figure. And if she had inherited more than just her mother's looks, Lucy might well have too high an opinion of herself to make life comfortable for either herself or those around her.

'Yes?' she demanded.

Hillary held out her ID.

'Oh right. I've been expecting you. Dad called. Come on in.' When she opened the door wider, Hillary could see that Lucy was wearing designer leggings of grey silk, ruched at the pockets and tapering to slim ankles. With it she wore an apricot jersey, obviously cashmere, and a set of dangling pearl earrings. Her hair was clean and looked as if it had been newly cut and styled, and her make-up was discreet and flawless. She also wore an expensive perfume, the name of which momentarily escaped Hillary.

The person definitely did not fit the surroundings, and Hillary was suddenly sure that the living arrangements had to be temporary. From what Sam and Vivienne had been able to unearth about the eldest daughter of their murder victim, Lucy had never married, but had lived with a succession of men, all of whom had been both older than herself, and wealthy.

Shades of her brother there, if Jenny was to be believed, Hillary mused. Of course, she wasn't sure that she did. For all she knew, Peter McRae was deeply in love with his partner. They'd certainly been together for nearly eight years now, which sounded more like a long-term and stable relationship, something that Lucy had been unable to find.

'Sorry about the flat. I'll be moving out soon,' Lucy said, giving Hillary a little eerie feeling, as if somehow the younger woman had been reading her mind.

Hillary looked around and smiled briefly. 'It's fine.'

But it wasn't so much fine, Hillary mused, as interesting. The general décor was old and dull, but a large, very new looking, wide screen plasma HD television sat in one corner. Another new-looking personal CD player rested on top of a plain battered wooden coffee table, along with several of the latest pop music releases. When Lucy indicated a chair, Hillary saw the sparkle of gold and diamonds on her wrist, indicating very nice bling indeed.

As Hillary slowly sat down in a well-worn but comfortable brown leather armchair, she had the feeling that Lucy McRae had been in a dry spell, but had recently, perhaps very recently, come into some money. And she made a mental note to herself to ask Sam or Vivienne to check around with the neighbours, see if any of them knew Lucy well, or where she might have got the money from for her little luxuries.

'Auntie Debbie said you'd been to see her.'

Hillary felt a jolt of surprise, and carefully squashed it. 'Oh? I didn't realize the family was still in touch with Mrs Gregg.'

'Well, we're not. Not really. I mean, she doesn't see Dad at all, and Peter's too happy living the good life to bother. But I reckon Jenny might touch her up for a couple of quid, now and then.'

'You know that for a fact?'

'Oh no, just speculating. I know my little sis, see.'

'But you yourself see your aunt regularly?'

'Oh, I wouldn't say regularly. But she's not banned from my doorstep or anything,' Lucy said, with mock-drama.

'I take it from that, that you don't think your aunt had anything to do with your mother's death?' Hillary asked bluntly.

'Nope. But I know you lot did,' Lucy said, sitting back in her own chair and crossing her legs. As she did so, a simple gold ankle chain glinted in the grey light filtering in through the dusty windows.

Hillary allowed herself to smile wryly. 'I take it DI Squires made his suspicions plain?'

Lucy laughed, a harsh, less-than-musical sound that made Hillary inwardly wince.

'Let's just say he shouldn't play poker.'

Hillary nodded. 'I asked your father if he believed in his sister-in-law's guilt.'

'Oh yeah?' Lucy went suddenly still. 'What did he say?'

Hillary's eyes sharpened on her. 'He said that he didn't know. Not for sure, one way or the other. But I got the feeling that he doubted it.'

Lucy shrugged. 'Well, we know her, see, and you don't. I just can't see Auntie Debbie taking a rolling pin to anyone.'

'And Jenny? Did she think your aunt did it?'

Lucy laughed again. 'You'll have to ask her. Nowadays I don't think Jenny thinks much of anything at all. No longer capable of it, if you know what I mean? The coke's cooked her brains. It's only a matter of time before they take those poor kids off her and put them into a home.'

'You don't fancy taking them on yourself then?' Hillary asked, more rhetorically than anything else. She could see for herself that the McRae children were hardly filled with the milk of familial kindness.

Right on cue, Lucy shuddered. 'Hell no! I'm never having kids,' she said emphatically. And there was now something as hard as diamonds in her voice. Hillary looked at her closely.

'The loss of your mother seems to have blighted you all, in one way or another,' she said carefully. She was treading a fine line here, and she knew it. The last thing she wanted to do was come off as if she was offering phoney sympathy. Or even worse, sounding like some know-it-all social worker or amateur psychologist. But she needed Lucy to open up more than she was currently doing. At the moment she was all brittle, cynical defiance.

'What did you expect?' she asked sharply. 'I came home from school when I was thirteen years old and found my mum murdered on the kitchen floor.'

Hillary nodded. 'Yes,' she said simply.

The flat, unemotional reply, as she'd expected, caught Lucy by surprise, and gave her pause. And in that pause, before she could have time to get her act together, Hillary said, 'Tell me about it.'

Lucy sniffed, then sighed, then shrugged. It was as if she had a catalogue of gestures to choose from and wasn't sure which one was appropriate. In the end, she shrugged again. 'Fine. As if I didn't say all of this, over and over again, at the time.'

'That was then,' Hillary said, 'now is now. Tell me what you remember, think and feel *now*.'

Lucy glanced at her again, suspicion and something like grudging respect clouding her face. Then she opted for the shrug again.

'OK. I remember it was hot and sunny. It was June, and I couldn't wait for the school holidays to begin. My last class was French, which I hated, but we were in the language lab, so that wasn't too bad. Me and Melanie Finch messed about in there, and got told off by snotty Forbes, but he didn't keep us in detention. Me and Peter caught the bus, and got off it together, but then he buggered off somewhere with one of his mates, like he always did, and I went down to the playing field.'

Hillary nodded. All of this had been in her original statement. 'Bit old for playing on the swings, weren't you?' she asked, with a slight smile, and Lucy grinned back.

'Bugger the swings. There was this girl, Janey Grey, who hung out down there and had all sorts of goodies that she was willing to share. She was a bit of a fat kid, and never popular, so I guess she felt the need to ingratiate herself.'

Hillary felt herself stiffen. 'Drugs?'

'Bloody hell no,' Lucy snorted on a laugh. 'This was twenty years ago, remember, in a little sleepy Oxfordshire village. Oh, I dare say anyone wanting drugs could have got them, but I was just thirteen. No, I'm talking about fags, or cider, or porn.' Lucy laughed suddenly. 'It was funny, because everyone's brothers were always salivating over *Penthouse* and what have you, but Janey had found some gay porn. So of course, all us girls hung out with her just to get a peek. None of us had seen a naked man before. Anyway, like I said, I hung out down there for a bit, but Janey wasn't around, and I got bored pretty quickly back in those days, and went home.'

Lucy suddenly drew up her legs under her, and rested the top of her chin on her bent knees. Her hands hugged her ankles and her eyes turned back to the windows.

But Hillary knew she wasn't seeing the cold grey March day outside, or the bleak Banbury housing estates beyond that. Instead, she was in a pretty village on a hot summer's day, walking back to the house that was her home, where she'd always felt loved and safe.

'I opened the gate and walked up the path. Everything was the same as it always was. Mum kept the garden nice, and we had sweet williams in the front and some love-in-a-mists and lilies and a couple of rose bushes. I stopped to smell my favourite one – a white rose. All the neighbours admired our garden.'

Hillary nodded.

'I went to the door and let myself in.'

'It was locked?'

'No. But it was shut. Mum was always home from working at the charity shop by the time us kids got in, so all I had to do was turn the handle.'

'Go on.'

'I went into the hall and slung my bag into the cupboard under the stairs, as usual. Then I went straight through into the kitchen. I always did. It would be hours until teatime and Mum had usually baked something – flapjacks were my favourite. I'd have a cup of tea and some cake or whatever.'

'It sounds ideal,' Hillary said, wondering if Lucy was accurately portraying her family life, or was remembering it as she'd wished it had been.

She was not one for introspection, however, for all she did was shrug dismissively. 'It was OK. So I went through as usual, and the first thing I saw was her feet. Lying on the floor, behind the big kitchen table. I thought she'd fainted or something. It was a hot day, like I said, and if she'd been baking, it would be even hotter in the kitchen. Of course, she hadn't fainted. When I went around the table I saw the red stuff on her head and in her hair, and leaking out on the tiles. It was splashed up some cupboards too.'

Lucy's voice suddenly stopped. She dragged her eyes from the window.

'I don't really remember much about the next bit. Sometimes I think I cried out her name, or screamed or whimpered or something, and sometimes I think I just stood there, saying nothing. Doing nothing.'

Hillary took a long, slow breath. 'That's the shock.'

'Yes. I remember going back outside, and standing in the doorway under the porch, in the shade. I don't know why.'

'Did you see anyone outside? Window cleaners, butcher's delivery vans, neighbours?'

Lucy frowned. 'I don't think so. Like I said, I'm not very clear on that. The next thing I remember clearly is hearing the garden gate go, and seeing Peter walking up. I stopped him from going inside, and then for some reason, I don't know why, I insisted we go a few doors down to Mrs Wilkins's place. She was a neighbour, lived on her own. Lost her husband, I expect, or he'd buggered off and left her. I always liked her, though. She was a lot older than Mum, but she always had a kind word for me.'

Hillary nodded. 'And then?'

'I told her and Peter together what I'd found. Peter wanted to go back, but I wouldn't let him. Then Mrs Wilkins must have phoned the police because a little while later they arrived, and Mrs Wilkins made this woman copper in uniform some tea, and made me and Peter drink some too. It was hot and sweet and by then Peter was all shaking and crying and what have you. I don't think I was. I can't remember crying or shaking anyway. I just sat there drinking this hot sweet tea. Then Dad came.'

Lucy sighed. 'Then we went to a hotel. Then we buried Mum. End of story. I wonder if Mrs Wilkins is still alive?'

Hillary wasn't about to leave it there, of course. 'I got the feeling, from talking to Jenny, that she always felt that Peter was your mum's favourite. And I guessed for myself that Jenny was probably your dad's. Are either of us right?'

'Both,' Lucy said flatly. 'Dad didn't think they would have any more kids after me. They had the two children, see, a boy and a girl – isn't that what everyone wants? One of each? So I think Dad thought that she, my mum that is, had decided enough was enough. So when Jenny came along she was always going to be an added bonus.'

Lucy shrugged, and continued, seemingly without rancour, 'Jenny was a "little girl" type of little girl if you know what I mean? Always looked cute as a button in pigtails with ribbons, and played with dolls and crawled onto Dad's lap like a bichon frise the moment he came home from one of his coach trips. Me, I wasn't that needy.'

Lucy shrugged again, and regarded Hillary sourly. 'Anything else you'd like to know about us McRaes?'

'Peter was your mum's favourite then?'

'Yeah, poor sod. Rather him than me. She was always more on his case than on ours.'

Hillary wasn't fooled by the supposed sympathy for her

brother. Deep down inside, Lucy must have resented every perceived slight, every little proof that she was second best to both her mother and father.

'Did you know about your Uncle Shane and your mother?' Hillary asked, and saw Lucy's eyes narrow suddenly.

'Of course not,' she said flatly. And far too quickly.

Hillary smiled. 'Now you're telling me lies,' she chided softly.

Lucy all but gaped at her, then laughed, then shook her head. 'Nope. As if I would.' But her eyes gleamed with mockery, and Hillary knew she was mentally challenging her to prove it.

Hillary tried again. 'Come on, Lucy, let's not play games. You must have felt like the odd one out in that family. And you were thirteen, and into gay porn! You're not telling me you didn't know what was going on. You're obviously as smart as a whip, and I bet back then, nothing missed your eagle eyes. Kids always are very observant, and I bet you loved spying on the grown ups. Hugging secrets to yourself, gathering power.'

Lucy forced herself to relax and let her legs back down onto the ground. Shit, this one was perceptive. She'd have to be careful.

'Sorry,' she shook her head. 'I had no idea she was having it off with Debbie's old man,' she said, deliberately crude now.

Hillary nodded. 'OK, play it that way if you like. Did you know she was also having an affair with Mark Burgess?'

Lucy shrugged and laughed. 'If you say so. Like I said, I was just a kid, and in spite of what you think, I had more important things to do than care about what my Mum was up to. I had just hit puberty, for Pete's sake. I was into boys, and pop music and growing up. My biggest fear was spots on my face. Mum's life was boring. Any adult was boring. My friends, what boyfriends we had in our sights, discos and trying to find ways of getting at some booze – that's what I was interested in.'

'So your mum was very discreet about her love life.'

'Must have been. Poor Aunt Debs had no idea Shane was sniffing around, and it's usually the deceived wife that's the first to suspect isn't it?' Lucy asked.

Hillary shrugged. 'Either that, or they're the last to know.'

'You think one of her men friends bumped her off, don't you?' Lucy said flatly.

'Don't you?'

Lucy tensed, then forced her shoulders to relax. 'Like I said, I've no idea.'

'How do you feel about it now?' Hillary pressed, sensing evasion, and not liking it. For the first time since being handed this case on Monday, she strongly suspected that she'd finally found someone who could shed some new light on it, and she didn't want to play ball. It could become very frustrating, if Hillary let it.

'What do you mean?' Lucy asked cautiously.

'I mean now that you're an adult. You'll soon be more or less the same age as your mum was when she was killed. How do you see your mum now, as an adult woman yourself?'

Lucy shrugged. 'Don't know. I never thought about it. Of course, our lives are totally different. She was married to Dad, but I've never wanted to get married. And she had kids. I'd rather die first! And our tastes are totally different, that's for sure. You wouldn't catch me sleeping with a butcher for instance – I've got more pride than that! I suppose I think Mum was just a bored housewife. A cliché, right? I don't blame her, exactly – Dad was away a lot, having fun abroad, and she was stuck with the house and the kids and the boring little part-time job. Why shouldn't she have some fun?'

Hillary nodded. 'Why not a butcher?' she asked silkily. 'I mean, why not a butcher, specifically?'

Lucy frowned at her, shifting uneasily on her chair, sensing danger. 'What do you mean? I just wouldn't, that's all. Thinking of hands that had been handling dead meat all day, all over me.' She shuddered. 'Ugh, no thanks.'

Hillary nodded. It was as she suspected. Lucy knew about her mother's lovers all right. She had mentioned Mark Burgess, but had never said what he did for a living. And why would a school child, who'd be at school most of the time when the butcher's van came around, even know that the name of the butcher her mother brought the family joint from, unless she had made it her business to find out?

'Do you have any ideas who might have killed your mother?' she asked carefully.

Lucy shrugged again, and her eyes went to the window once more. 'How should I know?' she asked blandly.

Steven Crayle tapped on Hillary's door and opened it without waiting for a summons.

The room was empty. It was vaguely annoying but then he didn't really blame her for spending most of the time out in the field – if he'd had this tiny cubicle for a work area, he'd soon feel the need to get out as well.

He'd read her notes on the case so far, and couldn't fault her groundwork. He'd wanted to stop by and discuss her opinions on how long she'd like to work on it before calling it quits, and felt an odd flutter of disappointment to find the room empty.

Well, empty of people anyway. But something else was here – and making its presence extremely obvious. Its perfume alone was filling the tiny space with heady fragrance.

Two dozen blood-red moss roses, arranged in a crystal vase, sat on her desk, taking up almost as much room as her computer and files.

Steven's eyes rested on them for a moment, and the flutter of disappointment hardened into something much more green-eyed.

'Who's the man then?' he heard himself say, and for a second, actually thought he'd spoken out loud, until he realized that the thought was so strong, it had sounded almost physical.

As far as he knew, Hillary Greene had spent her year and half's retirement cruising the waterways in her canal boat, and had only been back less than a week.

So she was a quick worker to have picked up a boyfriend already, he thought grimly. Or maybe she'd left behind her some

131

poor lovelorn schmuck who was now desperately trying to win her back.

He glanced behind him, but the rabbit warren was deserted, and he stepped into her office and checked the vase. There was no note. If they'd been delivered from the florists, there was usually a note.

Or had she brought them in herself?

Somehow that didn't seem very likely. Oh, he knew he hadn't known her for long, but he wouldn't have her pegged as the type who brought flowers in to work. Or pot plants, or personal photos either for that matter.

He shrugged, and retreated, closing the door behind him.

It was no business of his who left Hillary Greene flowers.

But in that, as it so happens, he was wrong.

Very wrong.

When Hillary returned to HQ she went to the communal office, and gave her team the rundown on her interview with Lucy. When she'd finished, there was a moment of thoughtful silence.

'You think she's holding back, guv?' Jimmy picked up on what she'd left unspoken at once, and she smiled at him. He really was shaping up into a first-class right hand man. Pretty soon they'd be finishing each other's sentences.

'Yes. Sam, Vivienne, I want you to go back to Banbury later, when people are coming back from work, and see what you can find out about her. She had some pretty expensive stuff at her place, and was wearing more than her share of bling. I think she's come into some money recently, and I want you to see if any of her neighbours can shed light on it.'

'Sounds like a waste of time to me,' Vivienne said, then flushed as both Sam and Jimmy looked at her. 'What? Doesn't it? What has it got to do with who killed her mum twenty years ago?'

'Maybe something, maybe nothing,' Jimmy said, with an edge to his voice. 'But when you're given orders, you do what you're told.'

Vivienne flushed again, and reached petulantly for her bag. 'Want a Nazi salute while I'm at it?'

'No, just a curtsy will do,' Hillary said, grinning widely.

Sam slunk by her in Vivienne's wake, not quite able to meet her eyes. No doubt he was embarrassed by Vivienne's insubordination, and was anxious not to get tarred with the same brush.

'Don't worry, she won't be here much longer,' Jimmy said, looking at the space vacated by the tempestuous teenager. 'Once she realizes that the boss isn't going to take her up on her generous offer, she'll be off.'

Hillary sighed, and leaned against the doorframe. She was not about to get side-tracked into gossiping about Steven Crayle's love life. She was far too canny for that! 'You've read Lucy McRae's file. What's your take on her?' she asked instead.

Jimmy frowned slightly. 'I think she's used to living off men. And from what you say, it's pretty clear that she's currently inbetween beaus.'

'Yes, that's how I read it too. But this sudden access to ready cash worries me.'

'Why, guv? It's obvious, isn't it? She's found another mug.'

Hillary nodded. 'Perhaps. That might account for the jewellery. But if you're a professional man-eater, like Lucy seems to be, you don't exactly just ask for cash, do you? She had a fancy TV and personal stereo. I didn't get a look at much else, but I'd bet she's got some other gear too. But if you're hooking a man, you've got to be far more subtle than that, right? Maybe you start off going on long romantic holidays – that he pays for. Then maybe you let him "help you pick out" a car, which he ends up paying for. You don't just say to him, "give me some dough, I want to buy a new telly", do you?'

'Not unless she's on the game, guv,' Jimmy pointed out. 'Just because her sister's a street walker, doesn't mean to say Lucy isn't a bit more upmarket. Perhaps her clients are a bit more discerning, that's all. You know, they go out, have dinner, back to her place, do the business and then he just happens to leave some cash lying around, which they both pretend not to notice. Then he goes back to the wife or the day job or whatever, and she pockets the dough. Until the next time. And both parties, if asked, will swear to the fact that they're just having a little affair. Nothing so sordid as being a pro with her John. Oh no, nothing like that.'

'Perhaps,' Hillary agreed. The scenario wasn't that far fetched, she knew. People liked to lie to themselves, as well as each other. 'But I just didn't get that vibe from her. I got the feeling she was in for the long haul – maybe on the lookout for husband material. She isn't getting any younger, after all. And if she is looking to her future, she's not going to blow it by being so obviously money-grabbing.'

Jimmy frowned. 'So what does that leave?'

Hillary shrugged. 'Maybe I'm reading more into this than there is. But I'm thinking … maybe blackmail.'

Jimmy let out his breath slowly. 'Bit of a leap, guv.'

'Oh yeah. Which is why I'm not going to put it onto paper yet. Not unless I get some confirmation. Tell you what, find out how long Lucy's been in that flat, and see if you can find out if she has got herself another mug. If she has – well, then fair enough. He's probably "helping her out" with her living arrangements. But if not – then I think we'd better keep a close eye on our Lucy. The timing on this thing stinks. We take a new interest in her mother's case, and now she suddenly seems to have found a sudden source of revenue? Add to that the fact that I think she knew all about her mother's lovers, and might know the names and identities of men we haven't even uncovered yet, and what have you got?'

Jimmy whistled through his clenched teeth. 'A recipe for trouble, all right.'

Hillary nodded. 'Exactly. Anyway, see what you can nose out, Jimmy.'

'OK, guv.'

Hillary went back to her office and found the roses on her desk.

Like Crayle not an hour before, she sniffed the sweetly perfumed air, and like Crayle, checked for a note. Unlike her boss, however, she was not surprised to find the flowers were strictly anonymous.

Her admirer was getting bolder.

Hillary slowly sat down behind her desk and eyed the flowers belligerently. Unlike most shop-bought blooms, these were an old fashioned variety that actually had a perfume. Thus, they were probably expensive. Did that mean her admirer had a relatively good pay cheque? Not necessarily, she knew. Obsessive types thought nothing of spending money they could ill-afford on the most ridiculous of things.

How had he got them down here?

She frowned over this for some time. Had he just walked in, as bold as brass, holding a vaseful of roses in his hands? Surely he'd have been seen by someone?

She checked the quality of the vase – cut crystal. Nice.

But there were plenty of ways you could smuggle them in. In a rucksack, the roses wrapped protectively in tissue paper, the vase stashed separately. The admirer could then fill the vase with water in the gents, then just have a few paces to negotiate, unseen, to her little stationery cupboard.

She wondered, briefly, if they could be from Steven Crayle, then swore at herself for being so stupid. Of course they weren't from Crayle.

Why would they be?

No. She had to face facts. In all probability she had herself, at the very least, a fan.

But far more likely, she had herself a stalker. And one who was just starting to step up the pace.

She felt her heart sink. This was just what she needed.

Andy Squires turned into the familiar parking lot of the HQ and found a space near the back. He whistled tunelessly as he made his way towards the building, telling himself that he wasn't nervous. He was just popping in to say hello. Strictly a courtesy call. He'd heard on the grapevine that someone in CRT was working on one of his cold cases, and he wondered if he could be of any help.

He took a deep breath, pushed open the doors and walked into the foyer.

The desk sergeant was an old crony of his, and recognized him immediately. They chatted for a short while, but desk sergeants were canny beasts, and without Andy having to ask him, he soon pointed him down into the depths where CRT hung their hats.

'Hillary Greene's the gal you want,' the desk sergeant called to his retreating back, and grinned to himself as old Andy waved a thanks. The poor old guy must be shitting himself, scared stiff that the wonder girl was going to succeed where he'd failed. Nobody liked to look a chump, retired or not. It was a shame that. He'd been a good copper had Andy Squires.

But not in Hillary Greene's class, and no mistake. They were currently taking bets on how long it would take the newly-back-in-harness Hillary Greene to solve her first cold case. He himself had a tenner on her bringing it in before the end of the month.

The desk sergeant heaved a sigh, and went back to his cross-word puzzle.

Jimmy looked up at the stranger in the doorway. 'Yes, sir, can I help you?'

Andy nodded. 'I was looking for Hillary Greene. I'm DI Squires. Sorry, ex-DI.'

Jimmy grinned and got up, holding out his hand. 'Sir, glad to meet you. I'm ex-job myself. Sergeant James Jessop. I know the guv was hoping to speak to you at some point. Hang on, I'll go and fetch her.'

He left, returning a scant moment later with a good-looking redhead.

Andy took a deep breath. So this was the legendary Hillary Greene. His palms felt slightly damp as they reached out to shake her hand.

CHAPTER NINE

Hillary stepped forward as ex-DI Andy Squires turned around. He looked to be in his early seventies, and was one of those lean men with an exceptionally rounded pot belly, probably due to drinking too much beer. He'd kept a full head of hair, but it was dirty-white in colour, with a yellowish tinge. If his hands had been the same colour, she'd have said it was due to nicotine staining. His eyes were vaguely dark, vaguely bloodshot, but he was wearing a clean pair of heavy-material black trousers, and his knitted dark blue sweater was equally clean.

'DI Greene,' Andy said, but Hillary quickly shook her head.

'Not any more. I'm a civilian consultant now. Call me Hillary.'

'Sorry. 'Course. I was in the Bull the other day, and I heard you'd pulled one of my old cases. I just thought I'd pop in and see if you wanted to pick my brains.'

'I'd love to. Jimmy, how about some coffee all round? Please, Mr Squires, take a seat.'

'Thanks. Call me Andy.'

They all sat and sipped the not totally unpalatable coffee for a few moments. 'So, you've been retired long?' Hillary asked affably.

'Nearly thirteen years now. Bloody hell, where's the time gone?' Andy moaned.

'You don't have to tell me,' Hillary said with a smile, as Jimmy snorted and echoed the sentiments. 'Me and Jimmy here, as you can see, just couldn't keep away,' Hillary added. 'You miss the job too?'

'Not so much as I want to come back to it,' Andy said after a few moments of thought. He looked faintly surprised to be hearing himself say it. 'Of course, I think about it often. Especially the ones that get away, you know?'

Hillary did.

'Anne McRae was one of them for you, I take it?' she asked, careful to keep her tone emotionless. The last thing she wanted was for him to get proprietorial or defensive.

Andy sighed. 'Yeah. I guess she is. I can still see her now – a pretty blonde lass, laying out on her kitchen floor, with the rolling pin that killed her laying beside her. It seemed so damned *wrong*, you know?'

Again, Hillary did. Every death you investigated was different. As a general rule, dead junkies made you tired and sad. RTAs made you depressed and grateful that it hadn't been you or yours in the mangled wreckage – which in turn made you feel guilty for thinking it. Domestics could make you angry. And then there were the ones like Anne McRae. The ones who just didn't fit. And Hillary could easily see why the death of a young mother of three, being bludgeoned to death in her own kitchen whilst in the middle of making her family a meal, would sit heavily and uneasily on the senior investigating officer.

'I've read and re-read the file, of course,' Hillary said, getting down to it, whilst Jimmy unobtrusively switched on a tape recorder. 'You liked the sister for it, right? Debbie Gregg.'

'Oh yeah. She had it all – means, motive and opportunity. And she was spitting mad with her sister. I don't know if that was because she still loved that useless husband of hers, or whether she was just floored because her younger, prettier sister had poached him from her. But I'd never seen a woman more bubbling with rage.'

'When did she find out about the affair exactly?'

Andy sighed heavily over his coffee mug. 'She claims she

didn't know about it until after the killing, when we were nosing around the neighbours and some of them put us on to Shane.'

'You think she was lying? That she knew long before then?'

'Oh yeah.'

'Giving her motive.'

'And she would have had access to her sister's house. And no alibi for the time.'

'Home alone, right?'

'Right.'

'And Shane Gregg?'

'Cast iron alibi.'

'What was he like?' Hillary pressed. 'It's a bit of pain not being able to interview him.'

'Right. He died in a car crash a couple of years later, yeah? To be honest, I wouldn't have pegged him as a ladies' man. I reckon he was going through a mid-life crisis or something. He swore up and down that Anne instigated the affair, and he just went where he was led.'

'You believe him, or was he just bullshitting?' Jimmy asked, with a man-to-man grin. Andy shrugged.

'To be honest, I never did make up my mind. The lady was dead, and couldn't defend herself. On the other hand, like I said, I didn't have Shane Gregg pegged as a sexual predator.'

'Right. You found no other evidence of her having any affairs?' Hillary asked, again careful to keep her voice emotionless.

'No. None.'

Hillary nodded. She was not about to tell him about Mark Burgess, or that she was sure that the eldest daughter, Lucy, almost certainly knew about other affairs her mother had had. It would smack too much of rubbing his nose in it, and she wanted him focused and co-operative.

'I'm surprised she seemed to be so popular,' Hillary changed tack. 'Attractive women, and especially ones who cheated on their husbands, tend to be disliked as a general rule.'

'Yeah, I know. But I couldn't find anyone who had a bad word to say about her, apart from her sister, of course. Oh, and her mother-in-law.' Andy rolled his eyes. 'What a harpy she was.'

Hillary blinked. 'There's not much about her in the files. This is Melvin McRae's mother we're talking about, yeah?'

'That's right – her own parents were both deceased. Her mother-in-law was in her late seventies at the time. I think she was at bingo or something when Anne was killed.'

'But she bad-mouthed Anne?' Hillary pressed.

'Oh yeah. Said she wasn't surprised at all to learn that she'd been sleeping around. She even made hints that the youngest child, Jenny, probably wasn't her real grandchild.'

'Crikey,' Jimmy put in. 'I bet that caused some feathers to fly.'

'Oh, she never said it in front of her son – she was too canny for that. But he can't have been oblivious to the fact that his mother and his wife never got on.'

'You checked her out?' Hillary asked sharply, then could have kicked herself, as Andy flushed angrily.

''Course I did. Put a constable on it. Like I said, she was at WI meeting, or jumble sale or something.'

Hillary quickly backtracked. 'Sorry, of course, you said.'

'Anyway, I didn't take her bile all that seriously. I got the feeling that Mother Theresa wouldn't have been good enough for her little boy. He was an only kid. Mother was a bit reluctant to let go of the apron strings. You know what I mean?'

'Got it. But apart from the disgruntled mother-in-law-from-hell nobody struck you as holding a particular grudge against the vic?'

'No. Everything seemed to point straight to Debbie Gregg. No one else had anything approaching a motive. It wasn't robbery. No strangers were seen hanging around the house prior to the murder, or entering it on the day it happened. And back then there were still plenty of neighbours around – it's not like it is nowadays, with everybody out at work. There were several old couples who had nothing to do but "people watch" as they call it nowadays. Plus a stay-at-home mum with two infant twins. It was a sunny day – folks were out and about in their gardens. Strangers would have stood out.'

Hillary nodded. Of course, she'd been a cop for too long not to know that that didn't necessarily mean anything. Anyone watching the house from a distance could gauge when it would be a good time to make his move; old folks slept in the hot summer afternoons, and a mother with twins had lots of things to distract her.

'What was Debbie's attitude to questioning?' Hillary asked curiously.

Andy sighed. 'About what you'd expect. At first she was all co-operative and anything-I-can-do-to-help. Then she got antsy when she figured out she was our prime suspect. Then she got herself a solicitor and finally stopped speaking to us altogether. Got defiant, got angry.'

'And you just couldn't place her at the scene?'

'No,' Andy said reluctantly.

'No forensics on her?'

'Oh, her presence was all over the house, but then it would be. She was family – she visited regularly. There wasn't much forensics one way or the other – apart from the stray hair found on the body – everything else was family.'

Hillary nodded. They went over it again for nearly an hour, with both Jimmy and Hillary wracking their brains for a new lead, but when Andy finally left, they'd come up with nothing helpful.

'Well, that's about it,' Hillary said, glancing at her watch as Jimmy came back from walking the retired DI out of the building. 'It's nearly five. Might as well call it a day.'

It was a novel experience for her to quit every day at five on the dot. When she'd been working before on a murder case, over-time – unpaid of course – had been the norm. But as she had to keep reminding herself, Anne McRae had been dead for twenty years.

Office hours meant nothing to her.

*

That night, she went into The Boat for the first time, and was promptly cheered by the regulars.

'Thought I saw the Mollern parked up beyond the bridge,' the landlord said by way of a greeting, pouring, without having to be asked, her favourite glass of Rioja and setting it down in front of her at the bar. 'Then, when you never came in, I thought you were ignoring us. Or maybe you'd sold the old girl on, and there was a stranger living aboard.'

'Sorry, John. I haven't been in because I've been busy getting stuff sorted out. I've actually got a job.'

The next half an hour passed pleasantly as each brought the other up to date on their lives since they'd last talked.

'By the by, I don't suppose you want to buy back that old car of yours, do you? You know, the one you sold my Colin,' the landlord asked, after he'd left her to serve a couple of pints of cider to two regulars who were organizing a dart's match.

Hillary felt her heart actually lift.

'What, Puff?' she asked, a tentative grin creeping over her face.

'Dunno about that. He calls her Junkheap,' John said, grinning at Hillary's outraged expression. 'Thing is, he's finally saved up enough cash for this little babe-magnet he's got his eye on, and is looking to sell it on. He'll let you have it cheap.'

'I should bloody well think so,' Hillary said, 'considering I practically gave it away in the first place.' Then, as the landlord was still spluttering with laughter, said cautiously, 'How much we talking about?'

The next morning, being a Friday, had that usual little air of excitement about it that told everyone that the weekend was nigh. When she bicycled in and locked up her trusty steed, the sun was beginning to peep through a layer of cloud, and several uniforms milling around in the lobby were full of the joys of spring.

She took off her coat and bag in her stationery cupboard, then walked in through to the office.

'Hello. Sam, Vivienne, I have a little job for you.'

Vivienne sighed audibly. Sam looked interested. Briefly she went through their chat with DI Squires yesterday.

'I want you to re-check the mother-in-law's alibi,' Hillary said. 'When we talked to ex-DI Squires, he said at first that she was at bingo, then he thought it might have been a WI meeting or a jumble sale. I got the idea he only put one DC on it, and he may not have done as thorough a job as I'd like.'

'Oh for Pete's sake, she was an old woman,' Vivienne said. 'She must have been dead for yonks.'

'Almost certainly,' Hillary agreed evenly. 'But that doesn't mean to say that she couldn't have killed her daughter-in-law. When I was your age, my sergeant had a case where a ninety-two-year-old committed murder. Spry old sod, the sort who could run marathons. He took exception to a seventy-two-year-old who was trying to get off with a woman he had his eye on. Just because they're a wrinkly, doesn't mean they can't kill.'

Vivienne sighed again, even more audibly.

Jimmy looked as if he couldn't make up his mind whether to get angry or laugh. Eventually he decided yet another reprimand would be a waste of breath, and let it pass.

'Go back over the file,' Hillary said, addressing Sam, 'and find out the details and then get on with checking it out. Interview whoever you have to.'

Sam nodded eagerly, and pounced on the file. Whilst he read and made notes, Vivienne did her nails.

Hillary went back to her stationery cupboard until she heard the youngsters leave. Then, with a sigh, she went down the corridor and tapped on Steven Crayle's door.

'Come in.'

He looked up as Hillary walked in, and leaned back in his chair. Today, she was dressed in a pale lilac pencil skirt and matching jacket, with a white blouse. He felt that instinctive quickening of interest which so annoyed him, and squashed it firmly.

'We're making some progress with Anne McRae, sir. You have five minutes?'

Crayle thought at once that he'd always have time for Hillary Greene, then frowned at the thought, and nodded.

Hillary frowned right back at him. 'I can always come back if you're busy, sir.'

'No, I'm not busy. And call me Steven.'

'Yes, si … Steven.' She took a seat and brought him up to date. She was concise but left nothing of significance out. Crayle listened to her voice, liking it, and listened to what she had to say, liking it even more. He had to admit – the commander had called it right. She was good. Very good. Already she was unearthing suspects that the original team hadn't been able to find.

When she was finished, he was tapping his pen thoughtfully on the desktop.

'You need to get Mark Burgess's DNA and compare it with the hair fibre,' he ordered briskly.

'Already got Jimmy on getting a warrant.'

'And you think the eldest girl – Lucy is it? – might have knowledge about the identity of some of her mother's other lovers?'

Hillary stirred. 'Let's just say, I think she's holding back on us. I'd like to take another crack at her later. I've got the youngsters investigating her recent activities. I'll ask Sam for an update on that when he gets back to HQ. I'd like a little more leverage before tackling her again. She's got a hard shell, and it'll take some cracking.'

'The mother-in-law seems a stretch,' Crayle said, watching her carefully.

'She probably is,' Hillary acknowledged readily. 'But until we know, she can't be ruled out. Doting mothers can go postal, as we both know. If she was reasonably fit, I can't see why she couldn't have hit Anne with the rolling pin. The victim wouldn't see her as a threat, and so wouldn't be on her guard. And you read the post mortem report – Anne McRae had a fairly thin skull. The ME didn't rule out a woman as a possible killer.'

Steven sighed. 'I'm not criticizing. You carry on doing it your way. Keep me informed.'

'Sir,' Hillary said, pretending not to notice when he winced.

'Call me Steven!'

'Yes si … Steven.'

Sam and Vivienne approached the village hall with eager steps. Although Vivienne wouldn't have admitted it for anything, she was feeling kind of excited to be out and about and doing real cop stuff.

Even if it was only lame stuff like this.

According to the file, Grace McRae had been playing bingo right there on the afternoon that her daughter-in-law was murdered. And the village hall in Middleton Stoney wasn't that far from Chesterton – maybe three miles, if that.

'Did she have a car, this old biddy?' Vivienne asked as Sam tried the door and found it locked.

'No. There was a minibus that took a load of them to the venue and then took them back. Damn, it's locked.'

''Course it is. Look around for a notice or something saying when it's open or who to contact if we want to hire the place,' Vivienne said bossily. 'So if she didn't have a car, she was stuck here, wasn't she? Unless our high-and-mighty boss thinks she jogged the three miles to Chesterton,' Vivienne laughed. 'I can just see it – a granny jogging along in that heat. I told you, this is a waste of time.'

Sam, who'd found a notice board and was busy jotting down the telephone numbers of anyone who had anything to do with the running of the hall, grunted vaguely.

Vivienne sighed and glanced around. Middleton Stoney was a small village, bisected by a busy main road. 'What a dump.'

'What's wrong with it?' Sam asked, using his mobile. 'I think it's quite nice.'

He'd lived with his parents on a large housing estate in Reading before attending university, and now he found himself rather enamoured of the Oxfordshire villages.

They were way out of his price range, though. 'It's quiet,' he pointed out, 'and that cottage over there is ... hello? Is this Mr Porter? My name is Sam Pickles. Mr Porter, I work for Thames Valley Police. I'm currently outside the village hall in Middleton Stoney.... You do? Oh good, I was hoping you could help me. I'm trying to track down who was running the bingo sessions that would have been held here twenty years ago. I know it's an odd thing to ask, out of the blue, but I was hoping you might know someone who was active around then.'

He snapped his fingers at Vivienne and mimed writing something down.

She rolled her eyes in a parody of long-suffering patience and reached for her notebook and pen, obediently jotting down names and tentative addresses as he relayed them.

She was already getting bored. It was all such a monumental waste of time!

Tom Warrington pulled off the main Oxford to Banbury road, and parked the car on the side of the narrow lane. He didn't want to drive into the hamlet proper, and wasn't particularly happy about leaving the car this close to his target either, but he had no other choice. Leaving the car on the main road would attract far more attention to it.

He glanced at his watch as he slid out from behind the driver's wheel and locked the car. Nearly noon. With any luck, everybody would be out at work. Just how busy could a place like Thrupp be anyway? He'd have to be very unlucky for anybody to notice the car, let alone take down its licence plate number.

He walked casually down the lane, trying to look like a tourist, and saw not a soul. At the canal, however, he saw that several narrowboats had smoke coming out of their narrow chimney stacks, and knew he would have to be careful. He could be observed. Not that he was that worried – on the canal, strangers came and went all the time. It was part of the transient lifestyle.

He walked casually past the pub and down the towpath, heading north, glancing at the lines of boats as he went. But none of them was named the Mollern. When he got to the last one in the line, he turned and strolled back, going in the other direction. He went under a low arched stone bridge, and past more boats.

At last, he spotted her boat. It looked different from all of the others, and he felt his heart swell with pride. Of course it was different. She'd hardly be likely to live in any old boat, would she? Hers was a soft subtle blue-grey colour, with old gold and white and black trim. Her boat looked elegant and sophisticated, unlike some of the others, with their garish reds, greens and blues.

Her boat was older than most too – no, classic – he corrected himself, and luckily for him, it was the second-but-last in the line of boats at this end.

As he walked on, he looked quickly down into the boat behind, but its little round porthole windows had curtains drawn over each of them. Perfect. As he'd hoped, the boat belonged to a fair-weather boatee. He knew from his research, that a lot of narrowboat owners only lived on their vessels in the summer. Winter on the canal was too much for most.

Unfortunately the very last boat in the line, the one directly in front of the Mollern had the curtains drawn back at the windows. But as he walked past it carefully and went on down the towpath for a way, he could hear no movement from within, and no sound of the radio or conversation. He turned around and took another careful walk back, and when he was level with the boat called not too loudly, 'Hello, anyone in?'

If anyone was in, he could always use his ID badge and say he was here to warn boaters about the rise in theft on the canal.

He called again, a little louder. 'Hello, on board Kingfisher?'

Nothing.

Perfect. The boat was empty after all.

He walked back to the Mollern, stepped confidently onto the deck and bent down to start picking the padlock on the double front iron doors.

'Good grief, that's twenty years ago now!' Penelope Mobbs said, looking from Sam to Vivienne, who were standing on her doorstep, and trying to look non-threatening.

Hers was the fourth name on the list of people the current care-taker of Middleton Stoney's village hall had given them, but since she still lived in the village, they'd tried her first.

Sam smiled back at her hopefully. 'Yes, ma'am. I know that. But Mr Porter said you were one of those who volunteered back then.'

'Well, you'd better come in then,' Mrs Mobbs said, standing back to let them pass. She lived in a tiny, rather dirty-looking cottage that faced the main road. Sam suspected that it was the road pollution that gave the cottage its grimy appearance, for inside it was all clean and tidy.

They crammed into a dinky little living room that was kept a shade too warm with a gas fire. 'Tea?' Mrs Mobbs asked, but was already half way to the kitchen before they could say either yes or no.

She was a woman in her late seventies, Sam would have guessed, and like most old people, she remembered things from years ago, whereas they couldn't tell you what they did yesterday.

Luckily for them, she recalled the bingo sessions well. She even remembered Grace McRae.

'She was a bit of a bossy woman, Grace,' Mrs Mobbs confided several minutes later, as they all munched down on some diges-tives. 'She was always going on about that son of hers – from the way she talked, you think he was something special, instead of a coach driver. But she made him sound glamorous, you know. "Melvin says Bruges is really old," and, "of course, he can speak several languages now." All that sort of thing. Like he was in the diplomatic service, instead of a plain old bus driver! But we used to just ignore her. It was easier than picking her up on it all the time.'

'She didn't like her daughter-in-law, did she?' Vivienne said bluntly. 'The one who was murdered.'

Penelope Mobbs's old lips puckered in disapproval. 'You shouldn't speak ill of the dead,' she admonished. Although whether she was telling off Vivienne for saying something about the now deceased Grace, or whether she'd been thinking of Grace, who shouldn't have had anything bad to say about her deceased daughter-in-law, neither Sam or Vivienne could quite work out.

It took him ages to get into the boat, but at last he was inside. Tom crouched down to avoid hitting his head and went down the three narrow iron stairs into the boat. His heart was beating so fast he had to gulp in air.

It felt weird. Everything was so narrow and tiny. And he felt low down too, and the ground under his feet felt just a little bit off. Of course, there was no ground under his feet – only water. It wasn't as if the boat rocked, exactly, because it didn't, but his mind and body could tell that this environment was something new to him.

He was not particularly sure that he liked it. This distressed him somewhat. Because Hillary Greene chose to live in it, it had to be good. There was probably a whole different cultural ethos to it, but he was still so new to it, it would take him a while to attune himself. Having satisfied himself on that score, he felt himself begin to relax and enjoy himself.

He breathed deeply and smelt *her*.

It wasn't just the light, floral perfume she used either, it was a combination of things – the aroma of her life. Soap and books, leather and wood. He moved forward, going into the small main living area. Books lined the walls.

Of course, she had a BA in English literature from Oxford. He perused them – the poetry, the Brontes, *Beowulf*. Stuff he could never have read or understood in a million years.

She was so clever, his Hillary. Cultured, brilliant.

He moved to the kitchen. Fresh veg in the tiny fridge, a small loaf of bread from a bakery – the kind with seeds.

Of course, she'd eat right. She didn't smoke, he knew, and never had done. She was probably a modest drinker too – in fact, he could only find one bottle of wine in the place – a good quality white.

What else? Hell, she had class, this woman. Not like the others.

He went to what he was sure must be her bedroom and stood outside the door, his hands literally tingling with anticipation. What sort of lingerie would she wear?

He slid the door open and looked inside the tiny bedroom – at the neatly made single bed, almost monastic-looking in its purity.

She never slept around – everyone knew that.

He'd heard it said that she'd been with another officer from Vice a while back, but he didn't believe it.

With a sigh of pure pleasure, he stepped into her tiny domain and stared down at the pillow. Just to think, eight hours ago, her head rested there, and she'd been asleep.

He closed his eyes, picturing it. Pictured him being there with her, the two of them pressed so close together, like a pair of spoons, on that tiny bed.

Hillary left early for lunch, and pedalled back to Thrupp. The landlord's son had agreed to bring Puff back in his own lunch hour, and she had a modest cheque in her bag, ready to hand over. She knew it was daft, but she was sort of looking forward to seeing her old car again.

She felt as if she was going to meet up with a long-lost friend.

Sam and Vivienne thanked Mrs Mobbs for her help and left her to her grimy cottage. In Sam's hand was the name and old address for the minibus driver. The volunteer world was a small one, obviously closely knit and friendly, and Sam wasn't at all surprised that the man who drove the minibus should be on her Christmas card list.

He drove to Bicester in less than ten minutes, but it took him twice that long to find the address in Glory Farm, a large, rambling housing estate that seemed designed by planners to deliberately baffle anyone wanting to either live or visit there.

Glenn Timmons was perhaps a few years younger than Grace Mobbs, but it was obvious from the moment he opened the door that his driving days were long over.

The man shook from head to foot.

Parkinsons Disease, Sam thought at once, who'd lost his maternal grandfather to the illness a couple of years before.

'Yes?' the voice wavered as did the rest of him. He was a tall, very lean man, covered in liver spots.

Beside him, he felt Vivienne shudder.

'Mr Timmons?' He showed the man his ID card, careful to hold it close to his face so that he could see it. 'We're with the police, Mr Timmons. Is it all right if we ask you some questions about when you used to drive the minibus for the old folks?'

Glenn Timmons looked astonished. 'D'yah what?' he quavered.

Patiently, Sam repeated himself. Beside him, Vivienne sighed heavily.

Hillary swung her legs off the bike whilst it was still in motion and put her foot to the tarmac of The Boat's parking lot, coming to a practised walking trot as she pushed the bike ahead of her before propping it up against the wall.

She glanced along the canal automatically towards where her boat was moored, but her eye was snagged by a familiar pale green outline.

'Puff,' she said, walking over towards the car and grinning widely.

The old Golf hadn't suffered much under new ownership as

far as she could see. For a car that was getting close to being twenty years old, it still, to her eyes at least, looked to be in fairly good nick. OK, so maybe her eyes were a bit biased.

But she hardly needed a fancy motor.

She gave the bonnet a friendly pat, and headed towards the pub. If the landlord didn't fancy paying for the drinks, she'd stand the old man's son a drink herself.

She'd half expected to find her car a mess of rust, with the trim coming off and the tyres bald. To find out that the young sod had actually looked after it had earned him a single malt.

Or whatever his particular poison was.

On her boat, a few hundred yards away, Tom Warrington lay on Hillary Greene's bed, holding her nightgown to his face and breathing deeply.

'Oh yes, I remember Grace all right,' Glenn Timmons said in his unnervingly uneven voice. 'Bit of a tartar, that one. 'Course, we all knew about that dreadful murder. Her son's wife. Terrible it was.'

They were sitting in his parlour, his daughter sitting opposite. She had come around to cook his lunch, and on finding the police – or their representatives – in situ, had decided to stay on.

She now listened openly, looking intrigued and half-proud, as if her father's input was up there with giving testimony at the Old Bailey.

Vivienne thought that she probably had a dull life, if this was the highlight of her day.

'Anne McRae,' Sam prompted.

'Yes. That was it.'

'Mrs McRae was at Middleton Stoney, playing bingo when it happened,' Sam added, wondering if he was giving out too much information. Surely he should be asking questions, not supplying answers? The trouble was, the old man looked so fragile and confused.

'Ah, that's right. I remember. I drove them. There was a bunch come from Bicester.'

'That's right,' Sam said relieved. 'You remember?'

'Well, I remember reading about it in the papers,' Glenn said tremulously. 'And the next week, Grace was holding forth about it. She did like to hear the sound of her own voice, that woman.'

'So you can definitely say that she was playing bingo when it happened?' Vivienne put in restlessly, wanting to get away from this place and this creepy sick old man as soon as she could.

'Yes. I suppose so,' Glenn said, rather uncertainly to Sam's ear.

'You remember her getting into your minibus to be driven back, Mr Timmons?' he pressed.

'Well, she must'a done, son. I took 'em there, and I brought 'em back. Unless'n she took the regular bus, like.'

Sam perked up. 'The regular bus?'

'Ah. The red 'un, the one the local bus company ran. Well it used to be red, probably a different colour now. It's still running though to this day, but for how much longer, what with all the cutbacks and so on, who can say? It's on a regular run from Oxford to Bicester, going through all the villages en route. That stops at Middleton Stoney. I knew some of the drivers who do the route, see.'

Sam felt his heart rate pick up.

'Did it go to Chesterton do you know?'

'Oh yes,' Glenn said, perking up. 'The next stop would have been Chesterton.'

CHAPTER TEN

H illary got back behind the wheel of her trusty – well, perhaps not *that* trusty – car for the first time in nearly two years and turned the ignition key. She half-expected it to cough like an asthmatic donkey before braying into silence, but it started smoothly first time. She patted the steering wheel in silent apology for ever having doubted it, and, leaving her bike propped up against the wall of the pub for now, turned and headed out of the hamlet.

She passed a car parked on the side of the lane without giving it a second thought, and was back at HQ within five minutes.

In the office, she asked Sam for his report. 'Start with Lucy McRae,' she began. 'You went back to her flat yesterday evening?'

'Yes, guv,' Sam said, careful not to meet Vivienne's eyes. Since it was unpaid overtime, Vivienne hadn't bothered to turn up, but since Hillary Greene hadn't asked him specifically if he'd been alone, he didn't volunteer the information.

Consulting his notebook, he scratched his head absently. 'She's only been living there for a few months – apparently the man she was living with died. None of the neighbours like her that much, guv – the women say it's pretty obvious that she thinks of herself as a cut above the rest of them, and that she's always on about finding somewhere better soon. And I got the feeling that though most of the men might fancy her, she wasn't interested in any of them. I sensed that one or two had tried it on and been well and truly told where to get off! I suppose none of them are rich enough for her blood, if you get my drift.'

Hillary nodded. It tallied with her own opinion of Lucy McRae rather well.

'And the bling?' she prompted.

Sam was already nodding. 'I found an old lady on the bottom floor. She says the delivery vans started arriving only a day or so ago – she can't remember if it was Tuesday, Wednesday or yesterday – time's a bit fluid to her, I think. But first a big fridge arrived, then the big-screen telly, then something else she couldn't identify.'

Hillary smiled. 'Right. We'll have to have another word with Lucy soon – see if we can pin her down about why she's suddenly so flush. OK, next. How did you get on this morning tracking down Grace McRae's movements on the day Anne died?'

Sam flushed in excitement. Jimmy Jessop watched him with a fatherly smile. No doubt he remembered, just barely, what it felt like to be so young and eager.

'It turns out the old lady could have done it, guv,' Sam said dramatically.

Hillary, apparently unimpressed by this revelation, merely nodded. 'Explain.'

'She was at bingo all right – a regular session was held at the village hall in Middleton Stoney. We tracked down several people who remember seeing Grace McRae there, and found the minibus driver who collected the old folks and took them there and back. But the thing is, guv, the minibus driver told us that there was a regular bus service that passed through the village, with the next stop being Chesterton.'

Sam paused for a breath. 'Trouble is, we can't find anyone, well not yet, who can say for sure that Grace McRae went back on the minibus. The bingo session would have lasted from one o'clock to two forty-five, and I've been onto the bus company, and they e-mailed me the timetable for the year 1990–91. And there was a bus that would have got her to Chesterton in time to kill her daughter-in-law.'

'Good – that shows initiative,' Hillary put in, making Sam blush with pride.

Vivienne said flatly, 'Actually that was my idea.'

'Then it was a good one,' Hillary said, smiling at her.

Vivienne smiled wryly. And thanks very much for that grudging pat on the back, she thought sourly. It was obvious to her that Sam Pickles, that long lanky piece of string cheese, was the boss lady's blue-eyed boy. Not that she cared. The only boss she was interested in pleasing was the hunky Steven Crayle.

'So we can't rule Grace McRae out,' Hillary mused.

'I don't suppose her DNA was tested against the hair that was found on Mrs McRae's body, was it?' Sam asked, then immediately felt stupid. If it had, it would be in the case file, and he knew damned well it wasn't. 'Sorry, silly question.'

'And in order to do that now, we'd probably have to get a court order to dig the old lady up,' Jimmy put in. 'I doubt we'd be able to find a sample of her DNA just lying around, not after all this time. She's been dead and gone for over ten years. And you don't even want to know about the paper work involved in getting an exhumation order.'

'Besides, the hair was almost certainly that of a male,' Hillary said. 'If I remember the forensic report clearly.'

'Of course, we've made great strides in DNA profiling in the twenty years since then,' Sam put in eagerly. 'We could turn the hair over to Sergeant Handley for an up-to-the-minute analysis. He loves that sort of thing. He's always boasting that he's got friends in all the forensics labs, and can pull strings to get quick results if need be.'

'Maybe,' Hillary agreed. 'But don't forget, we're running on a limited budget here, and that sort of testing costs a lot of money. I think we'll hold off until we get it tested against Mark Burgess. About that, Jimmy?'

'Yeah, guv. I've called him and arranged to get a mouth swab early next week. I've also managed to track down a judge for the warrant, but it probably won't get done today. And then it's the weekend, so we're probably looking at Monday sometime.'

Hillary sighed. 'When you're there, see if you can get Mrs Burgess to give a sample too – we might as well eliminate her properly.'

'Want me to get her included in the warrant?'

'Might as well, although I think it's highly likely she'd volunteer anyway,' Hillary said. 'If she refuses, I'll be very surprised.'

Jimmy grunted. 'Sounds as if you don't much like her for it, guv?'

'No. But don't let us get discouraged. We're making progress. Plodding away might not be glamorous and would make for a boring TV programme, but it's getting us there. And speaking of plodding away – Sam, Vivienne, I want you to go to Peter McRae's school. He was in some kind of trouble there at the time of his mother's murder. I want to find out what it was. You never know what might turn out to be relevant.'

She turned and looked at Vivienne, waiting for the snide comment. Perhaps sensing it, Vivienne kept her pretty red-painted lips very firmly shut.

Hillary smiled, nodded, and left them to it, giving Jimmy a passing wink as she went.

The McRaes had all gone to school in the nearby market town of Bicester. A large, sprawling comprehensive, it reminded both youngsters uncomfortably of their own school days, which were not that long past.

Feeling very grown up flashing their ID badges with the Thames Valley Police Service logo, they were quickly directed to the headmaster's secretary's office.

She was a middle-aged woman with a rounded belly, rounded face, and rounded greying bun perched high on top of her head. She reminded Vivienne of someone you'd see on a child's set of playing cards. Mrs Bunn the baker's wife, or some such stupid thing. But she had sharp blue eyes that watched them both carefully, and she said not a word as they explained, somewhat less than succinctly, what it was they needed. Since they tended to take turns in explaining what they wanted, the woman kept looking from one to the other, like a spectator at a tennis match.

'Let me get this clear,' she said, when they'd finally finished. 'You want to find out what kind of trouble an ex-student of ours was having in the summer of 1991?' She sounded both slightly disbelieving and incredulous, as if they might as well have asked her to produce Lord Lucan.

Sam felt his heart sink.

'Well, to begin with, Mr, er, Pickles,' she began sardonically, and Sam felt himself flush, 'I can't give you access to any student files. The data protection act, and all that – but I don't need to go into the finer details of that with you, do I? Being a *consultant* to the police and everything.' Her lips twitched briefly, and Sam saw in that instant how absurd he and Vivienne must look to her. Two teenagers, barely out of school, playing a grown up game of detectives. She must be fighting the urge to tick them off and send them back to their classroom with the advice to do better next time.

He realized he had to do something to retrieve the situation, and wondered what Hillary would do. But since he didn't have enough experience to figure out what that was, he decided to appeal to her better nature instead.

'Look, his mother was murdered, Mrs Usherwood,' Sam said quietly. 'The case is being re-opened. Our boss, Detective Inspector Hillary Greene,' he gave her back her old title without a qualm, 'is following every lead, in the hope of finding some-thing new. I think it's important that we all do our bit to help her, don't you?'

Mrs Usherwood blinked, then sighed.

'Let me see if we have a member of staff still with us who was around then. I think that's the best I can do.' She turned on her swivel chair and began to tap industriously on the computer.

'Yes, you're in luck. There are only two – Mr Portman, but he's out sick today. And Mr Cleeves.' She pulled up the classroom schedules and consulted her watch. 'He'll be finishing his geography class in ten minutes. That's in the big building at the front, right-hand corner 6B. If you wait outside you'll probably have a few minutes to talk to him before the next class arrives. In the meantime, I'll consult the minutes of the meetings around then, and see if I can trace any sign of Peter McRae having come to our attention. And if it was a disciplinary matter, it almost certainly will have done. Will that do?'

Sam stood up at once and smiled with relief. 'Thank you, Mrs Usherwood.'

Outside, Vivienne let out a long, whistling breath. 'Bad-tempered old trout,' she muttered. 'I had a cookery teacher like her. Hated her guts.'

Sam laughed and shook his head. 'Being back at a school gives me the willies,' he agreed.

They found 6B fairly easily and after hanging around the corridor for five minutes, heard the bell go, and stood aside as a hoard of noisy, bored 13-year-olds filtered by. They then pushed their way into the vacated room.

In the classroom, the walls were covered with colourful maps, along with photographs of erupting volcanoes, peaceful-looking glaciers, majestic mountains and aerial shots of river deltas and island atolls.

A man stood behind a desk. In his early fifties, he was tall, lean and with a full head of blonde-going-silver hair and pale blue eyes. Beside him, he could feel Vivienne going onto full sexual alert, and he felt a spurt of irritation wash over him.

What was it with her and older men? Didn't she know that little girls in search of a Daddy replacement were so retro?

'Mr Cleeves?'

'Yes?' The blue eyes sharpened on them and he smiled,

revealing even white teeth. Attractive crows' feet appeared at the side of his eyes.

Wow, what a dish, Vivienne thought, quickly pulling out her ID and taking charge.

'Ah, I thought you were a bit old to belong to my next class,' he mused. 'Please, have a seat. What can I do for you?'

Phil Cleeves watched the two strangers take a seat, and felt his heart rate accelerate. Their IDs said they weren't even proper constables, so it was ridiculous to feel this alarmed. But he couldn't help it. He didn't like the police. He never had, and over the years had been careful to avoid having anything to do with them. He sat back down behind his desk, his traditional seat of power, feeling the need to re-assert some authority.

'You were here twenty years ago, right?' Vivienne asked, sitting not on one of the backless stools, but on a desk instead. She let one long leg dangle, and made sure her skirt was hitched up high enough to show a little bit of thigh.

Phil didn't seem to notice.

'Crikey, that makes me sound as old as Methuselah. But yes, I've been here nearly twenty-two years now. For my sins.'

Again he smiled.

Vivienne smiled back.

'Do you remember a pupil called Peter McRae?'

Phil's palms began to sweat. He frowned slightly. 'Peter McRae? Good grief, do you have any idea how many pupils I've taught over the years? Why on earth should I remember one out of thousands? Unless, that is, he did something to bring himself to my attention. Is he in some trouble with the police? If he was a bit of a delinquent, I might be able to dredge him up from memory. What did he look like?'

'You might remember him, sir, because his mother was murdered when he was attending school here. Anne McRae. She lived in Chesterton,' Sam put in.

'Oh hell, yes!' Phil sat up straighter in his chair. 'I remember that all right. And now, yes, of course I remember Peter. A bright enough lad, but apt to be a bit lazy, mind. Yes, of course. I hope he's not in any trouble?' he asked, looking from Vivienne to Sam. 'You being with the police and all?'

'Oh no sir, nothing like that,' Vivienne put in quickly. 'We're re-opening his mother's case, that's all. It was never solved, you see.'

'Oh,' Phil said, feeling his shoulders slump with relief. 'I see.' So *that's* what had brought them here. 'Well, needless to say, I wish you luck. But I still don't quite see how I can help.'

Neither do I, Vivienne thought sardonically, but said brightly, 'During our investigations,' hell that sounded good, 'we've come across reports that Peter was in some kind of trouble at school. Naturally, anything that reflects on the McRae family dynamic at that time is of interest to us.'

She was rather proud of her vocabulary, and only hoped that, as a teacher, it was making a good impression on the blonde hunk.

Phil blinked. 'OK,' he said, sounding rather less than convinced by her premise. 'But from what I remember of Peter, well, of all the McRae children actually, he was a well-adjusted kid. They all came here, you know. Jenny McRae, now, she was the one for getting into trouble. She seemed to be perpetually in detention. And if I remember rightly she was sent home drunk once or twice as well. But not Peter! If he was in any trouble here at school I don't remember hearing about it.'

'What about the other one?' Sam asked. 'Lucy.'

'Don't remember her,' Phil said casually.

Vivienne sighed. 'So Peter wasn't about to be expelled or anything?'

'Good grief no. He was positively well-behaved compared to some. Bright enough too. He had his own little coterie of friends, who were nothing special, but then again, he didn't get caught up with the bad element either. I'd have said his school life was strictly average.'

'Did you ever meet his mother, Mr Cleeves? Sorry, what's your first name?' Vivienne asked.

'Phil. And I'm not sure. If she attended the PTA meetings, I might have met her. In fact, I must have, but I can't say as she sticks in my memory.'

And she would have done, Sam thought, if Anne McRae had come here on the warpath. He had a feeling that their murder victim had a way of making her presence felt. 'Well, thank you, sir,' Sam said, realizing that they weren't going to get any further here. Perhaps Mrs Usherwood would have found something in the school records for them.

Vivienne got reluctantly to her feet. 'Well, if you think of anything, Mr Cleeves, please give me a call,' she said, scribbling her name and private number onto the back of a standard Kidlington HQ card and handing it over.

Phil smiled at her and took it.

'I certainly will,' he glanced at the card, 'Miss Tyrell.'

Outside, a long queue of curious 15-year-olds watched them leave, one or two of the male ones calling out softly explicit comments to Vivienne, which she pretended to ignore.

'What a hunk,' she said, once they were out of earshot of the munchkins.

'Yeah, I could see you fancied him,' Sam said flatly. 'Come on, let's see what the gorgon lady has for us.'

But, alas, Mrs Usherwood had nothing for them. There was no mention in any of the school documents concerning Peter McRae. If he had been in any trouble, it had not become official.

That evening, Hillary Greene returned home, and found a large, pink envelope lying on the roof of her boat. It had no stamp or frank marks, and had obviously been hand-delivered.

She picked it up and took it into the Mollern, hoping that it might be a card or a note from the landlord or his son, congratulating her on re-acquiring her car.

Of course it wasn't.

It was a Valentine's card, albeit a very late one with a big silk-padded pink heart on the front.

Inside was the usual gooey, standard Hallmark piece of poetry, and a few printed words:

'For my true soulmate. I think of you always.'

It was, of course, not signed.

Hillary sighed, and put the card in her bag. She stood still, and looked around.

And then she began to search, carefully.

Nothing was missing. But by the time half an hour had gone by, she knew that someone had been on her boat.

She swore roundly and with feeling.

She grabbed a can of furniture polish and set it beside the sink, then poured some pine disinfectant into some hot water and set about cleaning her boat from top to bottom. One of the advantages of living in a small space was that it didn't require much cleaning, and after about only an hour, with the sheets changed, and every surface gleaming, she felt a little less violated.

But it was not exactly how she'd expected to spend her Friday evening.

Phil Cleeves wasn't having much of a good time either. Once he'd driven home from school, he spent the next hour tracking down someone he badly needed to speak to.

Then he had to have a stiff gin and tonic before he could pluck up the courage to ring the telephone number he'd finally uncovered.

To make the call, he drove into town and used a pub call box. He didn't want to use the public phone boxes in town, just in case a call could be traced through a telephone card, which was all that they accepted. And there was sure as hell no way that he was going to use his own landline or even a pay-as-you-go mobile.

'Hello?'

He hadn't heard the voice in years, but he recognized it at once and his heart began to beat again. It was the second time that day it had had so much exercise, but this time it had nothing to do with fear or apprehension.

'Hello. It's me. Phil.'

There was a moment of complete surprised silence, and then, 'Phil? Cleeves?'

'Yes. Look, I'm sorry to call you out of the blue like this, but I had to talk to you. I had a visit from the police today.'

For the next ten minutes he spoke, awkwardly at first, but then with growing confidence. Finally, after listening to what the other caller had to say, he sighed in a mixture of relief and exasperation.

'No, I know her murder doesn't have anything to do with us,' Phil said somewhat impatiently. 'But don't you see? With the case being re-opened and all, they might just bumble around and step on our toes. They've already been to the school. Who knows what they might do next. I just don't want to get involved, that's all.'

He listened and sighed. 'I know I'm not involved now. But things have a way of becoming ... well, dangerous. For both of us. I think it would be a good idea if we got our stories straight. Just in case we need to make a statement at any time. Yes. Right. OK. Fine, I'll do that. In the meantime, I think it's best if we don't get in touch again. Yes! I know *I* called *you*. I'm just saying, this should be the only time we have any contact.'

He glanced around at the noisy bar, suddenly feeling old and vulnerable.

He felt, in fact, like shit.

'Yes. OK. I.... Look, I'm sorry, right?' He listened to the voice on the other end of the line, feeling equal measures of nostalgia and regret. 'What for? Just ... for everything. That's all. OK, bye. Yes. Bye.'

He hung up and moved stiffly to the bar. There he ordered himself two more gin and tonics.

Tonight, for the first time in quite a while, he felt like getting extremely drunk.

*

The weekend passed uneventfully. On the Saturday, Hillary gave Puff a thorough clean, inside and out, and got a load of shopping in. She also retrieved her push bike and secured it onto the roof rack on top of her narrowboat.

She had Sunday lunch at the pub, and spent a few hours putting the final finishing touches to her novel.

During her 'retirement' she'd written a police procedural whodunnit. It wasn't even based loosely on any of her cases, being purely fictional, although the DI heroine might have had a passing resemblance to herself.

Apart from being a blue-eyed, svelte blonde, with a neuro-surgeon husband and adorable twins, that is.

It had been fun, and dotting the last few 'I's' and crossing the final 'T', she finally made up her mind to send it to a publisher.

It would probably come back with a nice little bog-standard rejection slip, but nothing ventured, nothing gained.

On Monday morning, she stopped off at the post office to mail her manuscript off to a large, popular publishing outfit that specialized in crime, and then drove on into work.

As she spied the HQ building looming up, she heaved a heavy sigh. Her first task of the day was not going to be pleasant.

She parked and walked down into the basement, going straight to Steven Crayle's office.

In her bag, she took out the card, then tapped on the door.

If she'd been in one of those television programmes she so despised, the last thing she'd do is tell her boss that she was being stalked. For some reason that totally escaped her – TV heroines were always doing daft things like that. They either wanted to prove they were as tough as the men, or that they didn't need anyone to sort out their problems for them. As a consequence, they usually ended up at the end of the episode in a nail-biting position whereby their male colleagues had to rescue them from the mad hatchet man. Or whatever.

In real life, of course, it had to play out differently.

'Come in.'

She opened the door and walked in.

It was still early, but she could see at once that the superinten-dent had already been in and working for several hours. His suit jacket was slung over the back of his chair, his tie was loosened, and he had his shirt sleeves rolled up. Paperwork was in the process of passing from his IN tray to his OUT tray.

She remembered the routine well.

His dark hair flopped in two wings over his forehead, making her fingers itch to push them back. She told her fingers to forget about it.

'Si … Steven,' she said blandly, when he glanced up at her.

She put the card on his desk and he stared at it for a moment. What the hell? A Valentines card?

He stared at it, then at her, then at it again. Finally he smiled. 'Well, I'm flattered, Hillary, and all that but—'

'Sir,' Hillary said flatly, in no mood for fun and games. 'I think I've picked up a stalker.'

Crayle's smile instantly vanished.

'A few days ago someone stole a comb from my locker,' she stated flatly. 'Then they left a vase of roses on my desk here. Then Friday night, I found that on top of my narrowboat,' she nodded down at the offending card. 'And someone had been inside. Nothing was missing, but things were slightly out of place.'

Using a pen, Crayle pulled the padded heart towards him. 'I'll get Handley to run it for prints. But if it's someone on the job, it'll be unlikely he was stupid enough to leave prints.' He paused for a moment, and then looked at her.

'You do think it's someone on the job, right?'

Hillary sighed and shrugged. 'How many civilians have access to the locker rooms down here?'

Crayle nodded. 'Not many. Cleaning staff?'

Hillary nodded. 'The padlocks on both the locker and the Mollern were picked. Ex-cons?'

'You've put a fair few behind bars, but none of them would be employed to work here. I know the recruiting regime can be a bit lax, though.' He sighed heavily. 'I'd better go through the files.'

Hillary nodded. 'My ex-sergeant, Janine, she had a stalker once,' she mused. 'Turns out it was a PC right here in the station.'

'You think history's repeating itself? What was his name?'

Hillary gave it to him.

'I'll check him out. But it's unlikely to be the same man.'

Hillary knew that too. It was unlikely, after the scare she'd put into him, that he would be looking at her as his 'true soulmate'.

'OK, I'll requisition a camera. We'll hide it and keep it fixed on your locker, that way if Romeo tries the same trick twice, we'll get a visual on him,' Crayle said. 'Want me to set one up in your office?'

'Hell no,' she said quickly. The thought of knowing that Steven Crayle could be watching her at any time of the day without her knowing about it would send her blood pressure sky-rocketing.

'OK. We'll find him. But I don't have to tell you that it might take a while. If he's done this sort of thing before, he'll be careful. And in the meantime, you know the drill.'

Hillary smiled crookedly. 'Be alert. Don't go out alone at night. Have a digital camera with me at all times, and take discreet pictures of anyone I see hanging around. Et cetera, et cetera, et cetera.'

Crayle grinned. 'OK, granny, here endeth the lesson on egg-sucking.'

Hillary nodded with a wry smile, and walked to the door. Crayle watched her go, and then stared down morosely at the Valentine's card.

So the flowers hadn't been from a lover. He felt glad about that. On the other hand, a stalker was bad news. There were stalkers, and there were stalkers. Some could be fairly harmless, some could be pests, and some real head-cases who could turn out to be murderously dangerous.

And the thought that someone, and probably a cop at that, had

Hillary in their mentally-deficient sights filled him with a mixture of anger and dread.

As Hillary had done less than forty-eight hours ago, he swore roundly and with feeling.

This was just what they needed.

'Jimmy, I want you to get cracking with the warrant,' Hillary said, a few minutes later. 'Then I want you to take Sam and Vivienne to collect the DNA samples from both of the Burgesses. It'll be good practice for them. It's time they had some practical experience of chain of evidence.'

'Right, guv,' Jimmy said. 'What are you going to do?'

'I'm going back to Jenny McRae,' Hillary said. But although Jimmy looked a question at her, she didn't elaborate. The truth was, she was stuck at a dead end, and when there was nothing else to do, a second interview with a witness was better than twiddling your thumbs.

But she didn't want to tell her team that. Just because she was disheartened, didn't mean she fancied company in her misery.

'Oh, you're back,' Jenny McRae said flatly, when she answered the knock at the door and found the redheaded police woman on her doorstep. She didn't sound particularly welcoming.

Hillary didn't take it personally.

From the back of the tiny flat, Hillary was sure she could hear children's voices.

'Kids in school, Jenny?' she asked, as the younger woman, who, at gone ten in the morning was still dressed in pyjamas and a dirty housecoat, led her into the kitchenette.

'Yeah, course,' Jenny lied. 'Cup of coffee?' she then asked, so loudly that she was almost shouting.

The sound of childish bickering abruptly ceased.

Hillary declined. She watched Jenny make herself some toast, and wandered over to a grimy window.

'I've talked to Lucy,' she said. 'I got the feeling that she knew about your mother's lovers,' she said, deliberately bluntly.

Jenny, in the act of putting jam onto some toast, froze momentarily, and then shrugged.

'Lucy likes to give the impression that she knows everything.'

Hillary smiled. 'Sisters, huh?'

Jenny shrugged.

'Do you see much of your Aunt Debbie?'

Again Jenny shrugged. 'Not much.'

'But she helps you out from time to time?'

'Maybe.'

'What about Peter?'

Jenny snorted. 'He wouldn't give me the drippings from his nose. He said he'd get me into rehab once, as if he was doing me this great big sodding favour. I told him, I didn't want rehab. I just wanted some cash for a score. I haven't seen him since.'

Hillary nodded, then remembering the assignment she'd given Sam and Vivienne, said, 'Have you remembered what sort of trouble he was in at school?'

Jenny bit her toast and chewed, frowning fiercely.

'Huh?'

'You said he and your mum were arguing about some trouble at school. This would be the summer time, just before she died.'

'Oh that. I don't know. Something about one of his teachers. He was being bullied, or something. I don't know. She was going to sort it out for him, and Peter didn't want her going anywhere near the school. Can't blame him. You make a fuss, and you only get picked on more.'

'Can you remember which teacher it was who had it in for him?'

'Nah. His French teacher, I think. Or the geography teacher. Or maybe it wasn't one of the teachers, but a gang of kids, and the teacher was trying to help him. Anyway, it was no big deal. Mum would have sorted it out.' She suddenly stopped chewing as she suddenly realized that, actually, her mother had never had the opportunity to sort anything out.

She swallowed hard, and threw the rest of her breakfast into the bin.

'Your sister is moving into a new flat,' Hillary said quietly. 'She seems to have come into some money recently. She talk to you about that?'

'Nah,' Jenny said. 'It'll be some man. Paying for it, I mean.'

Hillary nodded. 'Do you think she learned that from your mother?'

'What do you mean?' Jenny said, bristling.

'I mean, do you ever remember your mum having more money to spend sometimes? Did she have pretty jewellery that your father didn't buy her, for instance?'

'Oh that,' Jenny said dismissively. 'No, nothing like that. Lucy's a tart. Mum wasn't.'

When Hillary got back to HQ she filled in her morning's work in the murder book and began to read it from start to finish. It was something she periodically did whenever she was stuck for something to do, and she was glad that she did.

Because the first thing Sam had done on coming in that morning, whilst she'd been talking to Steven Crayle about her secret admirer, was fill in his contributions to it as well.

And in light of her conversation with Jenny, there was one particular item in it that stood out as deserving more of her attention.

CHAPTER ELEVEN

Hillary walked through to the communal office, but apart from Jimmy, it was empty. This wasn't all that unusual, since both the younger members of their team had other commitments. It was something she was finding it hard to get used to.

'Where's everybody?'

'Sam's in a class at uni, and Vivienne's working on something for Sergeant Handley.'

Hillary sighed. 'I didn't realize we had to share them with the computer nerds as well.'

'We don't normally, but they're short staffed with some big fraud cause, and need more hands on keyboards.'

Hillary nodded philosophically, then smiled, a cat-contemplating-the-cream sort of smile. Jimmy found it fascinating. 'So Handley owes us a favour then?' she asked slyly.

Jimmy grinned, instantly catching on. The more he got to know his new boss, the better he liked her. 'Planning on calling it in, guv?'

'I might be. I've just been reading young Sam's account of his visit to the McRae children's school.'

Something in her voice made Jimmy glance at her sharply. 'Found something?'

'Maybe, maybe not. Something in it struck me as possibly relevant. Have you got Sam's mobile number?'

'Sure.' He rattled it off as Hillary punched in the numbers on her own phone. It rang twice and was quickly picked up.

'Yeah?' the voice was Sam's but pitched low, and she realized he was probably in a lecture. She squashed any feelings of guilt quickly.

'Sorry Sam, it's Hillary. Sorry to bother you like this, but I've just got one quick question, then I'll leave you to it. This Phil Cleeves, the school teacher you spoke to yesterday. Would you say he was good looking?'

Watching her, Jimmy's eyebrows rose in surprise.

There came a soft snort on the other end of the line. 'Well, Viv thought so,' Sam said grumpily.

'Thanks Sam, that's all I needed to know,' Hillary said, and hung up promptly. She frowned thoughtfully then glanced at Jimmy. 'Fancy going back to school, Jimmy?' she asked softly.

'I should bloody cocoa,' the old man said. 'Best days of your life, my arse.'

Hillary laughed. 'Don't worry. I won't let them keep you in after class.'

Phil Cleeves was in the staff room when they arrived, it being just going on for the end of the lunch hour. The room held only two others, who both looked up curiously as Phil quickly ushered them outside.

'Sorry about that, but you wouldn't believe the gossip mill in this place,' Phil said, as he led them out into an open area opposite the school playing fields. 'I've already had several queries from the head and the deputy head about the police visit on Friday. The last thing I need is for them to think my being questioned by the police is going to become a habit.' A brisk wind was stirring, but the sun was out, and Hillary tucked her hands into the pockets of her jacket as they started to casually stroll across the grounds.

Hillary studied the geography teacher briefly. She could understand why he'd be attractive to Vivienne, who was obviously going through an older man phase. Although in his fifties, Phil Cleeves still had a lean figure, and was lucky enough to possess the kind of facial features that aged well.

Jimmy, remaining silent, wondered what the guv had in mind.

'My colleagues spoke to you before the weekend, I believe, about the Anne McRae murder case,' Hillary began.

'Yes. I assumed that was what this was about,' Phil said, with a brief smile. 'I can't think what else about me would interest the police.'

The instant he'd said it, he wished he'd kept his big mouth shut. At least he managed to stop himself from letting the sickly smile that wanted to come to his face show itself.

Hillary nodded. That was twice now he'd indicated how unhappy he was to be the object of police attention. There was probably nothing in that, of course. Professional people often didn't like to have attention drawn to them by the forces of law and order. Their reputations, perforce, had to mean a lot to them. But it still made her wonder if there wasn't something about the man that protested a shade too much.

'I'm sorry if it's awkward for you, sir, calling on your place of work. If you'd like, I can have a word with your superiors – inform them that you're simply giving us information that might be useful to us. If it wasn't you, it could just as easily be another teacher who was around during the right period,' Hillary said, somewhat less than truthfully.

Phil sighed. 'No, don't bother. They already know that – the head's secretary told them what you needed. It's just that, like I said, it'll be all over the shop by the end of the day that you've been back. I'll have hoards of 12-year-olds humming the theme tune to *The Bill* for weeks to come whenever I pass by.'

He laughed.

Jimmy and Hillary smiled obligingly.

'I just wanted to clear up one or two things, that's all,' Hillary carried on smoothly. 'You taught all three of the McRae children, at various times, or so I understand?'

Phil felt himself tense, then forced himself to nod casually.

'That's right.'

'And you can't recall any incident or trouble concerning Peter McRae?'

'No. Like I said before, he was a pretty average student. His sister Jenny got into several scrapes, but they were all after her mother died. The whole thing obviously affected her pretty badly. Well, I mean, it would, wouldn't it? It's a bad age to lose your mother under any circumstances, but to something like that … well.' He trailed off and shrugged helplessly.

Hillary nodded. 'You see, sir, during our inquiries, we've come across some evidence that suggests that Peter was having some kind of trouble here,' she indicated the buildings behind her, 'and that his mother was in the process or sorting it out. Naturally, we're interested in any kind of conflict surrounding a murder victim.'

Phil shook his head. 'I'm sorry, but I really don't recall anything about that – I told the other two as much. If there was trouble, it never came to my notice. Perhaps you should ask one of the admin staff to check the records of the meetings around that time?' he asked, eager to appear co-operative. The last thing he needed was the cops sniffing around his personal life.

'We already have, sir,' Hillary said. 'It's a good suggestion, but unfortunately, they can only tell us that nothing was made official.'

She was picking up an odd vibe from the man strolling casually alongside them, and she glanced quickly behind her at Jimmy, who caught her gaze and gave a quick nod.

So he was picking up on it too.

Perhaps it was the way in which Phil Cleeves was striving to be so helpful. Perhaps it was the very casual way he was behaving. But she would have been willing to bet anything that behind his calm exterior, the man was sweating buckets.

'But if Anne McRae had come here to, say, talk to a teacher about it, it might not have made the minutes of any particular meeting. If it was off the record, so to speak,' Hillary carried on. 'So you can see our problem.'

'Oh yes. But like I said, I can't help. Perhaps if you tracked down some of the other teachers who were around then, they could shed some more light on it?'

Hillary nodded. 'We might have to do that, sir,' she said. But she doubted she'd bother. Because whatever it was that was worrying Phil Cleeves, the thought that they might talk to his contemporaries didn't phase him one bit. Which meant that whatever it was he was trying to hide, none of his fellow workers at the time knew of it.

Of course, he might be trying to hint that if there had been trouble, Anne McRae hadn't been on to him about it, but she might have taken it to one of the others. But if that was the case, why not come right out and say so? He was obviously anxious to get rid of them, and casting suspicion elsewhere was a tried and true tactic.

But, in reality, had Anne McRae only talked to him?

'Did you meet Anne McRae, sir?' she asked smoothly.

Phil shrugged. 'Like I told the other two who came, I might have done, but I honestly don't remember it if I did.'

Hillary nodded. 'You'd have been, what, in your early thirties when Mrs McRae was murdered?'

Phil looked momentarily startled. 'What? Yes, I must have been. Hell, where does time go?'

'I know, sir. It flies, doesn't it. Mrs McRae was a very beautiful woman, sir. Even from just the photographs I have of her in her dossier, I could tell she must have had men eating out of her hand,' Hillary continued casually. 'Blonde, green-eyed, and from what I've been able to learn of her character from talking to those who knew her, she was confident and friendly.'

Behind her, Jimmy picked up his ears. So that was it. The guv'nor had Cleeves picked out as another potential lover of the murder victim.

'She sounds memorable,' Phil Cleeves agreed with a slight smile. 'But it was twenty years ago now, and there have been literally hundreds of PTA meetings since I started my career. Like I said, if I met the lady, I certainly don't remember it.'

If the teacher had any inkling what Hillary was hinting at, he'd chosen to pretend he hadn't.

'So you never became friendly with her?'

'No! I just said.'

'And you never visited her home?'

'What? No, never.' Phil looked at Hillary as if she was starting to lose her marbles.

'The original investigation found some evidence of DNA at the crime scene that hasn't been accounted for, as yet,' Hillary said smoothly. 'We're currently trying to eliminate as many people from our inquiries as possible. Would you be willing to give a DNA sample, Mr Cleeves?'

Phil Cleeves felt the relief sweep through him. So that was all they were after!

'Of course I don't mind,' he said with a genuine smile. 'Do you want blood or something else? I'm not really good with needles, but if it'll help—'

'Oh no, sir, a simple cotton wool swab inside the cheek will do it. Jimmy, you were going to take some more samples later on, weren't you? Do you have the kit in the car ready?'

'Yes, guv,' Jimmy said. He had indeed arranged to go and take some samples from the Burgess couple later on that evening. 'You want me to get it?'

'If Mr Cleeves has no objection to doing it right here and now?' She let her voice rise in query, and glanced at the man beside her.

Phil Cleeves clearly didn't have any objections.

Ten minutes later, and with the geography teacher's DNA neatly packaged and labelled in a little plastic tube resting in a kit in the boot, the two of them made their way back to HQ.

'So you think he and the vic were lovers, guv?' Jimmy asked, pulling up at a set of red traffic lights.

Hillary grunted. 'I did when we started off. A good-looking teacher would have been right up Anne's street, I reckon. And when Sam confirmed that he was good-looking, I thought we might be on to a winner. Now I'm not at all sure.'

Jimmy sighed, watched an old lady cross the road in front of them, and put the car back into first and set off again. 'He was certainly antsy about something, guv,' he said stubbornly.

'Oh yes. He was like a cat on hot bricks all right,' Hillary agreed. 'But did you notice the way he practically slumped with relief when we asked him for a DNA sample?'

'Yeah. Odd that, it's usually the other way around,' Jimmy acknowledged, feeling a little deflated. 'They start to get tense when you ask them about providing a sample, not the other way around.'

'Hmm. Which tells us what?'

'That he's got nothing to fear from any DNA we found on the vic's body.'

'And he flat out denied being in the house,' Hillary said. 'And you know what? About that, I tend to believe him. But something else had him worried. I could practically smell it on him.'

Jimmy nodded. 'You think he's got form?'

'Possibly. But he's a teacher, and surely they're vetted pretty thoroughly nowadays. Even so.'

'Want me to spent a couple of hours doing a background check on him, guv? I'm not meeting the Burgesses for a while yet, not until after the hubby's finished his rounds. I can dig around, see if I catch a whiff of anything interesting.'

Hillary nodded. 'Yeah. Good idea. Something tells me we're not finished with Mr Cleeves just yet.'

Tom Warrington was on the late shift, and up in his bedroom in his parent's neat little semi, he lay out his uniform on the bed. He'd just had a shower and a shave, and was dabbing on some expensive cologne, a Christmas present from some doddering old aunt.

He liked to look good, though. It was important to be considerate to your lover. He owed it to Hillary to be smart and presentable. After all, he didn't want the others to snigger at her behind her back because he had BO or something hideous like that.

He cupped his hands over his mouth and breathed hard. Hmm, no smell, but he'd brush his teeth anyway. He did this straight away, and then, once dressed, hesitated and glanced at his wardrobe. He looked down at his watch, and nodded. His father wouldn't be in from work for hours yet and his mother had gone shopping.

It was safe enough.

He reached into the wardrobe and pulled out a large, steel padlocked box. He undid the combination from memory – the numbers to it weren't written down anywhere – and then he sat back down on the bed, his heart pounding in anticipation.

His souvenirs. He did so love to gloat over them.

He hefted the box onto his lap and opened it up. Inside, were three folders. They weren't quite the official missing persons reports, only bits and pieces of them that he'd managed to Xerox on the sly, but even so, they were like gold dust to him.

He reached for a silky green scarf, the kind with long tasselled ends, and ran it through his fingers. Judy's. Silly little Judy's. If only she'd had a few more brains, things might have worked out very differently.

He sighed, put the scarf to one side, and reached in further. He brought out a pen. A pretty black and gold affair, with the person-alized initials on it.

M.J.V.

Ah, Meg Varney. Now Meg's problems hadn't been lack of brains, so much as lack of taste. Fancy turning him down, after all that he'd tried to do for her!

'Ungrateful bitch,' he muttered, but put the pen lovingly, almost tenderly, down beside the scarf.

The final memento was a twisted silver bangle. She'd always fancied herself as a bit of a gypsy, had Gillian. Silly really, she'd been so solidly middle class.

He sighed, and put his treasures back, and carefully locked them away.

179

With a bit of luck, he wouldn't need them any more. Not now he'd finally found the right one at last.

Of course, he'd thought each and every one of the others had been the right one too, at some point. But he'd learned from his mistakes.

Hillary was older than he was, and a copper too to boot. That's where he'd always gone wrong before. Choosing young girls with no experience. And none of them knew what it was like to be a copper – the pressure or the glory. But Hillary was different. She'd understand him, and be glad of a younger lover. She'd treat him right.

The box stowed away, he checked that he looked smart and neat in the mirror, then went downstairs and on in to work.

With a bit of luck, he might catch a glimpse of her at HQ. Now that he was in admin for a spell, he could always start inventing little errands that would take him down into Hades. And what a daft nickname that was for the CRT offices. Hades – it meant Hell. Ironic really, since it housed the only angel in the place.

His Hillary was already lighting up the gloom down there. All the station house was buzzing with how well she was doing on her first case.

Even Steven Crayle seemed to be unbending towards her a bit. It was well known that he hadn't been as pleased as he should have been to have her on his team, the stupid wanker. But even the gormless Crayle couldn't help but be impressed by her, now that he'd had a chance to get to know her a bit better.

Tom Warrington didn't like Superintendent Crayle much. He was too good looking. He always dressed well too. He was, in fact, very much the sort of man that Tom wanted to be.

And he didn't like him being so close to Hillary. Being her boss might give him an unfair advantage.

But he'd keep an eye out. And if it looked as if Crayle was trying to encroach on what was his – well, Tom would have to find a way to sort him out, that was all.

*

Hillary and Jimmy arrived back just as the afternoon to midnight shift was coming in.

She nodded at a couple of uniforms hanging around the lobby, awaiting their assignments, and carried on talking to Jimmy as they walked briskly by.

'Since Handley's in our debt, see if he really does have a fast track at the labs like he says he has, and see how quickly he can get some results back on the DNA samples,' Hillary said. 'The sooner we can rule out the Burgess pair and Cleeves, the better.'

'Right, guv.'

Tom Warrington loved the sound of her voice. It was beautiful and yet full of command at the same time. From the cover of his surrounding work mates, he watched her carefully as she walked by. The old geezer they'd assigned to her looked to be all right. He was an ex-sergeant, so he should know the ropes at least.

He continued to watch her until she was out of sight, but was careful not to make eye contact. Hillary wouldn't want everyone at the station to know they were together. She had her reputation to uphold, after all.

But he felt his heart warm with pride at the brisk, professional way that she conducted herself. He wondered who she had in her sights with the DNA comparisons, but didn't doubt that soon the whole station would be buzzing with the news that she'd caught Anne McRae's killer.

He simply couldn't see his Hillary failing.

When Jimmy left to meet the Burgesses, he noticed that Hillary was still at her desk, and checking out an address in the updated file. He glanced at his watch – it was nearly 5.30.

'You off then, guv?' he asked from the open door of her stationery cupboard.

'In a bit, Jimmy. You clocking overtime for this?'

'Nah, guv, didn't think I'd bother.'

Hillary grinned. 'Nothing better to do with your time, huh?'

'Look who's talking. You don't look like you're heading for home any time soon, either.'

'No. I thought I'd have a word with Peter McRae's best friend, Brian Gill. The one he was with on the afternoon his mum died. And after work's always the best time to catch someone in. He still lives locally. Woodstock in fact.'

Jimmy nodded. 'Best to always let one of us know where you are, guv,' he said quietly.

Hillary nodded. She didn't need to tell him that she could take care of herself – that wasn't what this was about. And he was right, of course. It was always best to have someone at work know where you were. You never knew when it might come in very handy. And she was glad Jimmy had her back. Sam was too young and green to know what was what just yet. Besides, as today showed, he wouldn't always be in the office or on the job.

'OK,' she agreed easily.

Jimmy nodded and they walked out together in companionable silence, parting in the car park to go to their separate ways.

Hillary approached Puff and felt a distinct sense of homecoming. Cruising the canals and writing the book had been a nice break, but it was undoubtedly nice to get back to normal.

Well, as near to normal as her life seemed to get, anyway.

Brian Gill lived in a new-build house on the outskirts of the historic town of Woodstock, about as far away from the famous Blenheim Palace and grounds as it was possible to get and still be in the same town.

According to the updated file, he was married, with two kids. It was his wife who answered the door. From inside the house, Hillary could hear the half-hearted bickering that usually accompanied bored offspring.

Hillary held out her ID.

'Mrs Gill?'

'Yes?'

'Sorry, it's nothing to worry about. I was hoping to have a quick word with your husband.'

'Brian? What's he done?' Mrs Gill was a large-boned woman who hadn't quite shed the fat acquired with giving birth to two children, but she had beautiful and very long dark brown hair and bright blue eyes.

'Nothing at all, Mrs Gill. I'm just hoping he can help me out with one or two questions. Is he in?'

'Yeah, he's in the study. Come on through.'

The 'study' was actually the space under stairs, into which a tiny desk had been squashed, with a home computer on top of it. Sitting on an ergonomically designed swivel chair placed in front of it, a fat man with a bald patch that looked very much like a monk's tonsure, turned and glanced at them in surprise.

'Brian, it's the police for you.'

Brian Gill blinked at Hillary, then back to his wife. 'What?'

'Nothing to be alarmed about, Mr Gill,' Hillary said. 'I'm Hillary Greene, and we've re-opened the Anne McRae murder inquiry.' She didn't bother to explain about the case never having been closed. It was simpler just to say that they were re-opening it.

'Oh, right, that. Hell, that must be twenty years ago now. D'you remember me telling you about it, love?' he said to his still suspiciously hovering wife.

'Is this about that old school friend you told me about? Someone killed his mum?'

'That's right,' Hillary confirmed, then paused, as from the kitchen came the sound of raised voices.

'Those kids, honestly,' their mother said ominously, and stomped off towards the sounds of battle.

Brian Gill grinned somewhat sheepishly. 'Sharon'll sort them out. I'm afraid she's the disciplinarian in the family. They walk all over me.' He got up and indicated to the left with one out flung arm. 'Please, Mrs Greene, come and have a seat.'

Hillary froze momentarily. Mrs Greene?

Mrs Greene?

Then she realized that her ID no longer said Detective Inspector, and she forced her legs to move.

Opposite the 'study' was a small lounge, where a settee and two matching armchairs flanked a fake fireplace. Brian Gill chose one of the chairs, she the other.

'So, what can I tell you?' Brian Gill asked curiously. 'I went over that afternoon with the police at the time. I remember my mum insisting she sit in on the interview. Made me squirm, I can tell you. It was a DI Squires who talked to me, I remember him well. Nice man.'

'Yes,' Hillary agreed. 'Perhaps you can tell me what you remember of that day?'

'Well not much really. I remember I was watching *Blue Peter* when Peter showed up, because I was trying to get a badge. I was a bit of a dull kid, I suppose. Mind you, I never did win the badge, but you don't want to hear about that. Sorry, yeah, right. The programme was about half-way through when Peter got there, and we watched the telly, then listened to some music, I think. I had some comics I'd read, that Peter wanted to borrow, and then he left to go home. I heard later what had happened. My dad told me. Got me to sit on the bed, all serious like – I was scared stiff. I couldn't think what I'd done wrong, you know? But then he told me he had some bad news about Peter's family. I just couldn't believe Peter's mum was dead. I mean, you don't think it can happen to you or a kid you know, do you. Not murder, I mean.'

Hillary nodded, her mind working hard.

'Was Peter in any trouble at school that day? Or had he been recently?'

'No. Not that I knew of, and he would have told me if he had been.'

'Who was his favourite teacher at school, do you know?'

Brian Gill laughed. 'His favourite? Well, I dunno. Maybe Miss Rodgers, the English teacher. We all liked her. And we didn't mind old Chewed-up Bones. Sorry, Tudor Jones. He was a nice old fart – always telling us stories about the war. Bit odd, since he wasn't the history teacher.' He laughed at his own joke, then suddenly sobered. 'Sorry. I haven't seen Peter in years. We lost touch after we left school. I hope he's doing all right.'

'Oh yes, sir, I think so. He's living in north Oxford now.'

'You've seen him? Oh, right, course you have. Sorry, I can be a bit dim sometimes.'

'On the contrary, sir, you've been very helpful,' Hillary said with a bland smile.

Jimmy returned to HQ to drop off the DNA samples before finally calling it a night and found Sergeant Handley still manning the computers. He often wondered if the technophile ever actually went home, since no matter what time of day or night Jimmy happened to be in the office, Handley could be found at his desk.

When he handed over the three DNA samples, he asked if there was any possibility of a rush job and Handley cracked the usual jokes.

But Jimmy rather craftily told him that he could have Vivienne Tyrell's services for the rest of the week if he pulled a few strings, and Handley admitted that he knew someone at the lab who suffered from insomnia, and owed him a favour. And the simple comparison of DNA samples was actually a very simple proce- dure nowadays.

'I ain't promising nothing, but if Omar is in, I'll ask him to do them tonight,' Handley had finally promised.

Jimmy thanked him, not mentioning that, in fact, nearly all of those in Steven Crayle's team would be more than happy for the luscious Vivienne to be poached away from them for the next few months, if they wanted the little madam that long.

At his station several floors up, Tom Warrington stared down at the pink requisition slip that had been handed down to him along with a pile of others.

Part of his new duties involved helping out the store clerks, and the name of Steven Crayle had caught his eye.

It wasn't often CRT requisitioned camera equipment.

It made him wonder what they could possibly want it for. The items they'd asked for made it clear that they wanted to place a hidden camera with a back-up battery somewhere. They'd also asked for a motion-sensor device.

As he set about getting the gear together, Tom Warrington wasn't sure whether to feel elated, angry, or disappointed.

Of course, Crayle could want the equipment as part of one of their investigations. But somehow he doubted it. He'd always had good instincts – it was what had kept him safe and out of trouble all this time, and right now his 'spider' senses were tingling a warning.

Besides, if CRT was launching an observation on a possible suspect, he would almost certainly have heard about it from scuttlebutt. He made a point to keep his eyes and ears open.

Which meant only one thing.

Hillary must have told Crayle about his gifts. Perhaps the super didn't like the thought of his star asset being left flowers and cards. Perhaps Crayle was worried that Hillary would get married and leave the CRT, which wouldn't suit him at all. Everyone knew that Hillary Greene was set to lift the CRT's solve-rate through the roof – that was why the commander had recruited her.

Or perhaps Crayle's reasons for being unhappy weren't professional at all; perhaps the superintendent was jealous and wanted to find out who Hillary's lover was.

But why would Hillary tell him about their affair at all? That wasn't very nice of her.

But maybe she hadn't. Perhaps someone else in her team had snitched on them.

He'd have to find out. And from now on, be extra careful.

CHAPTER TWELVE

The next morning, Hillary arrived at HQ on the dot of nine. She was still trying to train herself to keep strictly to the nine-to-five office hours specified in her contract, but couldn't shake a vague feeling of guilt as she glanced at her watch and hurried past the desk sergeant.

In her stationery cupboard down in Hades, she reached for the phone and telephone directory.

Her first call was to the BBC. Once connected, she spent about the next ten minutes playing ring-a-ring-around-the-roses with various departments and individuals, until someone in programme planning was finally able to put her in contact with a junior admin assistant in the department she actually needed.

This individual sounded at first amused by her request, then much more interested as she explained who she was and why she needed the information. And with the help of a database, he was able to tell her exactly what she needed to know. It only confirmed something she was already fairly sure of, but it was good to get it verified. Things were beginning to come together.

Hillary thanked him and hung up, then re-read several of the interviews logged in the murder book.

Yes. She was remembering it right. Something about the afternoon of Anne McRae's murder wasn't ringing true. Either someone was confused about their timing, or someone was out and out lying.

And Hillary thought she had a good idea of who it was.

But not, yet, why?

She leaned back in her chair and frowned. She'd have to re-interview several people again, and get them to sign fresh statements. That way, once the lie was nailed, the liar would have to do some fancy back-tracking. But by then it would be down in black and white. Not that that in itself might amount to much, unless she could find out the motive behind the lie.

And therein lay her problem. A massive problem. Because as things stood, it just didn't make much sense. Not murderous sense, anyway.

She sighed and walked through to the office. It was totally empty. She sighed again, and walked down the corridor and tapped on Steven Crayle's door.

'Come in.'

When she went in, the super was already on his feet and holding some electronic equipment in his hands.

'This is just in,' he held up the tiny camera towards Hillary, who nodded. 'I thought we'd fit it up in the locker room before the rest of the place got too busy.'

'Right, sir. I hope you're a bit of a techie, because I'm useless at that sort of thing.'

Crayle smiled. So, she actually admitted to not being perfect, did she? Well, that was something.

'No problem, it shouldn't be that difficult. The hardest thing is going to be to make sure it records your locker and only your locker. I don't want to set the CRT up for a sexual harassment suit because someone thinks we're getting our jollies from watching them change their clothes.'

Hillary grinned briefly. 'After you, sir.'

They made their way through the torturous rabbit warren to the locker rooms, where they found they were in luck. No one was there. True to his word, Crayle quickly found a good location for a hidden camera and the back-up batteries, and set it up.

Hillary, meanwhile, went to her locker, opened it, and froze.

'Shit. We might be too late.'

Crayle quickly joined her, and watched her take out an old-looking, square book. It had long-since lost its dust jacket, and was a faded blue in colour with gold-gilt lettering on it.

'Not yours, I take it?' he asked flatly.

'No,' Hillary said, reading the title and opening the cover. *The Romantic Works of Byron, Shelley and Wordsworth.* She sighed heavily. Her admirer wasn't exactly an original thinker, it seemed. First roses, then valentines, now romantic poetry.

'The Romantics aren't particularly my cup of tea. I'm a metaphysics kind of girl myself,' she said. 'Now if this had been the collected works of Dr John Donne …' she opened the next page, and glanced at the printed information.

'It's a first edition,' she said thoughtfully.

'Worth a lot?'

'Perhaps, but maybe not. It depends on how rare the book is. It looks like a pretty standard tome to me, though,' Hillary mused. 'I've got a friend who's a rare book dealer – I'll pass on the details and ask him.'

Crayle nodded. 'Your stalker knows about your degree in English then?'

'It would seem so, yes. But he doesn't know me well enough to know my personal tastes.'

'So he's not someone you're likely to know well – or even have met casually?'

'Right. Which is going to make catching him all that much harder.' Hillary glanced through the book thoughtfully, but nothing was written on it and there were no personal messages. So no handwriting sample.

Both she and Crayle knew that the majority of stalking victims had some prior knowledge of their stalker. A man they'd dated perhaps, and then rejected. Or a fellow worker at their job, who wouldn't take no for an answer. Stalking by strangers was usually the preserve of celebrities.

'No messages?' Crayle asked, going back to the installation of the equipment.

'No. At least he has respect for books,' Hillary grunted a laugh. 'If he was the sort to deface literature, I'd be inclined to throw the book at him,' she came out with the atrocious pun deadpan.

Of course, she knew that she was just desperately trying to downplay the sick sense of unease that was escalating inside her, and was grateful when her boss did the same.

'Nice to have a stalker with some ethics,' Crayle agreed lightly.

'I'm wondering if the timing on this is a coincidence though, sir,' Hillary said.

When Crayle had finished with the job in hand, and was satisfied that the equipment was working properly, he dusted down his hands fastidiously, and turned to look at her.

'What do you mean?' he asked curiously. He was wearing a dark grey suit, with a mushroom-coloured shirt and dark maroon tie. A neat gold watch shimmered at his wrist and he was looking particularly lean and elegant.

Hillary wished, somewhat sourly, that the man would develop a great big red spot, right on that classically handsome chin of his.

'Did he leave the poetry book in the locker just because it was time for his next little "gift" or did he know that soon he wouldn't be able to do so?' she explained.

Crayle glanced up at the now placed and hidden camera and frowned. 'You think he might know about the surveillance?'

'It's a thought,' Hillary said. 'We suspect he must be either on the force, or have civilian access down here. And if he was on the force, and he's done this sort of thing before, he'd have had plenty of practice.'

'And this does have the feel of someone who's done this sort of thing before, doesn't it?' Crayle agreed, rubbing a hand thoughtfully across his spot-free chin. 'And if he was a desk jockey, he'd have access to all kinds of info. Especially if he was in admin.'

Hillary nodded. 'So who would know that you'd ordered some camera equipment?'

Crayle sighed heavily. 'Store clerks, requisition clerks, office supplies, maintenance, the techies....'

Hillary nodded glumly. 'Right. It would be impossible to narrow it down much. Not to mention what would happen once they got a whiff of what we were after.'

Crayle nodded. 'It wouldn't take a clever little lad long to figure it out. And if they thought we had a witch hunt on for one of our own....'

Hillary shuddered. 'No. We can't go down that route. I don't want everyone looking over their shoulder because of me.'

She'd left the force in the first place because she didn't want to be the one who might possibly bring it into disrepute. And the last thing she wanted to do now was bring dissension to the ranks.

'So we'll just have to wait and see. Keep our eyes and ears open,' Steven said reluctantly. He knew it was stupid, but he felt the absurd desire to be her knight in shinning armour, and rescue her from the villain.

He gave himself a mental head-slap, and nodded to the door. 'We'd best get out of here before we start the gossips going in a totally different direction,' he grinned. 'If they find us both in here, having a secret little get-together, it'll be all over the place before we can say sod off.'

Hillary smiled grimly. 'So long as it doesn't get back to your girlfriend, sir.'

'I don't have a girlfriend,' Crayle said deliberately. 'And call me Steven.'

'Yes si ... Steven.'

'By the way, it isn't your ex-sergeant's stalker we're dealing with here. I've tracked him down to Barrow-in-Furness. He's got a job as a car mechanic. He hasn't been back our way since he left the force.'

Hillary nodded. 'That was always a long shot anyway.'

They were passing the communal office now, and as they approached the level of the door, she could hear the raised excited voices of both Jimmy and Sam Pickles.

She paused in the doorway, Crayle directly behind her.

'What's up?' she asked.

'Guv, we've only gone and got a bloody match on that hair!' It was Sam who spoke first, too excited to hold back and let Jimmy do the honours, as protocol dictated.

But it was to Jimmy that Hillary looked for confirmation.

'Guv,' he said happily. 'After I took the last samples, I brought them back here and joshed Sergeant Handley a bit, sort of betting that he couldn't get the results back overnight.'

Hillary blinked. Normally lab results could take days, or even weeks.

'Who's the match?' the voice came over her shoulder, and Jimmy's attention snapped up to that of the superintendent.

'It's the geography teacher, sir. Phil Cleeves.'

'Who the hell's that?' Crayle asked ominously, and Hillary sighed. Jimmy shot her an apologetic look, but it was hardly his fault.

'I'm sorry sir,' Hillary said at once, half-turning around to face her boss. 'I haven't had a chance to update you on that yet. The lead only came in yesterday, and it seemed a long shot.'

Crayle's eyes narrowed briefly. He was not about to upbraid her in the front of the troops, but it was clear that he was not happy.

'A long shot that seems to have paid off, it seems,' he said tightly. 'Why don't you come to my office and fill me in now?'

'Sir.'

This time he didn't suggest that she call him Steven, she noticed with a grimace.

Jimmy grimaced his support back, and Hillary called briefly over her shoulder, 'Jimmy, take Sam and go and bring Cleeves in.'

'Right, guv.'

In Crayle's office, Hillary quickly took him through the details. And as he listened, he began to feel more mollified. The break in the case had come suddenly, as she'd claimed. And he knew that sometimes that was the way of it. You could slog away for weeks, and nothing, and then suddenly some little spark sets something off that hands the case to you on a platter.

And she had been following his orders to keep him regularly updated.

'Sorry if you think I was a bit slow off the mark to tell you, sir,' she concluded. 'But I didn't expect to get any DNA results for days yet, and the connection seemed tenuous at best. In fact, if Phil Cleeves hadn't offered to give a sample, there was no way a judge would have given me a warrant for one. I was operating on gut instinct and hardly anything else.'

Crayle nodded. 'No, you're right. It makes me wonder why he volunteered to do it – Cleeves, I mean.'

'Me too,' Hillary said flatly. 'Even the most dozy villain nowadays knows that you don't volunteer anything – especially DNA samples.'

Crayle glanced at her quizzically. His thick dark hair was doing that bouncing around on his forehead thing again, and his brown eyes looked far softer than they had done just a few minutes before. She could feel her heart rate pick up a bit, and when his hand rose to rub his chin lightly again, it picked up just a bit more.

Hillary wished he would give over.

Then she wondered why she was so obstinately trying to fend off her libido. After all, there was no real reason for it. He didn't have a girlfriend. And he'd been very careful to let her know that he didn't.

And she herself was unattached.

He wasn't even technically her superior officer anymore – she was a civilian, no longer a DI, so her self-imposed rule about not having a relationship with a boss or fellow police officer didn't even hold water any more. Besides, it had been nearly three years since her fling with Mike Regis.

And that was a long time for a gal to be celibate. No wonder the handsome and available Steven Crayle was pushing all her buttons. So why not…?

'You don't like him for it, do you?' Steven said, making her reign in her horses abruptly.

'I don't know,' she said, caught on the hop by the blunt question.

'The DNA match puts him at the scene,' Crayle pointed out. 'And he denied knowing her?'

'Yes.'

'He also denied ever having been at the house at all, you said?'

'Yes.'

'So he must be lying?'

'Yes.'

'And the moment you heard about him, you wondered if he might be a potential lover of Anne McRae's?'

'Yes.'

'And you learned about him from one of the McRae children?'

'Jenny McRae, yes,' Hillary confirmed.

'She said, I believe, that she thought a teacher at school was giving her brother trouble, right? But she wasn't sure of the exact details?'

'Right.'

'So she could have got it a bit muddled. Perhaps she thought her brother was in trouble because she happened to see her mother and this Phil Cleeves together. She was only, what, eleven years old at the time? Perhaps she misunderstood the situation – thought they were arguing about something, when really they were indulging in a bit of foreplay?'

Hillary stirred uneasily. 'I just think we might be jumping the gun a bit, that's all,' she said at last. 'There's something else that's been bothering me, about the timeline of the murder. I've found some inconsistencies. I was going to re-interview all three of the McRae children again, today if possible.'

'That can wait,' Steven Crayle said decisively. 'This DNA hit is the first piece of new, solid evidence we've come up with. I want you to concentrate on that first.'

Hillary smiled grimly and felt the childish desire to give him a Nazi salute. No doubt about it, the man was getting under her skin. She had to admit it, he was damned sexy when he got all commanding.

'Hillary?'

Hillary blinked. 'Yes, sir?'

Her amber-coloured gaze met his, and suddenly he found it hard to breathe. Steven Crayle felt, in fact, the unmistakable yank of sudden, explosive sexual tension, and froze in his chair.

For a moment, he opened his mouth to say something to her – he wasn't sure what – but suddenly she got to her feet and headed for the door. 'You'll want to sit in on the interview, sir?' she reached for the handle and opened the door quickly. She looked suddenly all business, and he felt grateful that he hadn't made a fool of himself by blurting out something ... well ... embarrassing.

'Yes, of course,' he cleared his throat. 'Let me know when it's set up. I'll be in obs.'

Hillary nodded, stepped through into the deserted corridor and shut the door after her.

Then she took a deep, somewhat shaky breath.

'Bloody hell, Hill, get a grip,' she muttered to herself. Had she really been on the verge of jumping over that oh-so-neat-and-tidy desk of his and sitting in his lap?

No two ways about it, she definitely needed to find herself a lover.

The trouble was, she already knew there was only one real contender.

But did she really want to sleep with her boss?

Phil Cleeves stepped into interview room three and saw the red-headed woman rise to her feet. The older man who'd come to pick him up followed him inside and indicated a chair – the younger one had parted company with them in the main lobby.

He'd never been inside a police station before, because he'd always been very, very careful, and he didn't like being in one now.

'Please, have a seat, Mr Cleeves,' Hillary said pleasantly enough.

He tried to smile confidently, as he pulled out a wooden chair.

Hillary was very much aware of Crayle's hidden presence behind the two-way mirror on the wall, and she told herself firmly to concentrate on the matter in hand.

Luckily, she felt herself slipping very easily into the old routine. She set up the tape recorder, identifying herself and those others present, and stating the time.

Cleeves became more and more pale as the procedure progressed, and now he could feel himself actually sweating. He reminded himself that he didn't have a thing to worry about. This was all about Anne McRae, and he knew next to nothing about the woman, but even though all that was true, it didn't stop him from sweating.

'I don't understand what this all about. I was in class, for Pete's sake,' he heard himself say, and winced at the panicky petulance of his tone.

Hillary nodded. 'Yes. I'm sorry about that, sir. But there have been developments, you see, and we need to sort them out quickly.'

'Developments?' Cleeves felt a coldness snake up his spine. He licked lips that had gone suddenly dry. 'What kind of developments?'

Who had talked? How? Why?

'You remember you very kindly volunteered to give us a DNA sample, sir?' Hillary said, very cannily getting it down on tape that Cleeves had volunteered the sample.

'That's right,' he confirmed, making Hillary nod in relief.

Good. They now had irrefutable proof of that, should a barrister or solicitor try and cry foul later on.

In the obs room, Steven Crayle sat forward on his chair and nodded in silent approval.

'Well, sir, it seems as if it was a match, and we were wondering if you could explain that.'

Cleeves's lower jaw fell open. He looked, literally, stunned. Stupefied, in fact.

Hillary, watching him, felt all her old unease stir uncomfortably in her stomach. As before when talking to this man, she had the nasty feeling that she wasn't seeing the whole picture. Or, even worse, that she wasn't seeing the right picture at all. Because unless the man was in the same class as Olivier and Orson Wells, he was genuinely stunned by what he'd just heard.

'What do you mean, a match. A match for what?' Cleeves whispered. All the blood had drained from his face now, and he stared at Hillary with a look of horrified panic in his eyes.

'A single human hair was retrieved from Anne McRae's clothing on the day she was murdered, sir. We were never able to match it to anyone in her family or circle of friends, or with anyone who might have access to the house. The man who read the electric meter, say, or workmen who called to fit a gas boiler the week before.'

'I still don't understand,' Cleeves whispered.

'The hair matched your DNA, sir,' Hillary said calmly and firmly. 'On the day she died, Anne McRae had one of your hairs on her body. Can you explain that, please?'

Cleeves looked from her, to Jimmy, then to her again. His face worked silently for a minute, and then he managed a near-sneer. 'I don't believe this. You really do that, then?'

'Do what, sir?'

'Fit people up for things. I mean, I heard about it, you know, criminals and that, they're always saying that the police plant evidence to get a conviction, but I never believed it. But you really do, don't you?'

Hillary watched him closely. She was still feeling both puzzled and non-plussed, which was not something that often happened to her. Usually, interviewing was her speciality, if it could be said that anything was. Normally, she had a feel for people, and with a mix of instinct, experience and ingenuity, got a handle on a witness fairly quickly.

But Cleeves was throwing her.

Perhaps she'd been away too long? Perhaps she should have stayed retired.

In the obs room, Steven Crayle listened to the silence stretch, and wondered how she was going to play it.

Hillary slowly leaned back in her chair. 'Do you really believe that, Mr Cleeves?' she asked steadily. 'Do you really think that I, my colleague here, the technical lab personnel, my superiors, the CPS staff and everyone else involved, are all in one giant conspiracy to send you, Mr Phillip Cleeves, to jail?'

Cleeves opened his mouth, closed it, opened it again, then closed it again.

Finally, he shuddered.

'I don't know,' he croaked.

Hillary nodded, and leaned forward in her chair. She put her hand on the table in between them, not actually touching him, but implicitly offering comfort.

'All right, sir. Let's take it steady, shall we, and see if we can't work this out. Do you still maintain that you don't, and didn't, know Anne McRae?'

'Yes. That is, I may have met her, but I don't, I didn't know her. Not like you mean.'

'You weren't lovers?'

Cleeves laughed bitterly. 'No.'

Hillary shot a quick look at him. There'd been something ironic in that laughter. For a second something seemed to nibble at her mind but then was gone again. She forced herself to relax, and not to try and chase it. It was important to keep focused.

'Do you still maintain that you never went to Mrs McRae's house? Please, think about that before you answer,' she said, and carefully recited the address to him. 'You never had occasion to go there – perhaps to discuss one of her children? Perhaps to drop off something important that needed signing – a school report, a permission slip for a school trip that one of the children forgot to bring in, anything of that kind?'

'No, of course not,' Cleeves said at once. 'Teachers don't go traipsing around after students like that. If something needed to be signed and it wasn't, then that was that. We wouldn't go to somebody's house, for Pete's sake.'

Hillary nodded. But she didn't like that answer. For a start, she was offering him – or seemed to be at any rate – a way out. If Cleeves was guilty, why hadn't he pounced on it? Gabbled out that yes, that must be it? Of course, she would then be able to reel him in, and point out to him exactly what he had just pointed out to her. That teachers didn't do that sort of thing.

Of course, it was just possible that Cleeves was clever enough to realize the trap. But he didn't strike her as having a particularly cool head right at that moment.

And there was another thing that worried her. When he'd spoken, he'd sounded genuinely angry and petulant. And in her experience, witnesses only tended to sound like that if they felt they had a genuine grievance.

'Is there anything you'd like to tell me, Mr Cleeves?' she asked gently, surprising not only Cleeves, but also Jimmy and Steven Crayle.

The man opposite her shied away like a horse spotting a snake in the grass. 'What? What do you mean? About what?'

Hillary shrugged elaborately. 'Oh, I don't know, Mr Cleeves. You seem to me like a man who has something to hide. I thought it might be easier for you if you just got it off your chest.'

'Well I don't,' Cleeves said. 'And I want a solicitor.'

Hillary stiffened for a moment, gave an inner groan, then smiled. 'Certainly, sir. Mr Jessop, perhaps you can show Mr Cleeves to a telephone?'

She suspended the interview for the tape, gathered her folders together and left the room. Once outside, she stepped straight into the obs room, and watched from behind the protective glass as Jimmy led the geography teacher out.

Crayle was still sitting on his chair, and watched her as she came in.

'It was almost inevitable he'd call for his brief the moment things started to get hot,' he said, by way of consolation.

Hillary nodded. 'Yes,' she said absently.

Crayle watched her curiously. He'd heard from many people the various stories about Hillary Greene – from Marcus Donleavy, of course, but also from members of her old team, and Sam Waterstone, the newly promoted DI who'd taken over her case load. All of them had mentioned how good she was with witnesses. But from what he'd just seen, that reputation didn't seem to be justified.

Unless she knew something that he didn't.

'Something's bothering you?' he said, offering her the chance to talk.

Hillary sighed, and took the seat opposite him.

'Something's off,' she said, then waved a hand quickly in the air. 'I know, I know, that's not very helpful. But something just doesn't ring right about all this.'

'You actually believe him?' Crayle asked, trying not to sound incredulous. 'Come on, Hillary, he can't explain how his DNA got there. He flatly denies being in the house, when we know he must have been. We need to dig around some more – if he and Anne McRae were lovers, we're bound to find someone who remembers them being together. Her kids maybe? D'you think they could be deliberately keeping quiet about it? Didn't you say you thought that Lucy McRae in particular was hiding something? Perhaps she knew about it.'

Crayle suddenly leaned forward, his eyes shining with excitement. 'That's it! She knew about them, and has been blackmailing Cleeves – that's where her sudden windfall came from. And that's what Cleeves is sweating about now. He knows that once we find out he's been giving her money, it's all up.'

'Maybe,' Hillary said.

A knock came at the door and Jimmy poked his head through. 'Guv, he's made his phone call.'

Hillary nodded. 'All right. Put him back in the chair. We'll start again, once his brief turns up.'

But half an hour later, they were still waiting.

And another ten minutes after that, they were still waiting.

'I'm going to go back in,' Hillary finally said.

Crayle nodded slowly. 'OK. But be careful. You know once he's asked for his brief, anything he says now, even on tape, can be contested in court.'

Hillary nodded. 'Don't worry. I'll just get the name of his brief from him and see if we can find out what the delay's about.'

Somewhat reluctantly, she went back into interview room three. She'd been glad of the respite, if truth be told, but although she'd had time to think things through, she still hadn't any clear idea of just how to handle Mr Phillip Cleeves.

Jimmy, restless in his chair beside their suspect, looked up hopefully, and seemed surprised to see his guv'nor come back alone. She sat down and set up the tape again.

'Your solicitor seems to be lost or delayed in traffic, Mr Cleeves. Perhaps if you'd give me his name I can chivvy him along?'

Phil Cleeves looked exhausted. He'd spent the last forty-five minutes slumped in apparent despondency on his chair. Now he glanced at her and smiled somewhat grimly.

'I didn't call a solicitor,' he said with breathtaking calm. 'I changed my mind.'

'I see.'

She wrote down on the pad in front of her. DID HE MAKE TELEPHONE CALL? IF SO, TRACE IT. She then pushed the pad towards Jimmy, who read it, stood up and left.

For the tape she said, 'Mr James Jessop has just left the room. So, Mr Cleeves, perhaps if you don't want a solicitor after all, you can tell me what you did on the afternoon Anne McRae died?'

'I was at school, wasn't I?'

'Yes. But school got out at, what, 3.30? You could have driven to Chesterton and got there long before the school bus arrived.'

'Well I didn't. There was a staff meeting, which I attended, along with many others. I didn't get home till gone six. I remember because there was a bulletin about it, the murder I mean, on the local evening news.'

Hillary glanced quickly towards the mirror, but needn't have worried. Crayle was already out the door.

He used his mobile, and got on to Sam Pickles in the office. He told him tersely to get back to Bicester School pronto, and try to find out if any meeting had been held on 6 of June, 1991, and if so, who had attended and when it had broken up.

Back in obs, he was in time to hear Hillary Greene saying, 'And was there anyone at home who could verify the time you arrived?'

'No. I'm not married.'

'You've never been married, sir?'

'No,' Cleeves flushed. 'Why is that a crime too?'

'Not the last time I checked, sir,' Hillary said mildly. And again she felt a vague little niggle. Something was staring her in the face here, and she was too wound up to see what it was. Or too far down the garden path, going in the wrong direction. If she could just clear her head a bit, she was sure that Cleeves was telling her something important, whether he realized it or not.

Just what the hell was it?

'So ...' she began, and then something else hit her hard. It was something so basic and fundamental, that she couldn't believe it had taken her this long to twig to it.

Hell, she *was* out of practice.

In the obs room, Steven Crayle tensed.

Hillary slowly straightened up in her chair. 'Mr Cleeves,' she said calmly, 'can you tell me what your last lesson was for that day?'

'Geography. I only teach Geography and Environmental Studies.'

'Yes, I'm sorry I should have been more specific. I mean which form, which class, did you teach last of all?'

'4B.' Phil Cleeves said at once.

Hillary nodded. 'That was quick, Mr Cleeves. Why do you remember that so easily?'

Cleeves went pale again. 'I just do, that's all. I remember, because Peter McRae was in that class, and when I heard about his mother being killed, I sort of went over it in my mind, trying to figure out what the poor boy must have been doing when it was happening. And it must have been around the time when he left my classroom to catch the bus to go home. And, well … I realized what would be waiting for him when he got there. It sort of stuck in my mind.'

'Yes, sir, it would. Would you excuse me for a moment?' Again for the tape, she signed herself off and switched off the recorder.

In the obs room, Crayle was on his feet. The moment she stepped inside, he shook his head in frustration.

'Damn. You're thinking secondary transfer, aren't you?' he said.

Hillary nodded, and just then, Jimmy came back in with Sam and Vivienne in tow behind him. Both the youngsters looked excited. This was their first big case, and it was obviously hotting up.

'Sorry, guv, he phoned a pay-as-you-go mobile. No way we can trace it,' Jimmy spoke first.

Crayle sighed. 'We think the DNA sample could be a case of secondary transfer,' he explained, and Jimmy swore softly.

'What's that?' Vivienne asked eagerly.

'Peter McRae's last lesson was a geography class, which Phillip Cleeves taught,' Hillary explained. 'Any good barrister could argue the case that Phil Cleeves could have shed a hair onto Peter McRae's jumper, and Peter McRae then consequently shed it in the kitchen later. Which means….'

She trailed off, unaware of Vivienne's moan of complaint.

'I get it,' Vivienne wailed. 'We've just lost our best suspect.'

'Except he couldn't have,' Hillary heard herself say. 'I've been so bloody dense! No, he couldn't have,' she said, turning to look at Crayle urgently. 'Because she said he never went into the kitchen.' Her voice was sharp with anxiety now.

'Who didn't?' Vivienne asked, baffled. 'Who didn't do what? What are you talking about?'

'Lucy McRae!' Hillary yelled, still holding Steven Crayle's eye. She grabbed her bag and ran for the door. 'We've got to speak to Lucy McRae! Right now, before it's too late.'

CHAPTER THIRTEEN

L ucy McRae sat back on her heels and wiped a hand over her warm forehead. Around her were ten big cardboard boxes, containing the bulk of her belongings. Tomorrow was removal day, and she couldn't wait to get out of this dingy flat.

She grimaced at the sweat on her hands, then told herself it was all good aerobic exercise; whether you worked out at a fancy gym, or hefted goods about, it came to the same thing. It kept the fat away.

And that reminded her – now that she had some spending money, she'd have to find a good expensive gym, and join up for a month or so. Not so much to keep in shape, but because it was a good way to meet a well-heeled man.

Now that she'd got her deposit on a decent flat, a steady source of income had become a priority.

She sighed in annoyance when she heard the doorbell peal.

Visitors, when she was surrounded by such a mess. That was all she needed.

Reluctantly, she got up off the floor and traipsed to the front door.

Jimmy, Hillary and Crayle all piled into the super's car. Of course, Sam and Vivienne had wanted to come too, sensing the case was about to break wide open, but Hillary had had to veto it in no uncertain terms.

They were both too young, and more importantly still, untrained to tackle anything that might turn nasty.

Now as they buckled up, with Steven behind the wheel of his expensive dark blue saloon, he turned to look at Hillary in the passenger seat.

'Where to?'

'Lucy McRae's flat. Banbury.'

'Right. Now perhaps you can tell me what the hell's going on?'

Jimmy Jessop, sitting in the back seat, thought with a wry grin that he'd quite like to know that too. Things seemed to have happened at the speed of light.

First they were interviewing their prime suspect, Cleeves. Then they get hit with the secondary transfer problem. Then the boss suddenly reacts as if someone's lit a firework under her and they're heading out of the door as if they're fully paid up members of the Sweeney, instead of the more staid and sedate CRT.

'I think Phil Cleeves's phone call might have put her in danger, sir,' Hillary said, an eye on the speedometer. 'Do you think you can hurry?'

Crayle put his foot down.

'Why?' he asked bluntly.

'Because of the hair,' Hillary said, holding on to the side of the door as the powerful car overtook three cars in succession and slid back onto the side of the road just in time to avoid an approaching BT van.

But even though she was fighting back a growing sense of panic about Lucy McRae, another part of her had to admire the man's driving skills. She felt perfectly safe, even if they were hammering along at eighty miles an hour.

In the back seat, she heard Jimmy phone in their destination back to HQ, and ask that they not be pulled over by any traffic patrols. Hillary silently blessed him for not having to be told to do it. 'Do we need backup, guv?' he asked.

'I'm not sure. It wouldn't hurt, if there's someone available.'

'Right, guv,' he said, and relayed the message.

'I don't get it,' Crayle said, as Jimmy closed shut his mobile.

'What's the hair got to do with it? I thought you'd decided it had to be secondary transfer.'

'I have. I don't think Cleeves ever set foot in that house, and I believe him when he said that he and the vic were never personally acquainted. In fact, if I'm right about all this, then the thought of Cleeves and Anne McRae ever being lovers is downright laughable.'

Crayle cursed a slow moving lorry, and quickly negotiated a way around it. They were now approaching the traffic lights at Hopcroft's Halt and they were on red.

He didn't reduce speed quite yet, gambling that they were about to change.

In the back seat, Jimmy checked his seat belt was secure.

Hillary eyed the upcoming lights – which were still on red – and glanced at her boss. His face was tight with concentration, his prominent cheekbones touched with white, a sure sign of tension. But his hands on the wheel were steady, and her heart rate did a little skip that had nothing to do with fear of imminent death by RTA.

'Go on,' Crayle said, about to touch the brakes, when the lights changed to amber. They roared through at nearly eighty-five. There was a dual carriageway up ahead, he knew, and he could gain even more time there. The speedometer crept closer to ninety.

From the way Hillary was sat tensed forward in her seat, he had a feeling they might need every second they could gain.

It was odd, considering the fact that he might be putting his promotion on the line, that he never once thought that she might have got it wrong. After all, breaking the speed limit and going personally into a potentially risky situation would all be frowned upon by the top brass if he didn't get a good result out of it.

'I think Phil Cleeves is gay,' Hillary said flatly.

Crayle nodded, his eyes and concentration still fixed to the road ahead.

'Does that necessarily concern us?' he asked, and in the back seat, Jimmy wondered the same thing. They were, after all, into the second decade of a brand new millennium. Granted, school-teachers might still have a hard time of it being openly gay, but as far as he could tell, Cleeves was still in the closet, which meant a blind eye could be turned.

'It is if he likes his partners young,' Hillary said flatly.

Crayle swore. 'You think he's a paedophile?'

From the back, Jimmy spoke up. 'He's not on the radar, guv. I started checking him out as you asked me to, and nothing even remotely pointing to that has shown up.'

'No, I expect he's been very careful. But I think someone, a long time ago, might have got on to him.'

Jimmy and Crayle got it at the same moment.

'Anne McRae did,' Crayle said, being forced to slow down at last as they approached the village of Deddington.

'Yes, I think so,' Hillary said.

'Then … you think, her son, Peter?' Jimmy said thoughtfully, from the back seat. 'The trouble he was in at school? It was with Cleeves?'

Hillary nodded grimly and glanced at her watch.

Crayle saw her do so, and swore at the next set of red traffic lights ahead.

'Look, Pete, it's not as if I'm not glad to see you and all that,' Lucy McRae said, pouring her brother a glass of orange juice from the fridge. 'But as you can see,' she waved a hand around the box-strewn flat, 'I'm in the middle of packing. And thanks for that, by the way. The new flat's great.'

Peter McRae glanced around nervously. The block of flats had been pretty quiet when he'd arrived, and he guessed that most of the tenants were out at work. But there'd be bound to be someone around. Old ladies, or new mums with babies. Was it safe?

'Thanks, sis,' he said ironically as he accepted the glass of juice. 'I should hope it is. I had to practically clear out my bank account for it. Just because Seb's loaded doesn't mean to say that I am. I have to be careful, you know?'

For a moment, the two siblings looked at one another in perfect understanding.

Then Lucy shrugged. 'Not to worry, you'll be able to fill the coffers again soon. At least you've still got your meal ticket. I've got to look around for another one.'

Peter's free hand clenched hard into a fist. 'I happen to love him, Luce,' he said grimly.

'Yeah sure, whatever.'

Peter forced the rage back and he took a brief swallow of cold liquid. She'd always been so damned cavalier. He just couldn't seem to get it through to her that this was his *life* they were talking about.

He'd always suspected that Lucy knew about their mother. And when she'd come to him for money, just when the cops had reopened her case, he'd known it for certain. But even then, he hadn't felt all that threatened. After all, she was his sister, she wouldn't grass on him.

But now, now all that had changed.

He glanced around the tiny flat again, and outside the window. Traffic moved on the busy streets below. He'd have to keep her away from the window. He couldn't risk being seen. Or should he lure her away from the flat? But take her where? The thing is, Lucy wasn't stupid.

That was the problem.

Lucy had always been the brightest of all of them.

'We're coming up to Banbury, Jimmy. Do you know the road where Lucy's flat is?' Hillary asked.

Jimmy did, and leaning forward between the two front seats began to give directions.

'So you think that Phil Cleeves and Peter McRae had a fling going when he was still at school, and that Anne McRae found out about it?' Crayle said, wanting to get things straight.

'Yes. And she wasn't happy,' Hillary said, in what she imagined was probably a gross understatement. 'You remember, Jimmy, how everyone said that Anne was fierce about protecting her kids. And that she was the disciplinarian, what with the father being out of the picture so often, and was always the one who took care of any problems the family might have?'

'Yes, guv,' Jimmy agreed.

'So if she found out, or suspected, that one of his teachers was interfering with her son, she'd take the bull by the horns and not think twice about it, rather than waiting for Melvin to get home or going straight to the cops. You agree?'

'Yes, guv,' Jimmy said. 'I reckon she'd go straight to the source of the problem. Cleeves himself. Then, if she got no joy there, the school and probably only on to us as a last resort.'

'Right,' Hillary agreed. 'She'd be reluctant to make it official until she knew all the details. She probably wasn't sure how far it had gone, and her instinct would be to protect her son, and the family, from the trauma of a trial and any publicity unless it was strictly necessary.'

'Especially since she must have known that her son was gay anyway,' Jimmy said. 'He is openly living in a same-partner relationship now, right?'

'Yes,' Hillary agreed.

'So you think that Cleeves called Peter McRae just now,' Crayle said, nodding his head at the latest directions Jimmy was giving him.

'Yes. I think when we pulled him in on the DNA evidence, he panicked. I think he probably called Peter to ask him to verify that they'd had a last lesson together at school that day,' Hillary confirmed. 'And it wouldn't surprise me to learn that they'd been in touch before this. At least, since the inquiry had become active again anyway.'

'Yeah, that would make sense. Even if whatever they'd had going together must have quickly fizzled out, once Anne McRae died, they'd tend to stick together once the case became active again. If only to get their stories straight, should they need to.'

'Yes, but they'd have had to be careful. And, by the way, I don't think for one moment that Phil Cleeves knows what's really going on,' Hillary said grimly.

'Which is?' Steven said. He knew where she was going with this, but as they pulled up in a small parking area near Lucy's block of flats, he wanted to hear her confirm it.

'That Peter McRae killed his mother,' Hillary said flatly.

'Peter, what the hell are you doing?' Lucy asked, turning around from taping up the last of the boxes, to find her brother standing behind her with a pair of her tights in his hand. 'You a tranny or something?' she laughed.

Then she saw that her brother, her taller, heavier, stronger brother, was twisting the tights into a silken rope, and all thoughts of laughter fled.

She had just a brief moment of disbelief, before he was on her.

As she felt his hands on her arms, roughly turning her, she kicked backwards and heard him swear. But then saw the tights come down in front of her face, and she wondered if her mother, twenty years before, had felt the same sense of panic and bewilderment as she herself was feeling now. That Peter, Peter of all people, could be doing this to her.

And then sheer terror took over as she felt the tights close around her windpipe, cutting off her air supply.

'This is it,' Jimmy said, stopping outside the door and putting his ear to the wood. Crayle reached over him and was just about to ring the doorbell, when Jimmy raised his hand.

'Stop,' he said quietly. 'I think I can hear something.'

And then they all heard it – a muffled female shriek of sheer horror.

'Shit!' Crayle said, and tried the door. It was, of course locked. 'Out of the way,' he ordered Jimmy, who was more than glad to oblige. He was way too old, and his bones far too suspect, to go around breaking in doors.

Crayle stood back, and kicked the door with tremendous force.

Hillary hadn't expected anything to happen at the first attempt. It was only in badly-made films where the hero could kick open a door with a single blow. So when the door splintered and flew open she looked as surprised as she felt.

Crayle noticed.

'Karate,' he said tersely, even as he was running forward into the heart of the tiny flat. Hillary was still standing there with her mouth open when Jimmy went in next, and she pulled herself quickly together and followed them in.

She looked around at once for a handy weapon in case it was needed, and picked up a large black furled, steel-structured umbrella standing beside the ruined front door.

When she stepped into the tiny living room, umbrella ready to hand, the adrenaline was already kicking in, and her eyes instantly relayed everything it saw to her brain.

Lucy McRae, half-facing them, her congested face beginning to turn puce, the tights biting deep into the skin of her throat. Her eyes were open, but were beginning to get that glazed-over look that told Hillary she was about to lose consciousness.

Over her shoulder, the handsome face of her taller, blonde-haired brother. His eyes were wide and startled, as if they couldn't believe what they were seeing.

And launching himself at him, Crayle, whose foot came out and hooked around the back of his right knee, making the younger man fall backwards. He tried to save himself with his hands, and instinctively let go of his sister, who sagged onto her knees and into Jimmy Jessop's competently waiting arms. He quickly half-dragged, half-carried her out of the affray.

Hillary stepped forward, umbrella raised, but kept well out of the way of the flailing limbs. She'd only lend a hand if it looked as if Crayle was in trouble.

Which never happened.

Crayle quickly followed Peter McRae down, neatly turning him onto his stomach. McRae started to back-elbow furiously, but Crayle kept his head reared back and well out of trouble.

Then, from out of his back pocket he brought out a pair of handcuffs and, forcing McRae's arms behind him, neatly slapped them onto the prostrate man's wrists.

Hillary didn't know supers still carried handcuffs in their back pockets. And then she wondered – perhaps it was only Steven Crayle who did so.

And that thought made her go hot all over.

She shook her head and listened to her boss crisply read Peter McRae his rights. Then she turned her attention to Lucy and opened her mobile to order an ambulance.

It didn't take long after that to sort things out. Crayle and Jimmy went back to HQ with the prisoner to begin the process of serving McRae with a murder charge.

Hillary rode in the ambulance with Lucy.

Lucy had never quite lost consciousness after all, and in the back of the ambulance, with the eye of the paramedic watching over them, Hillary gently questioned her.

'Did you actually see him kill her?' she started off quietly, keeping her voice calm, but needing to get to the heart of the matter before shock had a chance to set in, or Lucy became hysterical.

But the middle child of Anne McRae was made of stern stuff – just like her mother, and she was game to talk, even though her throat still felt sore, and her voice was little more than a croak.

'No. When I got back from the park, I saw Pete out in the back garden. He was running away from the house. I thought it odd, but then just assumed he'd been having another row with Mum.'

She paused and the paramedic gave her a few sips of water to help ease her throat.

'Then, when I went into the kitchen and saw Mum, I didn't know what to think.'

She was lying on the stretcher, her head in a neck brace, her face pale, and her eyes haunted and wide.

'I went out into the back garden and saw that he'd taken his sweatshirt off. It was covered in blood.'

Lucy swallowed hard and winced. 'Mum's blood.'

Hillary tensed. 'What did you do with it, Lucy?'

'I kept it,' she said, with a brief, grim smile. 'I don't know if Pete even remembers that he was wearing it at the time. I think he took it off and dropped it because, as he was running away, he saw the blood on it and panicked. Either that, or he was clever enough to realize that if he was seen with blood on him, people would put two and two together. Or maybe he was just in shock, and reacted without thinking.'

'Perhaps he looked for the sweatshirt later and couldn't find it,' Hillary suggested, and looked at her steadily. 'Did you tell him that you still had it? Later, I mean, when you asked him for a loan. It is your brother who's financing your move to the new flat, yes?'

Lucy smiled. 'Yes. I mean, yes he did loan me some money. And no, I never told him I still had the sweatshirt. I'm not stupid, you know.'

'Is it safe?'

'Oh yeah. I put it in a polythene bag and kept it all these years. It's in one of the boxes back at the flat.' Lucy took a gulping breath, half-laughing, half-crying now. 'It's funny, but when he started to strangle me, I remember thinking, "That's no good, big bruvver, because the evidence to nail you for Mum's murder is right under your nose". I could actually hear it, like a voice in my head, saying exactly that. Isn't it odd what you think of when you're sure you're about to die?'

She started to cry in earnest then, and the paramedic said quietly, 'All right, that's enough for now.'

Hillary nodded and sat back in her chair. She had enough to be getting on with.

More than enough, in fact.

At the Horton Hospital, she hung around long enough to find out what ward Lucy was being assigned to, and had a quick word with the examining doctor, who didn't anticipate any real trouble. Then she stepped outside and got back on the phone.

First she called Crayle, who was back at his office.

'Sir, it's Hillary. Lucy McRae's going to be all right. The doctor wants to keep her in overnight to monitor her for shock and to make sure that her throat doesn't swell up and give her any breathing difficulties. But he doesn't think she's too badly off. I got a partial statement from her in the ambulance, I'll fill you in on that when I get back to HQ,' she added, mindful that she was on her mobile. 'But we need to get forensics to her flat right away. I have reason to believe we'll find valuable evidence there.'

'We were all witnesses to the attack on her, Hillary,' Crayle pointed out, 'but forensics are already on their way as we speak.'

Hillary didn't bother to correct him over the phone. She'd tell him the good news about the corroborating evidence for Anne McRae's murder when she got back to the office.

Speaking of which, she thought grimly, as she hung up, she was stranded in Banbury without a car. With a sigh, she started to hoof it to the nearest bus stop.

This civilian consulting lark might have its benefits, but right about then she could have done with having her old authority back, allowing her to order up a jam sandwich to take her back to HQ in style.

It was barely five o'clock, when Hillary returned to interview room three.

Inside, looking like a limp lettuce leaf, Phil Cleeves watched her approach the table and his shoulders slumped as she once more went through the routine for the tape.

In the obs room, Steven Crayle watched. Jimmy, Sam and Vivienne were all still in the office, trying to sort out the blizzard of paperwork that the fast-moving case had suddenly generated.

Nobody wanted the case to falter now because evidence was mishandled, or warrants weren't properly worded.

'Mr Cleeves, I have to tell you that we have, this afternoon, arrested Peter McRae for the murder of his mother,' Hillary began, and saw the geography teacher go paper white. For a second, she thought he was actually going to pass out.

'No! You can't have. I mean, you've made a mistake. Peter's a good boy. He wouldn't do something like that!' Cleeves protested.

'You know him well then?' she asked casually.

'No. Yes. I mean, I knew him. He was one of my students, I told you.'

'But he was more than that, wasn't he, Mr Cleeves?' Hillary said, careful to keep her voice flat and unjudgemental. 'In fact, I think you loved him, didn't you?'

Cleeves went rigid, and said nothing.

'He's a good-looking man now,' Hillary went on. 'As a 15-year-old I imagine he was especially golden. Just beginning to fill out, all gangling limbs, still innocent, but with the promise of the mature man yet to come. Am I right?' she pressed gently.

And the geography teacher folded. 'He wasn't that innocent,' Cleeves finally muttered. 'He knew what he wanted. And he was golden, yes.'

Hillary nodded.

'His mother found out about you.'

'There was nothing to find out,' Phil contradicted quickly. 'OK, so I'm gay. But I never laid a hand on Peter.'

Hillary sighed. 'Mr Cleeves, if we start asking around all your pupils, do you really think one of them won't eventually give you up? You've been lucky so far, flying under our radar, and being careful. And I daresay you were very careful to only choose the boys who made it obvious that they were gay too. Left the really young ones well enough alone, did you?'

Phil Cleeves swallowed hard but said nothing.

'Right,' Hillary said, as if he'd in fact agreed with her. 'But you know as well as I do, that one of them will talk. He'll be older, wiser, maybe a little bit bitter. Perhaps you and "one of your boys" parted not quite as well as you'd hoped? We only need to find one willing to dish the dirt. What do you do – drop them when they leave school?'

From the way the geography teacher's hands clenched into sudden fists, she knew she'd scored a direct hit there.

'Eventually we'll find some "golden boy" who doesn't remember you quite so fondly. Someone who'd be willing to get a little payback for the way his life hasn't worked out quite how he hoped, by making someone else's life a misery too. Namely yours.'

'I was always careful,' Cleeves said sadly. 'I always made sure they made the first move. And I took it slowly and carefully. It wasn't about sex, you know, it was about love. All my boys will remember me with affection.'

Hillary was careful to keep her face blank and her voice flat. 'Yes, sir, I'm sure they will. I dare say Peter will too.'

'Yes he will!' Cleeves said, with a spurt of sudden defiance. 'What we had was special. He was nearly sixteen when we first made love. And I was kind and gentle and he was grateful. It lasted for nearly four months. Four wonderful months.'

Cleeves suddenly slumped back in his chair. 'Oh, what's the point. You won't understand. Your sort never do.'

'And then his mother began to suspect what was happening, didn't she?' Hillary said firmly, ignoring the self-justification and self-pity. 'What happened? Did she phone you? Did she come to the school to talk to you?'

'Not the school,' Cleeves said quickly.

'Your house then,' Hillary pounced, and he reluctantly nodded.

'But she only suspected,' Cleeves said. 'I could tell she was on a fishing expedition. I told her that nothing like that was going on. I told her that I thought Peter saw me as something of a father figure. I made her doubt herself, I could tell.'

'Yes, I'm sure you were very erudite, sir,' Hillary said dryly. 'I need you to write out a statement, detailing everything about your relationship with Peter McRae, and everything you can remember about your conversation with his mother, Anne. I'll leave you alone to get started,' she said firmly, pushing a large writing pad and a pen in front of him.

And as he opened his mouth to demur, she added firmly, 'It's by far your best option, Mr Cleeves.'

'I want a solicitor,' Cleeves said.

Hillary nodded. 'By all means, sir. And I think, when he realizes that you could be facing charges of aiding and abetting murder, he'll tell you the same thing.'

Cleeves went pale. 'But I don't know anything about that!'

Hillary didn't try and reassure him, although in fact, she believed him – about that, anyway. She simply turned her back on him and left him. But in the obs room, she slumped wearily down into the chair next to her boss.

'Thing is, sir, I don't think he *did* have anything to do with the murder. He might, in his heart of hearts, have wondered, when he first heard about her death, whether his golden boy might have had a hand in it,' she mused. 'But he's obviously convinced himself over the years that it was a passing maniac who killed her.'

Crayle nodded. 'I agree. Still, it'll be a good lever to use to get him to get cracking on his statement,' he said with a grim smile. 'That was good work. You look beat. You want me to take McRae?'

Hillary shot a glance at him. Was he trying to muscle in on her collar?

But as she met his level brown gaze, she realized that he wasn't.

'No, sir. I'll take him,' she said firmly, and Crayle smiled and nodded.

He had expected nothing less.

'All right then, I'll have him brought through. And call me Steven.'

Hillary nodded.

'All right, Steven,' she said. And this time, she liked saying his name.

After all, if she was going to drag him kicking and screaming into her tiny single bed, they really did need to be on first name terms.

Commander Marcus Donleavy walked briskly down the stairs and into the foyer, on his way to the interview rooms. He nodded and passed a knowing, cheeky grin with the desk sergeant as he went by and slipped into the obs room.

By now it was all over the station that Hillary Greene had cracked her first cold case, and all those who'd had a bet down, were hanging around and wondering what their chances were of scooping the prize.

A female DI from Juvie was happier than most, since she'd got it down to the day, although several male colleagues were chivvying her that it didn't count unless Hillary got a confession today as well. They'd both opted for a day in the third week, and were holding out to win on a technicality.

Inside interview room one, Hillary Greene and Steven Crayle sat in front of Peter McRae. Steven, as the senior officer, went through the routine for the tape, and then leant back slightly in his chair, obviously handing the initiative over to the woman beside him.

In the obs room, Marcus Donleavy smiled in approval. He was looking forward to this. Now that she had her first taste of success under her belt, Marcus knew he had her back for good.

Just wait until they all went to her local for a celebratory drink tonight. He'd rib her something rotten about her so-called retirement!

Then he leant forward, concentrating hard, as it began.

'So, Peter, you might like to know that your sister is going to be all right,' Hillary began. 'Or maybe not. I went with her in the ambulance, and she was able to talk to me a bit. Of course, she was still shook up. She couldn't quite believe that you'd just tried to kill her.'

Peter McRae was sitting forward in his chair, his elbows on the table, his head in his hands. He looked utterly tired and defeated, and he looked up at her as she began to speak, his brown eyes bright with unshed tears.

'Of course I'm glad that she's all right,' he said. 'I never meant it to happen. None of it. I just panicked, that's all. When Phil called me and told me about you matching the hair to his DNA I knew the game was up. I had to go and see Lucy, just to beg her not to say anything. I don't know how it all got so out of hand. I just got so scared. I didn't want Sebastian to find out you see.'

With that, Peter McRae's eyes filled with water. 'I love Sebastian, and he doesn't know anything about … well, any of it.'

Hillary nodded.

'Let's start at the beginning shall we, and get things straight?' she said gently, determined to get him to stick to the facts. 'When you were at school, you had a relationship with your geography teacher, Mr Phillip Cleeves. Is that right?'

Peter nodded.

'For the tape please, Mr McRae,' Hillary said gently.

'Yes.'

'We have Mr Cleeves in custody, and he's making a statement now,' she informed him.

Peter managed a somewhat trembling smile. 'Poor Phil. He'll hate all this.'

'How old were you when it first started?' she asked gently.

'Fourteen. Well, nothing physical till I was fifteen, and then really only heavy petting. It was all so stupid!' he burst out. 'Mum took it far too seriously. We weren't hurting anyone, for Pete's sake. It's not as if Phil was some dirty old man pervert who was corrupting me. I was fifteen! I was learning who I was, and what I wanted, and Phil was kind, and, well, like a father to me. He was good to me. And it's not as if I didn't know that I was gay. I'd known that for some time. But Mum never would accept that.

She thought it was all his fault. As if Phil could make me gay! I mean, how stupid is that?'

Hillary bit back her anger, and firmly squashed the response she wanted to give. At fifteen, Peter McRae had been in no position to know what he wanted. And a man in authority over him had no damned business taking advantage of his naivety. Whether he was gay or not.

'When you left school that last day, you didn't go to your friend's house straight away, like you told us, did you? You went straight to your house.'

'How did you know that?'

'Your friend, Brian Gill, inadvertently told me. He said that he remembered he was watching *Blue Peter* when you showed up at his house. And I phoned the BBC. They said that *Blue Peter* aired at a quarter to five in those days. But you'd have got back from school at 4.30 by the latest. Yet when you showed up at Brian's, the programme was halfway over, meaning that there was half an hour to account for in your version of events.'

Peter shook his head in amazement. 'If you say so. I can barely remember much of what happened that afternoon. I was in a daze after … after it all happened.'

Hillary nodded. 'OK. Let's see what you do remember. You went straight home?'

'Yes.'

'Your mother was in the kitchen, baking?'

'Yes. She told me she'd been around to see Phil, to have a word with him. She made me so angry, bossing me around, telling me I had to stop seeing him. She threatened to go to the head, which would have meant Phil lost his job! Just how spiteful was that?' he asked, his voice rising with remembered indignation. 'She was hateful. You've got to understand, I was in love with Phil. Well, I thought I was,' he qualified, almost at once. 'Back then I was just fifteen. It was all so new to me. Everything felt so intense, do you know what I mean?'

'I understand,' Hillary said softly. 'You wanted to protect him?'

'Exactly,' Peter said, looking relieved. 'You understand. But Mum was like a force of bloody nature when she was riled. She just wouldn't listen to me. I told her over and over that nothing had happened – well, nothing really physical. I told her that I loved Phil, and he loved me, but she just got angrier and angrier, and said that I didn't know what I was talking about. She said she was going to fix everything. I began to see red. She just wouldn't listen to me!' his voice was almost a shout now in remembered anger and frustration, and Hillary let him get it all out.

'She was your mother, and you'd do as you were told,' she said flatly.

'Yes. That's it exactly. I was just so damned angry. She was going to ruin Phil's life, and mine too, and she just wouldn't listen to me!'

'So you made her listen,' Hillary said quietly. 'With the rolling pin?'

Peter McRae looked at her, his big brown eyes wide with horror. 'You won't believe me, but I don't even remember picking it up. The rolling pin I mean. But I must have done – it was there on the table. And then Mum was on the floor and there was this sticky red stuff all around – on my hands, on my shirt. I just dropped the rolling pin and ran.'

Hillary let him get his breath back. He was breathing hard now, and looking genuinely bewildered. 'I just wandered around for a bit, and then went to Brian's. I thought he'd take one look at me, and everything would be over. The police would come, and I'd go to prison. I didn't know if Mum was dead, or what. But he acted like nothing had happened,' Peter said, the remembered wonderment of it still in his voice. 'So I pretended that nothing had happened as well. I didn't know what else to do. So I sat with him watching the telly, and at some point, I wondered why he wasn't asking about the blood on me, and then I realized that I wasn't wearing my sweatshirt.'

'You took it off,' Hillary said, and glanced quickly across at Steven. She'd told him about Lucy McRae keeping it, and they'd had word just before starting the interview that forensics had retrieved it from Lucy's flat.

'Oh, did I?' he asked, without interest.

'Anyway, everything then happened pretty much the way I told you it did when you first talked to me,' he carried on, sounding exhausted now. 'I went back home, and Lucy was there. She never said anything about seeing me, but I know she must have done. Because a few days ago, she called me to ask for some money. And then … well….'

'Pretty much blackmailed you when you said no.'

Peter nodded miserably.

'So when you heard from Mr Cleeves this afternoon, telling you that his DNA had been matched to the hair found on your mother's body, you panicked?' she prompted.

'Yes. I knew it was only a matter of time before you'd figure it out. You see, I remembered saying that I never went into the kitchen that afternoon – and Lucy would have confirmed that she kept me from going into the house as well. So how could you find one of Phil's hairs on Mum? I hoped you might think Phil had done it, but I wasn't sure that that would hold water. I realized what must have happened, of course – that one of his hairs got on to me, and that when I … when Mum died, the hair must have fallen off me and on to her.'

'We call it secondary transfer,' Hillary said helpfully.

'Right. Anyway, you could ask me, and I could deny every-thing until the cows came home. But if you put pressure on Lucy, I thought she might crack.'

'So you decided to kill her,' Hillary said flatly.

And it was then that Peter McRae started to cry in earnest.

Tom Warrington hung around the car park until it was starting to get dark, but his patience was finally rewarded.

He saw Marcus Donleavy first, then Steven Crayle. All the big men, gathered around her, like little satellite moons orbiting a bright shining sun. He barely acknowledged the presence of the old man, Jimmy Jessop. And Sam Pickles, that long ginger streak, was no competition. Vivienne Tyrell barely registered on his consciousness at all.

He had eyes only for Hillary. There they were, in a group, all headed for their cars and ready to meet up again at Hillary's local for a celebratory drink. It was the tradition, whenever a murder case was successfully closed, he knew that.

And it was all over the station that she'd secured a confession from the killer – the murder victim's own son. Who'd have thought it? Well, except for Hillary, of course.

She was brilliant.

Amazing.

As the group split up, his eyes followed her hungrily. She looked tired, but triumphant. A conquering heroine. She looked so beautiful. He wanted to go to the pub too, but knew he couldn't risk it. Not quite yet.

But it was time, he thought, to step up his courtship of her nevertheless. The flowers and poetry were a good first step. But it was time to let her know just how strongly he felt.

As Hillary Greene got into her old car and drove away to join her team for a victory celebration, Tom Warrington began to think of ways to make her pay the proper attention towards him.

And he was good at that. After all, the others had all come to realize that he shouldn't be taken for granted. A pity they had learned the lesson too late.

But it wouldn't be like that with Hillary, Tom was sure.

Hillary was the one.

Now all he had to do was prove it to her.

And he was going to enjoy doing that.